WARRIORS OF THE WOOD

The Gardiens Book 1

WARRIORS OF THE WOOD

Susan Shepard

Alpharetta, GA

ISBN: 978-1-6653-0174-9 - Paperback
eISBN: 978-1-6653-0175-6 - ePub
eISBN: 978-1-6653-0176-3 - mobi

Library of Congress Control Number: 2021910735

Printed in the United States of America 0 6 0 8 2 1

∞ This paper meets the requirements of ANSI/NISO Z39.48-1992 (Permanence of Paper)

Map and crest artwork by Kyilee Mortensen @open_sketch_book

To my husband, Dave,
for your constant support in all my endeavors.

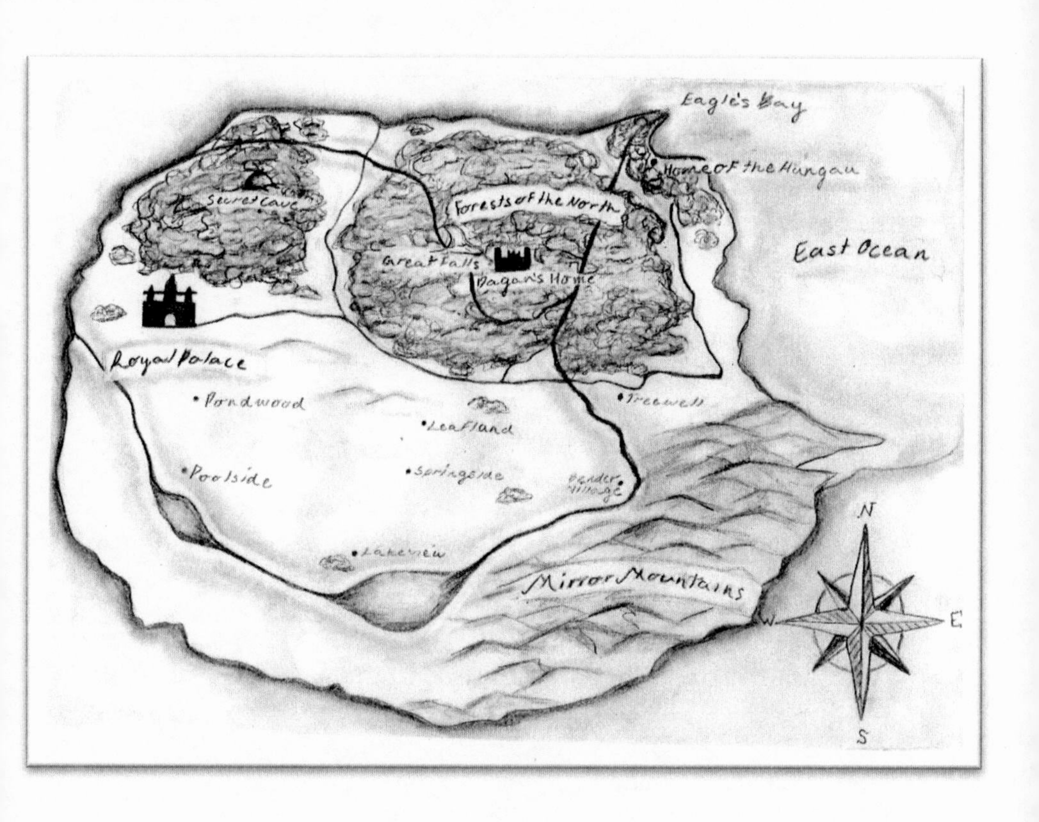
Eagle's Bay
Home of the Hungau
Secret Cave
Forests of the North
Great Falls
Dagan's Home
East Ocean
Royal Palace
Pondwood
Leafland
Treewell
Poolside
Springside
Bander Village
Lakeview
Mirror Mountains
N
W
E
S

Prologue

A fierce army—vast in number and intense in their hatred—laid siege to the country of Volcania. At first, their existence was but a whisper on the wind, a legend of scary stories passed down generation to generation.

They weren't a whisper anymore. Years past, in some long-forgotten war, the nation of Boulderland had hired a band of mercenaries from beyond the Unclaimed Territories. They were known for their ability to attack swiftly and quietly in any terrain. After the war, Boulderland's king refused to pay them. Incensed, the mercenaries turned on the king and his allies. They named themselves the Hungau, which in their original tongue meant, "The Destroying Winds." With their skills they roamed through the land attacking and plundering, recruiting from among the people of Boulderland, Volcania, and Cascadia to increase their ranks. Now, they were a force to be reckoned with.

Having successfully crossed the Volcanic border, small outlying towns became their next focus. Fires swept the nation and lives—regardless of gender or age—were snuffed out under the unforgiving flames of war.

The king of Volcania, Phillip Goldwyn, knew it was only a matter of time before the Hungau reached the towns surrounding his castle. His troops were already stretched thin securing the borders and evacuating the villages before more lives were lost. As a result of the evacuations, the citizens of Volcania had flocked to the castle for refuge. If the Hungau made it any closer, they would be lambs in the largest slaughter of Volcania history. The king was painfully aware he couldn't protect them for much longer. Help was needed.

He called for his battle commander and a runner. "Commander, I need your runner to get a note over the border to the king of Cascadia."

"Do we have time for that, Sire?"

King Phillip shook his head. "I don't have any other options. I can't protect these people on my own."

"Do you have the note ready?"

The king handed it over. "I'm asking for additional forces."

"I think that is wise, Sire."

He stood and looked out the window. Smoke filled the sky, making it look darker than it really was. That smoke represented his citizens being slaughtered, burned, killed. A burning anger of his own clutched his heart.

"Commander?"

"Yes, Sire?"

"Tell your runner to hurry."

The commander and the runner both hastened out. It would take two days to get the runner to the border of Cascadia and another three to get to the castle. Hopefully, Cascadia would anticipate their need and have their armies assembled and ready to march.

For nearly two days, the country of Volcania and her royalty watched as the Hungau moved farther inland. On day three, the sky blazed as red as the fires below, and the scent of burning earth surrounded them. King Phillip was losing hope that Cascadia would respond, let alone that the runner had even made it to the border. Finally, on day four, the Hungau could be seen from the topmost window of the castle. They were advancing, and fast.

The king turned to his commander. "Ready the troops."

The commander bit his lip. "Sire, we don't have enough to fight off the Hungau."

"I'm aware of that."

The commander, knowing what that meant, touched the ring

on his left hand. "Can I give them the option to desert? Many of our soldiers have families of their own."

"Do what you must."

The commander nodded and left to assemble what remaining troops were willing to fight. A few moments later, the commander barged back through the door.

"Your Majesty! The Cascadian king is here with his cavalry!"

King Phillip spun around. "Already? Take me to him!"

When he reached the war room, his heart leapt at the presence of the Cascadian king, his cavalry commander, and a few other men he assumed were military leaders.

"I have never been so happy to see you, Greyson Montcroix," he confessed. The two leaders shook hands.

"We're happy to help, Phillip. We anticipated our assistance and marched toward your border a few days ago. We caught your runner on the way."

"The Hungau will be here by nightfall." The Volcanic king pointed to his map. "They have almost destroyed my entire nation."

"We can stop them now," the Cascadian cavalry commander said.

"We brought another army with us. They are foot soldiers." Greyson turned to another man in the room. "This is Bernon Wells, the Gardien leader of the Forests of the North."

A large, burly bear of a man stepped forward. His face was serious, his eyes wise and patient. "We are experts on the Hungau and have fought them before. We are honored to serve alongside you during this battle."

King Phillip stared at the man's large, outstretched hand. "I've heard of the Gardiens before but have never had the honor of meeting you." He turned to Greyson and said, more quietly, "Are you certain they're an ally?"

Greyson gave the Gardien man a long look. "Right now, I am certain the Gardiens are as much an enemy to the Hungau as we are. It may have been against my better judgment to bring him here, but for now, I trust him."

Bernon gave the men a hard smile. "Our word is our bond; we are on your side. You don't have a choice to believe me. The Hungau are on your doorstep, and we are here willing to fight against them. Take that for what it's worth."

"Thank you for bringing your troops," Phillip said and gripped Bernon's hand. They certainly needed all the help they could get. Bernon nodded and stepped back.

"Let's come up with a plan," King Phillip said, and the men murmured in agreement. Before long, with the help of Bernon Wells, they devised a strategy that would halt the Hungau's attack and draw them into a trap.

As the men readied their troops and equipment, and prepared the citizens of Volcania for battle, Bernon pulled King Greyson aside. "There has been strife between us in the past, but I am happy to serve alongside my king and his armies."

Greyson eyed Bernon with an apologetic stare. "I confess I have not trusted the Gardiens over the years. You're a secretive lot."

"I assure you it is merely out of habit." Bernon smirked. "We are a peaceful people."

"Who specialize in military tactics and training."

"Also a habit. We have never threatened the crown and never will."

"What are you getting at?" Greyson huffed.

"When this is over, I want a treaty of peace between us. There is no reason why we should fear one another. The Gardiens are nothing like the Hungau, if that is what you are afraid of."

Greyson narrowed his eyes. "When this is all over, we'll discuss this treaty."

"I assure you I will not forget."

The two leaders rushed off to fight alongside their soldiers. The night passed slowly and solemnly. The cries of men in battle mingled with those who had fallen, their voices heard no more. As dawn crept ever closer, it became clear who stood victorious and who knelt in defeat. The royal armies overthrew the marauders, the Gardiens stood as the ultimate tipping point, and the Hungau were forced to surrender. The burial of the dead soon commenced. The Hungau warriors who survived were arrested for crimes against the crown, murder, and war crimes, and were banished to a corner of land near the coast called Eagle's Bay, where they could be watched by both Volcania and Cascadia.

Once the Cascadian armies and Gardien warriors returned home, Bernon sought the counsel of King Greyson to discuss the treaty that would be a step toward uniting the kingdom.

"You haven't forgotten," King Greyson offered.

"I told you I wouldn't."

"Why is this treaty so important to you?"

"For years we have been living in caution one with another. You question my people's allegiance to the crown, and we question whether you would act on your perceived threat. A treaty of peace would ensure you will not attack or displace my people from their homes, and that we would not go against the crown."

The king picked up his quill pen and thought a moment. The treaty he and Bernon had drafted sat on the table in front of him and outlined a potentially excellent agreement that would protect him, and in turn, the Gardiens. He turned to his chancellor. "What are your thoughts?"

The chancellor smiled. "I think you would be a fool not to sign it. The Gardiens are not dangerous, and their actions alone prove that."

Greyson returned the smile. He always appreciated his chancellor's candor. He turned to Bernon. "After your assistance and cooperation with our armies in the fight against the Hungau, I would be happy to grant a treaty between your people and mine," he said. "You have no history of instigating violence, and we are proud to recognize you as true citizens of Cascadia. This treaty states that we are to leave you and your people in peace and that you are not to defy the crown of Cascadia. The Forests of the North rightfully belong to the Gardiens, and we recognize the contributions your people make to our country."

In a triumphant, unifying move, King Greyson Montcroix and Bernon Wells both signed. It was a promise that would allow peace to reign throughout Cascadia without alienating one of her strongest assets.

The Gardiens of the Forests of the North, though secretive, had inhabited Cascadia many years prior to the royal line. Adept at weaponry, combat, and self-defense, the Gardien warriors played a crucial role in the history of Cascadia and continued to prove over and over that their loyalties rested with the crown and the country they loved. A century later, as one Gardien woman rose above the rest, that devotion to their king would demonstrate, yet again, how valuable they were to their nation, and to what lengths they would go to protect the crown and secure peace between the people.

CHAPTER ONE

ONE HUNDRED YEARS LATER

A billowing cloud of smoke rose high into the air. They saw it first, and then the familiar smell of burning wood reached their noses.

A Gardien team of four warriors had been sent out by their leader, Dagan Wells, for the sole purpose of discerning whether a certain report they had received was true. Wary of the Hungau, and not at all inclined to trust them over the past hundred years, this report had excited a flurry of anxious activity. It had come from a secret contact of Dagan's—the team didn't know his name and didn't ask. Dagan trusted him, and they trusted Dagan; that was all they needed.

The contact had informed Dagan that the Hungau were gathering their armies again. An attack to test their strength had been planned, but the contact didn't know when. He did know where. The team's job was to ride out to the small village of Treewell on the eastern coast where the supposed attack was to take place.

Despite their dormancy following the war in Volcania, the Hungau were now surrounded by fresh rumors. The Gardien team was fully aware of the fearful whispers that passed the lips of every citizen in Cascadia hinting at a Hungau resurgence. The rumors had gained strong momentum, but the Forests of the North shared a border with Eagle's Bay, so the Gardiens had regular run-ins with the former mercenaries. The skirmishes were always small and meaningless.

Four years ago, however, a single, terrible incident devastated the Gardiens, and sparked a turning point. Dagan's wife, Calida Wells, was savagely murdered by the Hungau while on a mission for the Gardiens. Her death had ensured the Gardiens' hatred, and it ran deeper than ever before.

Now, as the team approached Treewell, familiar fears manifested. The village was on fire and the citizens were panicked beyond their ability to act. The Hungau were much more active than anyone realized. They were back and had regained their strength and courage.

The team increased their pace to a gallop to reach the desperate village. What had started as a scouting party was now a full-blown rescue mission.

Maddox Ward, the leader of the team and one of Dagan's top military commanders, raised his hand and signaled for his men to fan out. If the Hungau were behind the fire, then they needed to be ready for battle.

The horrifying sound of screams reached their ears, but the awful scene before them forced them to swallow their terror and ride harder. Many Cascadian villagers were already dead and the bodies of the burned littered the ground. People who hadn't been injured in the fires were wounded by arrows and seaxes.

Maddox didn't know where to start. There were many wounded, but the fires burned hot and strong and were spreading quickly. To the south of the fires, many homes remained unsinged. In Maddox's mind, saving these homes and stopping the fires became the priority.

"We need to get the fires out!" he yelled to his team.

Two other Gardiens, Rawlins Emer and Casimir Atwood, veered to a nearby well and dismounted. As they organized nearby survivors to help draw water, their fourth team member, Danson Atwood, Casimir's brother, attended to the wounded.

Maddox braved the fires to look for any who had been caught.

The flames burned with an intensity he had never encountered. The heat made it almost impossible to keep his eyes open. He listened for cries, anything that would hint to a victim caught in the inferno.

The fires were too hot.

He pulled back and decided to use his energy to help Casimir and Rawlins contain the flames. As he ran down what used to be the main street, he caught a glimpse of a man running toward a nearby patch of trees.

The Hungau warrior wore a dark, sleeveless tunic. On each forearm was a leather guard, which Maddox knew carried deadly darts dipped in poison. Across the small of his back was the unmistakable outline of the seax, a large knife wielded expertly by the Hungau for generations. His dark breeches were wrapped in protective, pliable boots up to his shins and tucked by his right ankle was another dagger. With no end to their skill and use of weaponry, a bow and quiver was slung across his back. His hair was cut short on the sides, but a long tail of twists and braids fell down his back to his shoulders. His arms and face were covered with various muds and dyes to mimic the foliage of the woods.

What really caught Maddox's attention was the symbol on the warrior's left arm: a red X contained within a red circle. When the Hungau were ready for war, they marked themselves with this symbol. This warrior had it clearly painted for all to see. As he glanced back, he made eye contact with Maddox and a sickening smile crossed his lips.

A hatred that burned as hot as the fires beside him filled Maddox's chest. He scanned the treeline—where there was one, there would be more. He reached back and pulled an arrow from his quiver. It took no time at all to load his bow, and with the patience and skill of a stalking cat, he moved his arrow along the trees. Letting his instinct and training take over, his eyes zeroed in on the spot where he had last seen the Hungau.

The treeline was well out of range for most bowmen from his current position, but with only a flick of his finger, he released the arrow. Its whistling hiss sliced through the air and disappeared among the leaves. An instant later, a dead Hungau fell from the trees and landed with a dull thud.

Maddox smirked at the trees. That would be a message to all the Hungau. He knew they were there, and he was coming for them, each and every one. Calida had been like a mother to him after he lost his own parents, and he would not let her death go unavenged.

He turned his back on the woods and ran straight for the well. Tirelessly, they fought the fire while Danson organized the injured and dead. By the time the sun began to set, a light rain had started to pour. Maddox was exhausted and covered in ash and soot. They all were. The rain was a welcome relief, and soon the fires were out completely.

With the fires under control, Maddox turned to Danson. Duty far outweighed his fatigue.

"How many?" he asked.

Danson knelt on the ground and cradled a small bundle. He looked up at Maddox with tears in his eyes. "This boy was only three."

Maddox clenched his jaw and averted his eyes from the small body.

Danson released his hold on the young villager and covered his corpse with a blanket. "I have thirty bodies." His tired shoulders slumped. "I'm sure more were caught in the fires, but we won't know until we can organize the villagers and have them account for their loved ones."

"How many from wounds?"

"Ten died from seax and knife wounds."

Maddox swore. His eyes swept to the trees where he had seen the Hungau. "This was Hungau, you know."

Danson nodded. "We need to report this to Dagan and to the crown."

Maddox motioned for Casimir and Rawlins. "Rawlins, I want you to ride hard for the castle. Report this to King Montcroix."

"You got it."

"Casimir, will you stay and help Danson organize the remaining villagers? They'll want to know about the dead."

"What are you going to do?" Casimir asked.

Maddox mounted his horse. "I'm going to Dagan. He'll want to know immediately what has happened here today."

The men dispersed.

Rawlins' job was especially important. From Treewell, it would take at least two days to get to the castle, and he rode hard for his destination. When he reached the gates, the rain still had not stopped. He was wet and tired, and the dark of night had long been upon him.

He banged on the outer gate with his gloved fist. Rain dripped from his auburn hair.

"Who goes there?" a deep voice called from atop the lookout tower.

"My name is Rawlins. I seek an audience with the king. There has been an attack on the eastern coast."

The guards opened the gate and escorted him to the main castle doors. From there he was shown to a smaller side door where villagers could meet with the royal family. Usually, villagers had the opportunity to address their grievances on one day every week, called Grieves Day, but for such an emergency, Rawlins was granted immediate access.

When King Montcroix entered the receiving chamber, it was clear he had been awakened. Dressed in a long robe hastily thrust on over his bedclothes, the king still moved with a commanding grace that elicited a humble reverence from Rawlins.

He dropped to his knees and bowed. "Your Majesty, please forgive my late intrusion, but there has been a tragedy on the eastern coast."

"Please rise. What is your name?"

"Rawlins Emer, Sire."

"Rawlins, state your village."

"The Forests of the North. I come representing Dagan, the leader of the Gardiens. I have traveled from Treewell, Your Majesty, and I'm afraid the village has been destroyed."

The king stared at Rawlins for a moment. Rawlins knew the royal family had little interaction with the Gardiens, and his coming here, unplanned and unexpected, made his presence all the more shocking. If the king was shocked, he hid it well. Instead of asking about Rawlins' birthplace, he asked, "Destroyed?"

"By fire. Hungau warriors ransacked the village. By last count there are thirty dead, but I expect that number has risen."

The king sat on his throne. His tone became clipped, guarded. "You expect me to believe the Hungau are responsible for this?"

Rawlins furrowed his brow with a slight shake of his head. "We saw them leaving the village during the fire." He took a step forward. "About four years ago they started coming out of the woodwork, Your Majesty. Today they sent a clear message. They are out to attack again, and we must stop them."

"The Hungau have been dormant for a hundred years," the king retorted. "This was not the work of the Hungau."

"Your Majesty, I was just there! I saw with my own eyes—"

"What you saw was merely a terrible accident," he spat. "The Hungau are not active and our nation is safe. They remain in Eagle's Bay, as they have been ordered to do. You are wasting my time."

The king stood, a clear signal that Rawlins was dismissed.

"Will you even ride out and attend to Treewell?" Rawlins clenched his fists.

The king glared at Rawlins. "As sorry as I am to hear of all those deaths, what's done is done. What can I do? I appreciate you riding all this way to inform me of the situation. Our citizens are strong and capable, and they will rebuild their village, no doubt."

"But Sire!" A handful of guards came forward with swords drawn at Rawlins' outburst. He took a step back. "You must reconsider your decision."

"We've had a dry season," the king said, just as a clap of thunder echoed through the room. "Fires are bound to happen."

Rawlins was ushered out. The door was shut behind him.

He stood on the street, in the pouring rain, and surveyed the lush, green country surrounding him. A dry season? No one would believe that. He mounted his horse and rode back to the Forests of the North to give Dagan his report. The royal family wouldn't be coming to help. The Gardiens would have to fight the Hungau on their own.

As Rawlins rode through the night over the familiar countryside, he couldn't shake the incident at Treewell from his mind. For the first time he could remember, he felt a genuine lack of respect for the king he had been raised to revere. He just hoped he could hide his feelings from the villagers when the time came to tell them no aid or protection from their ruler would be forthcoming. They needed to look after themselves.

He dug his heels into his horse's flanks and rode hard, the thundering gallop matching his frustration step for step.

Miles away and still working tirelessly to help the poor villagers of Treewell, Danson had a solid count of fifty-nine either dead or missing. Twenty-five of those were unaccounted for, and it was presumed they had been lost in the fires.

He rubbed a hand through his light-brown hair and clenched his teeth to keep from shouting. So many lives had been lost, but for what purpose? Hungau history was fraught with plunder and sedition, and Danson hated them for it. The Gardiens had always been taught to care for others and to be solid, loyal members of their country. Danson looked at the poor, dead boy he recovered earlier. The Hungau only seemed to care about themselves.

The sun had risen long ago, and just as he put the last sheet over the last body and handed the list of the deceased over to the village's leader, a man on horseback rode into what remained of the village.

"We need help!" the stranger shouted.

The man slowed his horse and Danson stepped forward. "What's happened?"

"Bender Village is under attack!"

Danson cursed. "Hungau?"

"They attacked at dawn."

Danson mounted his horse and rode to the other end of the village to fetch his brother. "Casimir!"

Casimir looked up from his work. "What's the matter?"

"Bender Village is under attack!"

They wasted no time. After giving instructions to the village leader to relay a message to inform Maddox where they had gone, they raced hard to help the tiny ocean village. When they arrived, they could see they were too late. The entire town was on fire and no screams accompanied the flames.

Neither of them dared to voice what they knew in their hearts to be true.

Casimir looked at Danson. "I can't stand here and watch it burn," he said with a clench of his fists.

Danson only nodded. They moved closer to access the nearby well. In quick, urgent movements, they drew water to fight the flames. No one came to help them, save for the one man who had first warned them.

After some time on their own, Maddox appeared, having returned from his previous assignment. Casimir and Danson were grateful to see him.

"Where are the villagers?" Maddox shouted over the roaring of the flames.

"They're gone, Maddox. They're all gone." Danson turned away from the horrifying scene.

Maddox's eyes widened. He looked at the flames. "Men, this fire is too great. We can't get close enough to fight it or we'll also be consumed. We have to let it burn."

Casimir threw the wooden bucket he had been using and it shattered against the ground. He cursed. "I'm going to kill those Hungau if it's the last thing I do."

Maddox placed a hand on his shoulder. "I'm with you. But we need to get back to Dagan first and make a plan."

The team stepped back and watched the fires burn the once thriving town into nothing but cinders and ash. The town had housed nearly a hundred people, and not one of them had survived the Hungau onslaught. Reluctant to abandon the village but with no one left to save, the team mounted their horses to return home. Dagan would know what to do.

Deep in the heart of the woods where he lived, Dagan Wells stood at the door of his manor. Inside he was anxious, but the calm on his face would never betray him.

The Forests of the North had grown dark while he waited for his team, and though the peace of Cascadia had been disturbed, he felt safe among the confusing maze of trees and foliage. No outsiders knew how to find him or his people here, for the forested walls and vegetative cover protected them. Few had ever dared to cross their borders, though he often sent Gardiens to keep track of what happened outside this impenetrable, verdant fortress.

The clopping sound of horses approaching met his ears. The team returned to the Forests of the North, and Dagan gathered them as the Gardien Council.

They met in Dagan's council hall and relayed to him all they had seen and done. After recounting his unsuccessful conversation with the king, Rawlins asked, "Should I report Bender Village to him as well?"

Maddox shook his head. "Word is spreading of the attacks. I'd be surprised if the crown doesn't already know."

"That's what doesn't make sense," Casimir said. "Why wouldn't King Montcroix come investigate?"

Rawlins stiffened. "He blamed it on dry weather, remember?"

"I know you're all frustrated," Dagan said. "You have good reason to be. While you were gone, my contact brought more news." He took a deep breath. "The Hungau are planning an attack on the royal family."

A tense quiet stole upon the Council.

"With the king's lack of response, is that really a bad thing?" Casimir clenched his jaw.

"I agree," Rawlins said.

"I understand King Montcroix's actions are perplexing and reprehensible, but before we are sure of his reasons, let's refrain from speaking ill of the crown," Dagan chastised them. "If the Hungau attack the castle and bring down the royal family, they will take over Cascadian lands."

"I wouldn't let it get that far," Maddox vowed.

Dagan smiled, but it did not reach his eyes. "Neither would I. We need to act. We need to speak to the king, and we need to do it soon. Maddox, you've been watching the king's movements; is there anything that would work in our favor?"

"For the next three days he's supposedly traveling on the road south of our forests in an effort to reach out to the villagers."

Dagan turned to the one member of the Gardien Council who had not yet spoken. Willing to give her a little more training in political and diplomatic procedures, he decided that speaking with the king would be a good start.

"My daughter," he said, addressing the dark-haired beauty who resembled her mother exactly. "Go meet with King Montcroix. You know his location and can request an audience with him as he travels. Maddox will go with you."

Samara Wells, daughter of Dagan and heir to the Forests of the North, looked at her father with excitement in her eyes. "I would be honored to serve the Gardiens in such a capacity."

The Gardien Council adjourned and postponed any further action until Samara could meet with the king. They could only pray he would listen and accept the truth.

Chapter Two

Samara and Maddox took to the Forests on horseback. Raising horses in the Forests of the North proved a great asset to the Gardiens' ability to maneuver through the terrain; the horses were just as familiar with every rock, bump, and curve on the path.

After traveling for a day and spending one night on the road, they reached the western edge of the Forests. They had decided to approach the road from this side because it ran parallel to the Forests for one mile before taking a bend to travel east to the sea. It was considered a southern road by the Gardiens, while the rest of the country deemed it the North Road.

Samara dismounted her horse and looked up at the bright sun. Shielding her eyes, she carefully calculated how far the day had passed. The sun was not yet in the middle of the sky.

Maddox took a giant drink from his goatskin flask and surveyed the country around them. "Doesn't seem to be much activity around here."

"Do you think we missed King Montcroix?"

Maddox shrugged. "We'll rest here for a spell and then continue our mission."

Well-packed and ready for any contingency, Samara dug into their bags and pulled out bread and preserved cheese. "Here." She offered Maddox his share.

Maddox took it, raised it in the air as a thank-you, and dug in.

A mission to seek an audience with the king wasn't inherently dangerous, but Samara felt vulnerable without the protection of her woods. She glanced at her friend; he seemed perfectly at ease. Then again, Samara knew how often he traveled past the Forests' borders to fulfill assignments for her father.

"Why did my father let me go on this mission?" she asked.

Maddox paused midbite. "He felt you were ready."

Samara eyed him suspiciously. "Seems a little strange he let me go," she pressed, "considering the ban he's had on me for the last four years."

Maddox looked over a far hill. "It's true that he worries for you."

Samara wanted to roll her eyes, but she suppressed the urge. Her father had forbidden her to go on any missions beginning four years ago, when her mother's last assignment had proved fatal. It had not escaped her notice that suddenly he seemed willing.

"Come on, Maddox. You're the commander over his entire military, and you sit with him in every meeting and council. Why is he letting me go?"

Maddox finally faced her, a subtle grin on his lips. "I had to talk him into it," he admitted.

"Really?"

He nodded, without the slightest hint of shame. "I told him you were ready months ago, but his concern for your safety halts any clear thought."

"So, you're my nursemaid," she surmised. Irritation flared inside her.

"I don't think that title suits me, and you're hardly a baby."

Samara turned away. Maddox had been one of her best friends her entire life; to be treated in such a childish way at the age of twenty-two embarrassed her.

"Samara." Maddox stood, sensing her distress. "He was close to saying yes. Offering to accompany you sealed the deal. You're welcome."

Samara looked at her friend. "I am grateful," she said. "I just wish he'd trust my abilities."

"He does; that's why he has me train you nearly every day. So he doesn't have to worry about you."

Samara took a bite of her bread. It was no longer warm, but it filled her hungry belly with much-needed nourishment. "But he still worries."

His brown eyes met hers. "Yes, he still does, but you can't really blame him. You're the only family he has left."

All the Gardiens were trained in self-defense and combat. Those who exhibited exceptional ability made up Dagan's military. Maddox, whose own parents had passed when he was fifteen, trained hard and became an exceptional warrior. At the age of twenty-two, he took over Dagan's military as the lead commander and had been the commander for the last six years. Maddox personally oversaw the training of every Gardien man, woman, and child and handpicked each warrior he thought would fit best in the military. Samara's uncle Tristan, her mother's brother, helped Maddox oversee these tasks. Danson, Rawlins, and Casimir made up Maddox's leadership team.

Countless memories of her involvement in past missions flooded her mind. She had been a part of the team then, but since her father's ban she felt less and less needed. Samara had been training since she was young, and her lack of participation made her feel overlooked. As she grew and as Maddox began to excel, her father placed him as her personal mentor, and they trained almost daily. She didn't understand why her father had lost confidence in her skills.

"Don't worry, Samara. He'll come around in time."

She glanced up at Maddox, who still stood above her. "You'll help him get there?"

Maddox smiled wide. "I'd do anything for you. Especially if I know you are ready. Trust me, you're ready. You have great skill."

Samara reached out her hand and he helped pull her up. "You're not just saying that because you're my best friend, are you?"

Maddox laughed. "Of course not. I wouldn't deem anyone mission-ready unless I truly believed they were. Although, my knowledge and skill do add to my certainty."

Samara slugged him in the arm. "You can be so boastful."

He winked at her and returned to his horse. Samara watched him for a moment. Truly, Maddox was anything but boastful. He was thorough and confident, yes, but never boastful. He cared about every Gardien in the Forests, and Samara knew he viewed Dagan as a father. Dagan had stepped in to help him when he lost his father, and Maddox was loyal to Dagan in every way. He was a caring man despite his tough demeanor.

Samara stole an apple from her pack and looked around. "It certainly is quiet."

Maddox followed her gaze. "Yes. I'm afraid the king would have attracted more attention if he had come this way." He turned to her. "What do you think we should do?"

Samara thought about their options. "Let's do some tracking and see if we can determine where he might be. If we meet any citizens on the way, we can ask around."

Maddox nodded. "Lead the way."

Grateful for the opportunity to put her training into much-needed use, she mounted her horse and began a slow westward trot. If they traveled another day, they would reach the castle. As they made progress across the green, grassy fields of Cascadia, the wind shifted. She glanced at the sky, but it was clear.

"If a storm is coming," Maddox said, "we'll probably hit it on the way home."

She glanced at the sky one more time before focusing on their path. She kept her eyes peeled and her senses alert. When she glanced back at Maddox a time or two, she found he did the same. When Maddox was on a mission, he remained vigilant until all was complete.

As the path took a turn and headed southwest, they came to a fork. If they took the northern fork, they would head toward the castle. If they continued on the southern fork, it would take them to several outlying villages and a bigger town called Pondwood.

Samara looked at the ground for any indication of recent travelers. There were prints in the dirt, and the grass on either side of the trail had been bent toward the southern fork.

"What do you see?" Maddox asked her.

"A large party passed through here," she deduced. "Horses and a carriage."

Maddox pointed out the tracks. "Big wheels," he observed.

"Royalty?"

Maddox gave her a curt nod and looked toward the southern fork. "They must have headed to Pondwood first," he said. "Looks like we have company."

Samara looked down the road and saw a small wooden cart drawn by a single pony. There appeared to be only one driver, a villager by the looks of his dress. Maddox drew his horse beside and slightly in front of Samara's in a clear show of protection.

"Did my father ask you to protect me?" she asked in a low voice as the cart drew closer.

"You are the princess of our people, Samara," he replied without looking at her. "Your father doesn't always have to ask."

His response surprised her. Once upon a time it might have even given her hope that he had feelings for her that surpassed friendship. But her feelings had long since passed, and she saw him as the brother he always had been.

As the cart approached, Samara sat straighter in her saddle.

"Good afternoon, sir," Maddox called first.

"Good afternoon," the man said in return and slowed his cart.

"We're seeking an audience with the king," Maddox informed the man. "Is his party far from here?"

"You just missed them in Pondwood. They probably made it to Poolside earlier this morning."

"Thank you for the information," Maddox said.

The man stared hard at Samara. "She looks familiar. What is your name, miss?"

Maddox stiffened, but Samara felt perfectly at ease. The man was older and had a cart full of cabbages. He was hardly dangerous.

"I'm Samara Wells," she said with a smile.

The man's eyes widened. "Of the Forests of the North?"

She nodded once. "Yes, sir."

He stared at her, then climbed off his cart and went to the back. Maddox's hand shot for the hilt of his battle ax, but the caution was unnecessary.

In his weathered hand the man carried a beautiful head of cabbage. He approached Samara's horse. "If I may?"

"Of course."

He held the cabbage up for her to take. "As a gift," he explained. "The Gardiens have helped us on more than one occasion, but no one has ever seen the Wells daughter."

Samara was touched by the old man's sincerity. "Thank you for the cabbage," she said with gratitude. "It will greatly aid us on our journey."

"The honor is mine," he said with a bow of his head. "I remember when your father brought you to the castle as a babe to record you. It was the event of the year. No one will believe I met you!"

Samara laughed. "You are very kind, sir. We hope to help protect the people against the Hungau. That is why we travel today."

The man shuddered. "What happened on the coast has us all feeling vulnerable." He scanned the trees. "But I will sleep better knowing the Gardiens are out and about. The Hungau are a murderous lot. They have no right to live."

Maddox met her gaze, and a secret passed between them. Samara believed the Hungau were guilty of many crimes, but her very existence was proof that not all of them deserved such a fate. "Thank you again for your help, sir, and for the cabbage," she said, deciding to ignore his comment. "It was a pleasure to meet you."

"You as well, my lady." He nodded again to Samara then to Maddox.

Maddox dipped his head and watched the man retreat down the road where they had just come from.

"Let's go to Poolside," Samara said with excitement. "We may catch the king yet." She spurred her horse into an easy trot. It was several moments before Maddox caught up to her.

"You did well back there," he complimented her.

"With the old man?"

"Yes. Even when he unknowingly insulted you."

Samara studied him. "I was just talking. I thought it best not to let him know my ancestry. I have to believe I'm more Gardien than Hungau."

"You are a Gardien," Maddox assured her. "And you weren't just talking. It was something else. You have a way with people—you're personable and quick to forgive."

"Well, thank you." She didn't know what he meant. Having a conversation with a villager didn't seem like an extraordinary talent, but maybe kindness was. Maddox was also kind, but his wary and battle-hardened demeanor, she supposed, could be intimidating to some.

They trotted down the road, and just as the sky reached midday, they heard shouts. Uncertain where the voices were coming from, they glanced all around them until they saw a villager running in their direction.

"What is he saying?" Samara asked.

"Not sure. Get a weapon ready."

The sudden feel of arrows in the quiver on her back reminded her of their presence. She was so used to carrying them that she rarely felt them anymore. Her bow was hanging from her saddle on her right side and she unhooked it with her hand.

As the villager drew closer, his words became clearer. "Hungau! Hungau have been spotted east of Poolside!"

Instantly energized, Maddox whipped his head to Samara.

"I'm going," she said.

"No, you're not." The grip on his reins was as tight as his resolve.

"Maddox, you said I was ready."

He gritted his teeth and looked back toward the villager. "We need more information."

Samara didn't disagree, so she rode with Maddox toward the now running villager.

"Hungau!" he shouted.

"Where were they spotted?" Maddox asked.

The man was out of breath. "East of Poolside in the woods. The king just left."

"Are you from Poolside?" Maddox continued his questioning.

"I am. I decided to raise the warning bell. We don't need another massacre."

"Is the king vulnerable?"

"He's surrounded by knights, about twenty count, but word has it the prince was seen leaving the castle grounds."

"By what route?"

The man pointed north. "By the North Road."

Maddox cursed silently.

"You can't handle this alone, Maddox," Samara said. "The king is vulnerable to the south and the prince to the north. You need me."

He finally faced her and sidled his horse alongside hers. "I'll ride toward Poolside to search for the Hungau and try to speak to the king," he ordered. "You head north and see if you can find the prince. He doesn't need to be out with Hungau in the area."

"Yes, sir." She looked toward the north, her focus already on her mission. She forced herself to ignore the excitement rising in her chest.

"Samara."

Maddox's tone caused her to turn.

"Please be careful."

His brown eyes pierced hers so intently that the reality of the potential danger she faced settled over her. Her excitement became subdued.

"I'll be fine," she reassured him. "I'll head toward the North Road and look for the prince along there."

"If you don't find him, you head back to the Forests and straight to Dagan. Do you understand me?"

Maddox was no longer speaking to her as a friend, but as her commander. She would be expected to obey every order.

"Yes, sir."

His eyes lingered on her a moment longer, but they needed to get moving. "Head out," he said. "If you make it back to Dagan before I do, tell him where I am."

"You be careful, too, Maddox."

"Don't worry about me. I'll be fine. Just keep yourself safe." He turned his horse and started in the opposite direction.

"I will," she reassured him again.

"Good. I don't want to be the one to tell Dagan you're dead," he added, more gravely.

She rolled her eyes. "Then I'll tell him."

This got Maddox to turn back with a smile, and with a spur of his horse, he took off down the road.

Samara did the same, but in the opposite direction. She wasted no time getting to the North Road. The thrill of receiving such an assignment propelled her to her destination. That, and the desperate need to protect the crown and speak with the king. King Montcroix needed to be warned of the threat against the royal family.

As she made her way back toward the Forests along the northern road, she searched diligently for the prince. There was not a man in sight for miles around. Her horse, Taiga, was one of the fastest Samara had ever known, and his speed was unsurpassed. She kept him at a quick pace and retraced the steps she and Maddox had made earlier that day in record time.

As she rounded the bend that caused the road to straighten east toward the sea—the southern road to the Gardiens—she spotted the old logging mill nestled in a grouping of trees. Seeing no one around her, she entered the Forests to her left and led her horse to a small clearing where he could rest and eat the luscious grass.

She exited the Forests from the same point she had entered, crossed the road on foot, and ran straight for the mill. A low branch hung within arm's reach, and she used it to hoist herself up. She scaled the trunk and found a position on the roof of the now abandoned building.

It was there on her perch that she waited and searched the road below her. If the prince came this way, she would be the first to see him.

Chapter Three

As Samara crouched like a cat on the roof of the old mill, a sprinkle of rain started to fall on her shoulders. She turned her face to the sky to welcome the warm water. Dark clouds rolled in from the east, threatening the surrounding land with dull rolls of thunder and quick flashes of light. Apparently, the winds had finally brought the storm.

The view from high on her perch revealed no other travelers in either direction. So far, not a soul had wandered past her, but she could have missed the prince entirely. The mill gave her a great vantage point, but if the prince had turned toward Pondwood instead of maintaining a course on the North Road, she was in the wrong place.

She groaned. Maddox had assured her father she was ready for a mission. Could she have messed up already?

Maddox had also said to head straight home if she didn't find the prince right away. She eyed the road once more, debating her next course of action. She could stay here and watch the road from above, or she could return to her horse and ride until she found him. The tall trees surrounding the abandoned mill kept her well-hidden from the road, allowing her to relax her defensive stance. She rolled back so she now sat cross-legged and again wondered if she should go home or continue her search.

I can wait a bit longer, she thought. Regardless of what Maddox had asked her, she wouldn't leave the prince unprotected. Not only did they need to protect the prince, they needed to speak to the king. The Gardien Council was relying on her to fulfill both missions.

The wind picked up. She glanced down the path a second time to see if anyone was coming. Squirming in her outfit, she thought of her leather boots getting soaked by the rain—they would take days to dry out. She turned her gaze to the ever-thickening gray clouds. The rain descended harder now, more determined, but she matched it with her own resolve to finish her mission. Wet clothes would dry.

Samara's choice of style was vastly different than what was worn by the nobility. For comfort and ease of movement, she wore a pair of dark-brown breeches that fit tightly around her curvy waist. A pair of snug, brown leather boots, almost at the height of her knees, pulled over her breeches. A brown belt matched her boots and was home to a medium-length dagger, her number-one weapon of choice in close combat. Her forest-green, short-sleeved tunic had crisscrossing ties up the front and was slightly open at the neck.

Breeches were the logical choice for her duties as a Gardien. She only owned one dress, and it happened to belong to her mother. Female Gardiens generally did not wear dresses, but nobles within the royal court would notice her lack of formal wear. Fortunately, she rarely had to deal with them.

The sight of a horse coming up the road caught her attention and, with an instinct bred from years of training, she returned to her crouched position. The horse and rider crested a small hill, the horse a flash against the green. The horse's hair was pure white—soft and shiny like newly spun silk. The small amount of sunlight left in the sky glistened off its silky coat in such a way that made it glow.

She analyzed the horse's decorations next. You could tell the station of a rider depending upon how the horse was decorated. Where red and gold ribbons should have been attached to the snaffle bit to act as reins for a royal rider, there were plain brown leather ones instead. She concluded that this man was not royalty and rolled her eyes with impatience.

A second horseman appeared over the hill. Given his simple brown cloak and the rearward position of his horse in relation to the first rider, she recognized him as a servant. His horse was brown and smaller than the white horse. The rider himself looked lesser in stature compared to his companion. Although she had already concluded the first man was not royalty, she determined he must be a noble. Like the royals, some noblemen also had servants.

The first horseman, someone of rank, wore a plain red cloak over black riding breeches and a white tunic. Attached by a black belt, a long and decorated sword clung to his side.

She rolled forward to her knees and knelt there, frustrated that this man was not the prince she had been waiting for. She looked at his plain reins and then at his sword. The handle was beautiful, decorated with carvings and jewels. A perfect twist of the gold metal finished the look. In fact, it was *too* decorated. The fact that he had a servant made her think twice about her assessment.

The man had brown hair and olive-colored skin. Her eyes swept back to his sword. Unable to see any indication of rank on his person, the only thing to do was stop him. He could have seen the prince while on his travels and she could ask him about his location.

As the horsemen drew close, she held her breath and slowly let it out. With another breath, she reached over her shoulder for an arrow with her right hand, and gripped her bow firmly in her left. She jumped off the mill's roof and grabbed the limb of the nearby tree to help her swing down. Landing on her feet in front of the two horsemen with her bow drawn, she aimed at the nobleman's heart. They pulled their horses to a stop in front of her. Surprise at her sudden appearance crossed their features.

"Who passes this way?" She shifted her aim between the men. Her long, dark, wavy hair blew in the wind as the rain let up and made way for more sunlight.

The man on the white horse kept his hand on the hilt of his sword. "We are but travelers passing through."

"From where?"

"From a town not far off." His eyes flicked to his riding companion, but when they found her again, he tilted his head with curiosity. He guided his horse to circle around her, taking a special interest in her clothing. "Now, what may I call this fair lady who attempts to prevent our passing?"

She pulled her bowstring back harder and glared at him. "What is your name, sir? I must know who *attempts*," she put emphasis on the word, "to pass this way. I am looking for the prince of Cascadia." Reminded of her mission she felt her confidence rise, but he didn't answer her. Instead, he watched her intently from his horse. She noticed his gaze and was struck by the emerald shade of his eyes. They were expressive, deep, and conveyed his emotions. They pierced through her.

His eyes swept her clothes, her shoes, and her long, soft hair. He watched her fingers and how gracefully and effortlessly they held the bow and arrow in place. He took in everything before his focus landed on the dagger at her waist. A brief smile of admiration flashed across his face.

It was true her dagger was beautiful. The smooth, double-edged blade was topped with a polished silver handle etched with red and black swirls. A single ruby rested in the center of the pommel. The dagger had belonged to her mother and was one of few possessions Samara held dear in her heart.

The man rested his hand on the hilt of his own sword and stared at it, as if to compare the two weapons. He still did not say anything.

"Your name, sir," she commanded louder. Nobleman or not, he wasn't being helpful, and she was running out of time. If the Hungau were in the area and the prince was outside the palace, he was too vulnerable.

The man snapped out of his thoughtful state and looked at her with a glint of . . . what? The intensity in his eyes told Samara he was considering something. In the background, the servant had reached for his sword but did not draw it—as if he were unable to follow through without the command that would further elicit his actions.

Who are these men? Samara thought. "I ordered you to speak," she repeated.

"Why do you seek the Prince of Cascadia?" the nobleman asked.

"Hungau have been seen in the area and I worry for the prince's safety. Have you seen him on your travels?"

"Hungau? You must be mistaken."

"I assure you the mistake is not mine. I have asked you two questions, which you have not answered. State your name and tell me if you have seen the prince," she ordered.

At her comment, the nobleman lifted his chin and cast a quizzical brow, making it clear he was unsure what to make of her words. He even looked amused, as if he knew something she did not.

"You do not know to whom you speak, lady," the man in the red cloak said with a hint of humor. With perfect agility, he jumped down from his horse and took two steps toward her. He was a muscular man built for fighting. It wasn't farfetched to think he was a well-trained knight of Cascadia, and when her confidence wavered, she straightened her shoulders. Her energy spiked, and she prepared for the possibility of a fight.

"Your name, nobleman," came her impatient reply.

His body tensed for a moment before he relaxed again. His demeanor was calm and controlled. His eyes, however, betrayed all sorts of emotions: amusement, enjoyment, a secret . . .

"With your arrow drawn you must be ready to fight," he surmised.

"Perhaps."

"Even against two armed men?"

She had no choice but to be suspicious of his motives. He was a man of large stature and looked ready to defend himself in any fight, let alone against a woman, but she shook these thoughts from her mind as she recalled her training. Instead of backing down, she squared her shoulders and nodded.

With an unconvinced glance, he turned his back and strolled to his horse, pausing only for a moment to remove his cloak and place it over the saddle. He removed his sword belt, revealing another, smaller belt with a dagger. Setting his sword aside, he unsheathed his dagger and swiftly turned. With a quick step and a thrust of his arm, he struck out to disarm her.

He was fast, but she was prepared. She sidestepped and parried his thrust with her bow, tossed it aside, and with a flick of her wrist unsheathed her dagger. Catching him off balance, she closed the distance. As his dagger came down upon her again, her own blade rose to meet it. There was a clang as metal struck metal, both weapons stopping a handsbreadth from her throat. Standing taller than her by a head, he leaned into his position. She responded in kind by using both of her hands to apply counterpressure. His eyes betrayed his surprise at her quick reaction and his jaw clenched as he applied a bit more force.

Despite his intention to overpower her, his dagger faltered. As the experienced fighter he seemed to be, his choice to use it instead of his sword was foolish. He was holding back and did not give the fight his full strength. Irritated and confused by this insight, she realized he was clearly enjoying himself, and his movements were precise.

The servant took a step closer and drew his sword.

"Don't move," she yelled to him. "You come any closer and your master dies."

The servant halted and lowered his sword, but he kept it firmly in his hand. She could feel his eyes on them as he watched carefully from the side.

She fixed her gaze on the stranger with emerald eyes and he stared back at her. "You need to leave," she warned him.

"It appears, my lady, that you carry the disadvantage and speak unwisely." He looked over her features, their faces only a breath apart. His eyes again came to rest upon hers. "Perhaps I should explain why." Before she could respond, he released his dagger and took a step back.

What had been allusive before was now right before her eyes. On the left side of his tunic was a familiar emblem: a shield divided into four quadrants, each holding a different image. In the first quadrant was a griffin, in the second was a winged lion, the third held the scales of justice encircled by a laurel wreath, and the fourth contained a sword crossed by two yellow Cascadian roses—their country's flower. A phrase draped across the bottom of the shield read, "Deo, Patriae, Libertas." *God, Country, Liberty.* At the topmost part of the shield, the wings of the legendary phoenix framed the symbol of a crown.

Samara could not contain the gasp that escaped her lips as she was forced to acknowledge she had made a terrible, terrible mistake. "'Travelers passing through,' yet you wear the crest of the king?" she accused.

"Are we not in Cascadia?" he grinned. "My king is but your king as well."

"And with what title shall I now address you?" She asked, but she wasn't sure she wanted to know the answer. Wearing that crest made him more than a noble; he was likely a member of the royal family. Her plan had taken a detrimental turn.

He leaned against his horse and looked her square in the eye. "Let's just say I'm with the royal party. Now," he said with finality, "what is your name, lady? Speak."

Samara couldn't speak—having confirmed he was with the royal party only made the butterflies in her stomach come to life. Who was he? Was he related to the king? Was he a friend of the king? *Who?* Was this man the prince?

If he was related to the king, she had made a grave mistake indeed. She was certain any threat to kill a member of the royal family was not easily forgiven.

"You refuse to cooperate with a request as simple as your name?" he pushed, addressing her silence.

She pursed her lips and stared hard at the man who had just attacked her, deciding whether she should comply. *He could be a member of the royal family*, she reminded herself. Even so, he hadn't yet introduced himself, and Maddox told her to be careful. Her first name would do until she discovered his identity. "Samara," she finally said without looking away.

"Samara," he repeated, looking thoughtful. "Your name holds great meaning." He bowed and let a small smile cross his face. "At your service, my lady."

"What do you know about my name?" she said, surprised at the stranger's knowledge. He was an educated man, and he wore the crest of the king. As Samara pieced together the puzzle, she became more convinced of his status. This did not bode well for her, and she stepped away from him. The more she interacted with him, the more foolish she felt—his commanding presence and mysterious manner, combined with the high probability of his royal relations, made Samara wish she were somewhere else. However, she also felt a desire to learn more about him. It wasn't every day she met a royal, fought with him, and lived to tell about it. She struck that last thought from her mind; today was not over yet.

"Your name," he replied, breaking her from her thoughts, "means 'watch' or 'outlook.' Its roots are Cascadian."

She raised her eyebrows. His education must have been the royal kind: extensive and thorough.

Almost reading her thoughts, he replied, "There are a few of us in the castle who have some intelligence."

Without knowing his title or name, she still wasn't quite sure how she should interact with him. The man must have seen her hesitation despite her attempts to hide it.

"I mean you no harm, Samara." He sheathed his dagger and held out his hands, palms up.

The gesture was meant to make her feel welcomed and safe; it did not work. "So, picking fights with women and refusing to identify yourself when asked is something you do regularly?" she chastised.

A small smile crossed his lips. "Occasionally."

The dagger, she still held before her, debating whether she should sheath it. She glanced at the servant who still watched her with his own sword close by, and then looked back at the man. She sensed rather than knew he was not angry with her. Convinced, she replaced her dagger to her waist.

"Your name, please?" she asked.

He looked back at his servant. The servant shook his head, but he ignored the other man's caution. "Nickson Montcroix," he said with a hint of resignation.

Dumbfounded, she stared at the stranger in front of her, but she had a place and there were rules to follow. She averted her eyes and cast them to the ground, but she couldn't repair what she had just done to the king's own son, the prince of Cascadia! Embarrassment threatened to seize her, but she fought it.

"It appears I owe my prince an apology." She lowered her knees to the ground and took a bow, placing the palms of her hands on the ground. "I'm sorry," she swallowed hard, "Your Highness." She resisted the urge to smack herself in the forehead as she thought about what her father would say. He certainly tried hard to raise his daughter, but no amount of training would undo the mess she had created today.

Without looking up to see, the prince moved forward and crouched in front of her. She had threatened and fought with him—she could be hanged for something like this. The more she thought about it, the more frustrated she became. He had knowingly trapped her by not revealing his identity at the start.

"My lady, what urges you to such a quick surrender?"

The edge of his voice contained a hint of suppressed laughter as he spoke and an angry heat rose into her cheeks, but she kept her head bowed and her eyes averted out of respect for the crown. "Not surrender," she clarified, "respect." With more anger and defiance filling her limbs, she looked up into his face. "To the *royal* family."

The prince's full smile grated on her patience. Angry and embarrassed, she considered letting him handle the Hungau on his own. He was more than capable. She grabbed her bow from the ground, stood and turned, unable to take his gaze any longer.

"My lady, I'm sorry. I didn't mean it." His hand flew to her elbow, but his hold was gentle.

She spun to face him. "I could be hanged for the way I behaved toward you. You, a member of the *royal family*."

He was unrepentant. She turned again, and this time marched away.

"You still haven't explained why you think the Hungau are out to find me." He folded his arms. "Unless you have a different reason for stopping me."

She stopped in her tracks. Her frustration and embarrassment had almost caused her to forget the reason she was here in the first place. She turned back. "It certainly wasn't to play fighting games in the middle of the road."

The prince laughed. "You gave me no choice, my lady." He bowed his head to her. This time it was genuine.

Stunned by the gesture, Samara's anger fled. Traditionally, a bow from royalty was reserved as a respectful acknowledgment for people of equal status or station. Most did not receive a bow, even with position. Gardien though she was, she certainly did not expect to receive such a kind action from a person of royal blood.

There was no reason why he should bow to her, but the action engendered a mutual feeling of approbation between them. Being respected by a man who acquired respect by law made Samara feel well above her position.

A smile played at the corners of her mouth. The prince seemed forgiving of her earlier mistake, and despite his position, had shown deference. She was a Gardien and could have gone her entire life without ever seeing one of the members of the royal family, let alone receive a bow from one. Considering how events had played out so far, their unconventional meeting was a stroke of luck. One, he was safe and not in any harm. Two, if she could take him back to meet her father, they could discuss the growing problems with the Hungau.

They were still exposed in their current position on the road and a short explanation would have to do. "Your Highness, we must get you to safety. The villagers are feeling vulnerable with Hungau spotted in the area, and my companion has ridden toward the king to speak to him and help protect him."

Nickson shook his head. "The king has his guard to keep him safe. He has traveled by way of Pondwood to see to the people. What happened to those villages is tragic," he said, "but civil disputes are not unheard of within our country, and the Hungau remain in Eagle's Bay as they have been ordered to do."

"Civil disputes?"

"Yes, in Treewell and . . ." the prince trailed off. "My lady, why do you think I'm in danger?"

"Your Highness, what happened in Treewell and Bender Village were not civil disputes."

Nickson furrowed his brow. "Forgive me, but I don't believe you're correct."

Does he really think the decimation of those villages was caused by the villagers themselves? Samara thought. *His Highness's ignorance of the Hungau threat to Cascadia makes him vulnerable. This, along with the threat of attack, definitely puts him in danger.* She eyed her surroundings, whether to seek out the hidden Hungau or to seek answers to this perplexing development, she wasn't sure.

Without any real answers, leading the prince out of the open was the best thing to do, and given the good and forgiving nature of the man before her, it would be wise of her to befriend him.

"If Your Highness has no other plans for the day, I would be happy to show you around my land."

"Your land?"

Samara bit her lip. If she was going to befriend him, she had to tell him the truth. "Well, my father's land. I will inherit the Forests after he passes."

Recognition dawned on Nickson's features. "Your father is Dagan Wells? You are Samara *Wells*?"

"Yes, Sire."

Nickson bowed again, though much lower than the first time. "No one has ever seen his daughter," he considered with surprise. "But rumors have told of a beautiful maiden, as fair as the sun on a summer's morning."

Samara could only laugh. "I'm afraid I am far from legendary. Any rumors you may have heard are largely untrue."

"Hmm, I disagree. They do you no credit," he complimented.

She smiled in spite of herself. "What else do these rumors say? Hopefully, they tell of a fierce competitor, hunter, and warrior."

"After our encounter, I'm sure I can spread the word." He smirked. The prince then glanced at his servant.

Samara followed his gaze. She had forgotten the servant was even there. "Your servant may come with us to see my father," she invited him.

"We appreciate the invitation, but I have an errand of my own for him." Nickson turned to his servant. "Marshal, ride back to the castle and tell my father I will be visiting with Dagan Wells. He needn't wait for me, and I will report back when I return home."

The servant nodded without saying a word and climbed onto his horse. He rode off and left Samara and Nickson standing there on the gravel road alone.

"Shouldn't he come with us? I would hate to get the Prince of Cascadia in trouble by being alone with him, unprotected," she hinted.

Nickson feigned insult. "Were you absent during our fight? I am more than capable of defending myself," he teased. "And I don't care what anybody says. I like Marshal, but I'm tired of being followed around. I am far more interested in that tour you promised me. No one steps foot in the Forests of the North."

"Perhaps people are afraid," she offered.

"Afraid?"

"Yes. The Forests of the North are haunted," she lowered her voice. "There is a legend that says all of the dead spirits of the Gardiens return to the Forests to guard and protect it. That's why they call us Gardiens."

He chuckled. "I'm fairly certain that is far from true."

"Perhaps it's not," she said, catching his eye. "You ready for your ghost tour?"

Nickson's eyes sparkled with excitement. "I must confess, I am very intrigued to see what the Forests look like."

Anxious for this time that lay ahead with the prince of Cascadia, a shiver of excitement worked its way up her spine. "Let's go to the Forests, Your Highness. You're going to love them."

Chapter Four

They moved east down the road at a steady pace, Nickson leading his horse by the reins. All former traces of urgency and danger seemed to fade away in the wind, but Samara had not lost her focus and kept her eyes peeled just in case. Dark clouds continued to roll across the sky, but their presence was in direct contrast to her mood.

She looked at the prince out of the corner of her eye. "Are you positively sure you want to be alone with someone who is three times less your station and also capable of killing you?" she said, half teasing.

He gave her a sidelong glance. "With someone so beautiful, I don't see the downside."

She stopped and looked at him. "That is the second time you have mentioned my beauty," she pointed out. "Am I to understand that the prince is the biggest charmer in all of Cascadia?"

Nickson folded his arms and put a hand to his lips as if in thought. "Is this your opinion of me?"

Samara studied him. "Hmm. No. I find you much more genuine."

Nickson beamed a triumphant smile. They continued walking.

"By no means am I beautiful. There are women at court who would qualify for the beauty you seek. Perhaps they would be better served by your affections and compliments."

He cringed. "Thank you, but no. I find that the women at court are boring and dull. They can't even buckle their own shoes."

"And you prefer?"

"A woman with much more ability," he stated, giving her another sidelong glance to gauge her reaction.

The prince was an interesting person; much different than she imagined a prince would be. He was formal, that was true, but it was necessary for his position. From what she could gather, he also had a rebellious, individual side. She found it refreshing and unlike anything she expected of a nobleman.

He's not a noble, she reminded herself. *He's royal.*

She looked up at him and found him staring, his green eyes bright and intense. She analyzed them, and what she saw was a clear, transparent honesty. It was the kind of honesty human beings were drawn to—where men could trust, and women felt safe.

Samara had heard many good things about the prince, but had never had the chance to see if they were true. He was always described as a man whom men were willing to follow into battle, a man of integrity and kindness. During their fight, if she could call it that, she recognized a drive for action that she often felt in herself. He may be kind and sincere, but he was also competitive and intense. She was struck by his ability to balance the opposing characteristics. She envisioned a horse being controlled by its rider. The horse was power, aggression, and nobility, but the rider was kindness, direction, and safety. The prince was truly a master, it seemed—not just of people, but of himself.

They walked a few paces in silence and for not one instant was it awkward. For having just met it was fairly comfortable, but her earlier behavior was inexcusable and she needed to apologize.

"I—" she began, just as Nickson also started to speak.

They looked at each other and laughed.

"I apologize for what happened back there," he continued. "It was unfair and rude. I thought you were a common thief."

"The fault is all mine. I assumed you weren't royalty, but even if you were just a nobleman, I should have more respect."

"Now, I know you don't mean that. As rich as they are, you and your family are probably far more respectable than most," he said.

"Thank you," she replied. "By the way, your horse is a beautiful creature."

"Thank you. Her name is Kalia. I've had her for four years. She's one of the better horses in the stables. One of my best friends, you could say."

Samara understood the sentiment exactly. Her horse, Taiga, was her best friend, but surely the prince had others, human others. "What brings you so far east of your home, Your Highness?"

"I was going for a ride. It's a time for me to be alone, save for the one servant my father insists I bring along."

"You like to be alone?" She recalled her childhood excursions exploring the Forests and land around Cascadia. If she had not been able to roam as a child, she wouldn't have been able to live as freely. With her father's current ban, however, she had been feeling trapped, more so than any other time in her life.

"It's better than being surrounded by servants, and guards, and cooks, and false friends, and, you know, the whole scene of royalty. What about you, my lady? What brings you here?"

"Call me Samara, if you will," she offered with the hope he wouldn't find her too impertinent.

"Samara." He dipped his head and smiled at her.

She looked away—his eyes captivated her enough as it was. "This is my father's land," she began, waving her hand across the road and toward the Forests. "The Forests of the North are safe ground for my people due to the Treaty of Peace."

"Ah," Nickson replied. "The treaty."

"My people dwelt here many, many years ago," she said. "One hundred years ago, the king of Cascadia—"

"My great-great-grandfather," Nickson interrupted with a smile.

Samara smiled. "Your great-great-grandfather was a brilliant leader. Because he worked with the Gardiens, we have maintained an alliance."

"Cascadia is fortunate," the prince agreed. "We've had a long reign of peace."

"Except for the Hungau," Samara tried again. "They are a terrible people. We were experts on the Hungau when the treaty was signed, and we still are. We've fought them before." She glanced up at Nickson, gauging his reaction. He looked doubtful.

"You speak of the Hungau as if they are still conquering nations. They are legendary, yes, but hardly a threat now."

Samara shook her head. Rawlins had told her the king's explanation of the fires that claimed Bender Village and Treewell. He didn't believe the Hungau were to blame, but with so many eyewitnesses and the word of the Gardiens backing up the claims, how could the royal family ignore something so obvious?

"The worst enemy is the enemy you know nothing about," she said. "Over the last fifty years the Hungau have rebuilt themselves. My family has had close experiences with them, and they continue to thrive. They conquered, Your Highness, and they still do."

Nickson clenched his jaw. "Samara, perhaps the affairs of the kingdom are best left to the members of court."

Samara was completely taken aback by his comment. An image of her mother on the day of her death hit her and the memory surfaced despite her desire to keep it locked away.

An angry flame within caused her face to flush. It had been a painful time for the Gardiens, and her mind wandered to that time four years ago . . .

Samara rode Taiga hard. She, with a few others, raced to where the scouts had reported trouble at the border. They sent a messenger to bring backup. She was the fourth member of the rescue team that had been organized to help the other Gardiens in distress.

Her mother's team.

She steered Taiga to the location and came upon a gruesome scene. The scouts were too late, and so was Samara.

The stench of burning bodies almost made her turn back. As they approached the southeastern border of the Forests of the North, they could see four large stakes driven into the ground. Four victims were hung and burning—three she recognized.

The fourth was shriveled, burned, and blackened like a piece of overcooked meat. The smell was even worse. The Hungau war symbol, a red X within a red circle, had been painted on each one. The biggest one had been painted on her mother.

Her mother.

Her mother was burning before her very eyes. Already dead.

"When do I get to see this land of yours? Or meet your father?" Nickson interrupted her horrifying thoughts.

Samara stopped short. The anger refused to subside; she had been a witness to the terrible truth that the Hungau were indeed back. For Nickson to brush her aside so easily stung, but what she felt toward the Hungau would not be satisfied. "Maybe this was a mistake," she said.

Nickson was caught off guard by her change of attitude. Samara couldn't help it; just thinking about what had happened to her mother made her feel angry all over again. "It's been ages since anyone stepped foot in our forests, and the treaty defends our right to prevent passage."

He stepped closer to her, his eyes ablaze with sudden, helpless frustration. "Am I a threat?" Hurt clouded his tone.

Samara averted her eyes. She thought carefully before she spoke. "I would hope not, Your Highness, but you tell me."

"I'm not a threat," he observed, "but you are angry with me for something, and I know not what."

She did not look at him. If she did, she might blurt out everything she was feeling. She wanted to raise her voice and accuse the prince of leading with his eyes closed. She wanted to ask why he didn't believe her about the Hungau. Her mother's death was a sure testament of the Hungau's thirst for violence and domination. Would her mother have died for nothing?

"I know my place with the royal family." She fixed her eyes on him. "And it isn't here, walking with you down a road with no protection for your sake and with no escort for mine." These were not her real reasons, but they would do, for now.

It was apparent that Nickson was confused by the sudden turn their acquaintance had taken, but she didn't care. The anger still burned as hot as the memory.

"Samara, will you please explain to me what I have done?"

His boots were as high as her eyes would go. She forced herself to breathe slow, deliberate breaths to calm herself down. As silence reigned between them, she considered the outcome of her actions. If she alienated him now, she would never understand why the royal family seemed uninterested in listening to any claims concerning the Hungau. If she didn't take him to her father now, who knew when their next opportunity would be? Being emotional wouldn't help her get answers, or help the villagers get aid from the crown, so she forced her emotions away from the front of her head and away from her heart, letting them come to rest in a safe corner of her mind. By doing so, she regained her focus on the mission she had started that morning.

"Forgive me, I am not used to outsiders coming to the Forests. I feel protective." This was partially true.

Nickson didn't respond right away. The friendly line they had crossed earlier had been put back in its place, and neither knew how to respond. Their first awkward silence surrounded them.

"I would like to see your land," he tried again, but with less enthusiasm. "If now is not a good time, I will return to the castle."

Answers to all the Gardiens' questions wouldn't happen in a single moment. It would take time. Determined to be patient, she again shoved her emotions aside so she could be rational. "I would like you to meet my father and see my home," she stated. "Come, we will enter over here."

She led the prince through a small opening in the trees, and their world transformed. Thick shrubbery and evergreen pines engulfed them. The speckled bark of the aspen and birch trees tangled with the fountain-shaped elms. Tall fir trees twisted and twined with the billowy ash. The friendly white flowers of the dogwood trees dotted the landscape here and there, only to be overcome by vines of ivy. The immediate solitude and quiet that surrounded them was a comfort to Samara. So dense and lush were these woods that it disoriented any traveler. The road they had left behind disappeared upon their entry, as did the world outside this mysterious green realm of never-ending foliage.

"Samara," Nickson began, but he stopped when his voice was swallowed by the environment. He touched the soft leaves of a nearby tree. "Samara, there are many kinds of trees and shrubberies here," he said, astounded. He took two steps forward and stopped to look behind him. They were barely ten paces from the forest's edge, but the entrance, seemingly distant because of the entanglement of plant life, was obscured from their view.

Thunder rolled above them, and he glanced up to check the sky. The denseness of the foliage obscured his vision so much that he could not see the sky to tell how far the storm was.

Samara watched his uncertainty and his bravery fight between themselves. She knew the effect the forest had on those who didn't know it well, and she smiled to herself when she saw the prince unconsciously put his hand on the hilt of his sword.

"The trees have eyes and ears," Samara said, and placed her hand on the trunk of a nearby tree. "They know whether you are friend or foe."

Nickson fixed his gaze on hers. "And what do you say? Am I friend or foe?"

"I think I will do like the trees," she said, "and wait." She pointed to a hidden path. "Come this way."

Nickson's footsteps were tentative and careful, but he followed behind her. "Are you sure these woods are safe? You do know where you're going?" he asked.

She smiled. "If you get lost in these woods, I am the only person who could find you again. But don't worry, you won't get lost with me. Not in these woods, at least."

Nickson looked around him. "It certainly is dark, though it must be after noon."

Samara nodded. "These forests offer us excellent protection. Now, are you ready for the journey?"

"Journey?" he questioned.

She led him to the tree where her horse was tied. "I met your horse this morning, and now I introduce you to mine. This is Taiga." She approached her large, ebony horse and gently stroked his head.

"He's beautiful," Nickson admired him.

"He's fast and reliable. He was a gift from my mother, and one of my best friends, you could say," she said with a smile.

Nickson smiled. "We certainly agree on that point."

Samara bowed her head. "I will lead you and your horse through the Forests. We'll move as quickly as we can, but you'll need to follow my trail exactly. I would not want Kalia to get injured on this terrain. If we push through today and tonight, we can get there by midnight. If you feel Kalia is not up to the journey, I can go fetch another horse for you. In that case, it would take us two days."

Nickson interrupted her. "Pardon me, but two days?"

"Yes," she said, her tone playful, "two. Will Kalia be all right? Taiga can maneuver the terrain quickly and show her the way."

The prince glanced at his horse. "She's battle-trained. If she has a good leader, she'll do fine."

Samara untied Taiga and grabbed his reins. With graceful movement, she jumped onto the beast's back and steered him toward home.

Nickson mounted his horse and stepped in line behind Taiga. "Lead the way, my lady."

"It's Samara," she corrected with a grin. "Yah!" she yelled to Taiga while kicking her heels into the horse's sides. The beast took off with lightning speed, and the prince's horse fell into step behind them without missing a beat. Taiga, sure-footed and agile, knew the forest ground and surrounding trees better than Samara did. Nickson seemed more than capable of keeping up; Kalia was in good hands. As they sped through the forest together, Samara smiled to herself.

They continued to ride for a time on invisible roads only

Samara could see, trotting at various paces depending on the incline and shape of the land. The horses never faltered and rarely slowed to a walk.

Soon, they approached a vast, grassy field, and it was here where Samara stopped. A river in front of them stretched twenty paces across: the swift current flowing to a tree line's edge and disappearing into green shadow. Sunlight bathed the area with warmth, reflecting off the water like many small jewels.

"The storm seems to have passed. We'll stop here. I assume you are thirsty," Samara offered. She jumped off her horse and approached the river.

Nickson nodded. "Yes, my lady."

"Samara," she corrected him.

She dipped her leather water flask into the stream, the cool water lapping around the flesh of her wrist. Nickson's eyes were on her back, and her thoughts drifted to the possibility of spending a night on the road with the prince. With Maddox, or any other Gardien, traveling overnight was always expected, especially on a long journey. The prince, however, was an entirely different circumstance. Grateful for the fortunate turn of the weather so their trip wouldn't be unnecessarily delayed, she determined they wouldn't have to sleep if they pressed on. When she stood, she saw that his eyes had not moved.

"Are all Gardien women as capable as you are?" he asked.

Samara approached him with the water and handed it to him. "A good majority. These forests have taught me a lot."

He shook his head. "Ladies first," he replied. He held the pouch out to her while she hesitated to take it. Only after the prince took his drink should she also drink from the same flask.

Nickson noticed her hesitation. "You worry about station, yet it is I who am the guest here." He held up the water again. "Drink."

She licked her lips, unable to ignore the dryness of her mouth, and took his offering. She took a long drink and then held it up for the prince to use. Inside, she wondered if he really would drink after her.

Nickson locked eyes with her, almost as if he had heard her unspoken question, and took the leather pouch. He took an even longer drink and replaced the cap. "Thank you," he said.

For a moment, all Samara could do was stand there with astonishment. How could a man of his status bear to drink after someone who was of lesser station? It didn't make sense.

It wasn't until Nickson spoke that she realized she had been staring. "Is something the matter?" he asked.

"Um, no." She looked away. "No, I don't think so," she said as she turned to take care of the horse.

"Good. Should we get moving? How much longer will we be traveling?"

Samara adjusted the saddle straps as Taiga took a drink from the river. "The sun is setting, and it isn't far. We have a short way to go. First, we'll cross the river. If you want to stay on Kalia, I'll maneuver you through the water."

Nickson climbed on his horse, but when he saw Samara take her place on the ground holding Kalia's reins, he objected.

"I will lead. You don't need to get wet."

"Thank you, Your Highness, but there is a stone path under the water. I have crossed this river many times and know how to get safely across without getting more than the soles of my boots wet." She smiled.

Nickson studied the water. "If you are certain."

Samara picked out the familiar rock path and led their small party through the water. When they reached the other side, she mounted and continued to lead them through the trees. As they emerged from the other side, she stopped.

"Here," she said, and they both jumped down. She brought him to the rocky edge of a cliff. Far off to their left was a beautiful, cascading wall of water that fell into a large, bowl-like valley. The cliff, which seemed like a barrier, was like a giant step to the next level of the land. The forest continued to grow down the side of the mountain on which they were standing and continued as far as the eye could see. Far off in the east, the glassy ocean surface stretched to the horizon. Nickson looked on in disbelief.

"I don't believe it," he whispered. "It's beautiful."

The cliff stretched and curved to their left. It always made Samara feel like she was standing on the highest point in the world.

"I had no idea this existed."

"That's because no one does, Your Highness." She stretched her hand out toward the valley. "You are about to enter the heart of the Forests of the North."

He let his eyes linger for a moment on the majestic scene before he turned to Samara. "All of Cascadia is impressive to me, but these forests capture her essence entirely."

A shimmer of pride ran down her spine. She loved her home and its beauty and felt privileged in this moment to show it to someone else. As she watched the prince admiring the scenery, she weighed her options. She could talk to him now about her important business, or she could wait until they were in the presence of her father. She looked down into the bowl where the council would be waiting for her and then back at the prince. She decided she would wait. She wanted him to be in good spirits when he met her father.

As they journeyed on, the comfortable companionship returned between them. They didn't talk as much; both enjoyed the quiet solitude of the forest as they rode, but as they neared her father's home, an anxiousness fluttered within her about the exchange that would occur between him and the Gardien Council. She didn't want him to feel bombarded when he sat down in her father's council hall, especially when his beliefs of the Hungau were completely wrong.

"Is everything all right, Samara?" Nickson asked.

Samara stared at him in surprise. "How could you tell?"

"I'm not sure," he answered. "You just look like you have a lot on your mind."

She stopped and took a deep breath. "The Hungau started

those fires in Bender Village and Treewell, Your Highness. Your family is in great danger, as are all of the citizens of Cascadia. My father received word that they are making preparations for an attack. He sent me and his military commander to speak to your father, but we were delayed when Hungau were spotted. You had been seen leaving the castle and we split up—I was to protect you and my partner went to your father. The Hungau are a growing threat, and the Gardiens believe we should be working together to stop them. My father will want to discuss this with you."

As she explained, Nickson's jaw grew ever more tense. He jumped down from his horse. "You and your partner heard my father was out visiting the villages because of the fires?"

Samara nodded. "Since organizing a meeting would have taken a while, and we are still a few days from addressing grievances at the castle, the fastest idea we could come up with was to meet him on the road."

Nickson was silent as he assessed her explanation. When he didn't respond, she continued.

"Not only did we receive a reliable report from a reputable source, but the townspeople are whispering. There are dark rumors of a revolt against the king and his royal family."

Nickson rubbed a hand through his hair. "You must be mistaken."

She put her hands on her hips. "You're not concerned? You don't believe me?"

"Samara, I would like to believe you. It's just, well, the villagers have been disagreeing over source water for a while. My father sent the royal guard to investigate these reports of the Hungau and he found nothing. What he did find were disputes. He's been dealing with these grievances for months, and if there is a rebel force threatening the crown, we have our cavalry. I'm not worried."

"These rebels," she said with urgency, "are warriors and murderers." She looked at him directly. "They will stop at nothing. We've had problems with them before."

"And your people are still intact," he argued. "I don't think this needs to be discussed with the king. We've dealt with these rumors about the Hungau, but there is no evidence or proof."

The prince was uninformed about the threat against his own country, but even her understanding of that didn't ebb her rising anger. "What do you need in order to believe what I am telling you? Gardien warriors saw Hungau rebels around the villages during the attack. The villagers are seeing them periodically around Cascadia."

Nickson looked deep into her eyes, but he was not seeing her. His eyes were far away, looking at some moment long since passed. "My lady, listen to what you're telling me," was all he would say.

He knew nothing about the Hungau; otherwise, he would summon the appropriate concern. She decided to further explain. "Your Highness, do you understand why this is bad news?"

Nickson shrugged.

"There is a rebel group after you and your family. This isn't just any rebel group. It's the Hungau."

"The Hungau," he scoffed, "are the reason I'm hesitant." He shook his head. "You really believe they are able to conquer my country?"

"Yes."

Nickson rubbed another hand over his hair and removed his cloak. His eyes were unfocused, still lost in thought.

"Your Highness, I am sorry to bring you bad news—" she began.

"There is no proof the Hungau are in motion," he interrupted.

Samara's jaw fell slack in disbelief. "No proof? Is my word not enough? Are the cries from the dead not enough?"

"No offense against your honesty, but before a war is decided upon, one must see some proof!" he exclaimed. In a moment of frustration, he muttered, "You could just as easily be trying to rob me."

"Rob you?" she said, flabbergasted. "I could have killed you back on that road if all I wanted was your gold."

"You misunderstand me, Samara. I was only trying—"

She was too angry to let him finish. "I should not have brought you here. Your naïvety and lack of experience mean death."

"'My naïvety and lack of experience'?" he shot back. "At least I am not as naïve to try to convince the king that he knows nothing about what is happening on his lands. You will never get him here to discuss matters of war when there is no war to be had."

"I got you here, didn't I?" she challenged.

"Only because I came of my own free will."

"My father sent me out to speak to the king. I would have succeeded and would have—"

"No, Samara. You made one foolish mistake."

She paused. "What?"

"You're trying to tell the king you know better than he does, and you would have done it in public. Had you done that, he would have turned the royal guard on you. We're talking ten, fifteen men who would have forcibly removed you."

Samara pursed her lips. *Well, when you put it that way*. Out loud she said, "I forget, are we talking about my ability as a fighter or your lack of willingness to trust me?"

"I do trust you." He pinched the bridge of his nose. "Which is something, considering we have just met."

Silence prevailed between them for a few moments.

Finally, he broke it with, "I am not naïve. I understand your concerns, but I need evidence. I need a reason to engage in war. I need proof what you say is true."

"My father would like to discuss these things with you, if you will still meet with him."

He gave one swift nod.

"I want there to be an understanding and a sharing of information between the two of you. My word is not enough, but perhaps my father will be able to convince you. If you want proof, we'll get you your proof."

Nickson crossed his arms. "I will stay. Politically I agree that meeting your father would be beneficial, but I also have several conditions."

"Several?"

He gave her a look, and she averted her eyes. She was starting to forget who she was talking to. It wasn't like he was one of her good friends. "I apologize, Your Highness. Of course we will fulfill your conditions."

"Condition one," he began. "Stop calling me 'Your Highness' and start calling me Nickson. Condition two, I want you to stop averting your eyes when we speak; we are not at court and it doesn't come naturally to you anyway." He smiled. "There is a time and a place for such rituals, and here on your father's land is not one of them. Are we agreed?"

Samara couldn't help but smile. "Even though we have just met, you have me pegged fairly well," she praised. "Looking someone in the eye allows me to read them. Habit, I guess." She did not add that when she did avert her gaze, it was because sometimes his eyes were too intense for her. They made her feel like *he* was reading *her* and successfully seeing right through.

As if he could read her thoughts, he locked those vibrant green eyes on her own. She inadvertently turned away. Nickson closed the gap between them and rested his hand on her shoulder. Surprised, she looked up. He lowered his eyes to meet hers.

"That, Samara, is exactly what I do not like. It bothers me that someone as beautiful and skilled as you places herself below me simply because of who my father is. I do not see myself as better than you. As far as I'm concerned, you are heir to this land, and if we would like to use that as our definition, that would make you a princess. I see you are independent and you may or may not hold a secret disdain for people of royal blood, as well as for nobility." He smiled. "If I were not the prince, you would be staring me down like a lioness."

Captivated by his sudden proximity, Samara fell speechless. The very touch of his royal hand, his challenge for her to treat him as an equal, and his observant nature of her made her feel light and free to do as she pleased no matter his station. It was true, she did not like the concept of stations and privileges, but for a prince to be asking her for equality was unexpected and refreshing.

And impossible. Samara's bubble burst.

He seemed kind enough, knowledgeable and respectable, yet he had no need for the constant reminders of station. That *was* refreshing, but regardless of his charm and insistence, his conditions did make her uneasy. He was still a prince. His requests for normalcy would never be granted simply because of his bloodline. Calling him by his first name felt wrong, and her father would never allow it. But, looking him in the eyes seemed simple enough.

"Your High—" she stopped when he glared at her. "I mean—"

He still held her shoulder. "Say it," he challenged her.

Samara bit her bottom lip.

"Please?"

"Okay. Nickson." The name rolled off her tongue so naturally it surprised her. Nickson's triumphant smile took her breath away and for a moment they remained close, a feeling of enjoyment between them. Samara pondered this new level of understanding—by all accounts it was breaking the social rules. As the moment extended itself, the touch of his hand became warm and very noticeable. He was much too close.

They moved away from each other at the same time.

Samara reached into her pack and pulled out the cabbage head gifted to her by the elderly villager. She pulled a few leaves away from the rest and handed them to the prince.

"Let's eat before we get back on the road," she proposed.

Suggesting this to him made her heart pound prodigiously. They were close to her home, but a part of her wanted to keep this openness with Nickson for a moment longer. Sensing that desire in herself scared her, for she didn't know why she was enjoying this time with him, tense though it could be.

"I think that's a great idea." He took the cabbage. His eyes looked dark green in the dimming light, but the sparkle she had seen before was still there.

As they sat to eat their share of cabbage and bread, Samara searched for something to say. She remembered his earlier touch and reached for her shoulder absentmindedly. The night around them was quiet. They could still hear the river off in the distance, and the gentle chirp of crickets circled them in a musical embrace.

"Nickson?" She finally found the courage to speak, though she kept her voice soft.

"Yes, Samara?"

"You don't believe the Hungau are responsible for the fires, and neither does your father. Why is that?"

The crickets stopped chirping, as if they, too, wanted to hear his answer.

He swallowed some bread. "We've discussed the reports. My father has had spies watching them for years. They have not reported any Hungau movement."

Samara did not see how this could be. Her people had watched the Hungau as well, and they were definitely on the move. Something about his response left her unsatisfied and tumultuous. Questions flooded her mind.

Nickson stood and came to kneel in front of her. "I will talk with your father and the Gardiens, but I can't predict what will come of it. I would still like us to be friends, Samara." Concern etched the features of his face. Whether it was for their friendship or for the war rumors, Samara couldn't tell.

"We've only just met," she reminded him. "But, a friendship with the crown would be beneficial."

An affable and pleasant smile spread across his face. "I must agree to that."

Samara took a deep breath. He radiated warmth all over and she felt privileged for the time they got to spend together. Then she realized how late it was.

"We'd better get going," she said, somewhat breathlessly. She glanced at the star-studded sky through a break in the trees. "We're almost there."

Nickson followed her gaze and cleared his throat. "Yes, let's get going."

Before long they approached the manor of Dagan, leader and commander of the Forests of the North. Over a small creek lay a wooden drawbridge—the only entry point into the structure. The creek, a branch of the waterfall they had viewed earlier, surrounded the entire house, creating a natural moat. Around the river was a tall fence made of logs that had been cut down and tied together. The tops had been shaved into sharp points, but the vines and foliage of the forest covered most of it.

The clip-clop of Taiga's hoofs sounded across the wooden bridge as Samara trotted him into an inner courtyard beyond the entryway. The spacious inner court was home to a large stable for Dagan's horses. The front of the home had three long steps leading up to a front porch. At the top of the platform was a large, black, wrought-iron door. The outer walls of Dagan's home were made of large brown bricks, tightly fit and expertly molded together. It was within the courtyard where they stopped and dismounted their horses. The absence of light cast dark shadows along the house, and all seemed quiet within.

Suddenly, the front door opened, and light flooded the courtyard. "Samara?"

Rawlins descended the steps and approached them. Nickson jumped down and waited to be introduced.

"Who is this?" Rawlins asked.

"This is Prince Nickson," Samara explained.

"Your Highness," Rawlins bowed. "Welcome to Dagan's home."

His words were welcoming, but the firm set of his chin told Samara how frustrated he was with the crown. "He is here to speak to my father," she said.

Rawlins turned to her. "Your father is not happy."

She paused; she did not want to discuss this in front of Nickson. "Why?"

Before Rawlins could answer, an incredibly angry Maddox exited the house.

"Samara, where have you been?" he hissed.

Unsurprised by his sharp emotions, she tried to speak calmly. "I found the prince and brought him to meet Father." She gestured to Nickson.

Nickson inclined his head respectfully then looked Maddox right in the eye. "And you are?"

"Maddox Ward, Your Highness. Welcome to Dagan's home." He bowed.

Nickson stepped close to Samara until their shoulders almost touched. "I'm afraid her lengthy absence is my fault. I insisted she show me around the Forests as we made our way here."

Rawlins' eyes widened, and he and Maddox exchanged a glance.

"I'm glad she could be of service to you, Your Highness, but her orders were to return home as soon as possible. Dagan is deeply concerned."

"She was a perfect guard and hostess," Nickson insisted. "May I meet with Dagan?"

"Of course, Your Highness," Rawlins said and led him through the door.

Maddox motioned for a stable hand to come get the horses. "You're going to get us both in trouble," he whispered to Samara.

She pushed Maddox toward the door so they could follow Nickson and continue their conversation. "I did as I was asked and returned with the prince so we could have that audience with the king. If anything, I would think everyone would be happy."

"You should have sent word."

"I would have if I could," Samara retorted.

"Dagan is extremely worried."

"He wouldn't be if it were you or Rawlins out there," she fired back.

"Samara," Maddox warned. "You knew of his concerns before we left. Don't be surprised if he reduces your duties."

"Circumstances warranted a change in plans. You could easily testify to that."

"I'm on your side, here," he said. "And yes, I did explain that to Dagan."

"Then there is no need for concern. I'm home and the prince is safe. How is the king?"

"He's fine. We never could find the Hungau the villagers had supposedly spotted, and I didn't get a chance to speak to him."

They entered Dagan's house, the place of her childhood. It felt good to be home.

Nickson stood in the foyer.

"He insisted on waiting for you," Rawlins explained.

Samara looked at Nickson and found him smiling. "This is quite the house," he commented.

"I grew up here." Her eyes wandered the length of the walls. "I love this place."

They were standing in a beautifully decorated and open entry. An ornate rug filled the floor and elaborate, colorful antiques of masks, paintings, and weaponry decorated the walls alongside equally spaced stone pedestals. On top of these were colorful vases, jars, and statues.

A door to their left housed a large kitchen; to their right was an even bigger dining hall. The table was a giant slab of grayish-black stone, the top smoothed out and the edges chiseled with a beautiful pattern. The seating around the table consisted of vast, wooden benches. Spread atop their length for comfort were thick, wool blankets handmade by the Gardiens. The home had the essence of the outdoors, with extra protection from the elements, and gave the atmosphere an open, natural, and earthy quality.

Directly across from the main door was a giant staircase. It rose straight back, then teed off to the right and to the left. Underneath the staircase was a back hall that also housed two passages going right or left. Samara led Nickson up the big staircase and turned right. They moved down a well-lit hallway and opened the third door on the left.

In the center of the room was a large table and chairs, but Samara's attention was focused on the back of the room, where there stood a wooden desk. Hovering over the desk was a man. He had dark hair, like Samara's, and exceptionally large hands. His shoulders were wide and his stature, also large and somewhat threatening, reminded her of an ox—an animal most would not trifle with.

Dagan glanced up when they entered. He stood, revealing an even bigger frame. His brow had a certain dignified look that people could not ignore. He was wise, intelligent, and extraordinarily successful. When he saw his daughter, however, the smile that crossed his face revealed the true Dagan: loving, patient, and kind. Samara ran to him and his strong embrace enshrouded her.

"Welcome home, my daughter," his commanding voice boomed. Dagan turned to Nickson and bowed. "Your Highness."

"Sir," Nickson replied with a significant bow of his head. "It is great to finally meet you. I am truly honored."

"Thank you, Your Highness. We are honored to have you in our company." Dagan turned to Samara. "My daughter, are you well?"

The look of concern Maddox had warned her about finally manifested on his features. As she looked into his eyes, she could see the immense worry he had been carrying from her delayed return.

"Father, I am well. I felt it best to wait for the prince to ensure his safety."

He hugged her once more. "You must be famished, Your Highness. Would you like a refreshment?"

Nickson shook his head. "I am mostly just fatigued. Your daughter fed me throughout our journey. She was a phenomenal escort. Your land is beautiful; it has been a privilege seeing it firsthand."

"Thank you, Sire. As you and Samara must be quite tired, we will postpone our discussion for tomorrow. There is much to talk about."

"Samara has given me the high points," Nickson said, but his tone was skeptical. "We will discuss tomorrow."

"I will have Rawlins show you to a room. Rawlins?"

Rawlins stepped from the rear of the room, ready to escort the prince to his sleeping quarters.

"Thank you," Nickson said. "Samara, thank you for your company this afternoon."

"It was my pleasure," she said with a smile.

He smiled at her in return, letting his eyes linger on hers for a moment longer, and he departed Dagan's chambers to follow Rawlins.

"Samara," Dagan said when the prince had gone, "I was very worried about you."

"He nearly relieved me of my duties," Maddox said with a smirk.

Samara looked back at her friend. "We both know he would never do that. Everything was just fine, and the prince is safe. I felt it better to get him here so we could have a discussion with the crown. The most important thing for us to do is let the crown know the reality of the situation."

Dagan took a deep breath. "I am glad he is here, but what matters is that you are safe. Get some rest. We'll meet with the prince tomorrow and hopefully figure things out."

"Good night, Father."

"Good night."

Maddox followed her out of the room and down the hall. Samara ignored the stiff set of his jaw, but when he didn't speak right away, she decided to break the silence.

"Whatever it is you're thinking, just say it."

"I told you to come right home if you couldn't find the prince."

"If I hadn't waited, he wouldn't be here now. And we wouldn't have the audience we've been wanting."

"True," he agreed, "but you disobeyed an order."

She stopped and turned to him. "You told me you believed I was ready and capable, but you seem as worried as my father."

Maddox studied her, as if deliberating whether he should speak what was really on his mind. Finally, he said, "I do think you're capable, but as your friend I'm allowed to worry about you, too. What happened four years ago left all of us shaken. Your mother—"

"Don't, Maddox," she whispered.

"Your mother was as much my mother as she was yours," he pushed.

She forced herself to make eye contact with him. "What happened to my mother will not happen to me," she insisted. "I wish all of you would see that."

He grabbed her by the shoulders and forced her into a bear hug. "I do see that, Samara. Still, I do worry. Happy? I admit it, I worry."

She laughed softly. "Well, stop. It's all for nothing."

He let her go. "Get some rest. We still have training tomorrow, and I'm going to push you hard."

"You would," she said and released a moan.

He laughed. "Good night. Welcome home."

"Thank you, Maddox. Good night."

Maddox left her to her room, and she fell asleep with little effort. She didn't stir until the following morning.

CHAPTER FIVE

Nickson entered the council hall with a commanding air. His formal demeanor had returned, but Samara found she liked how he carried himself. He was very much a prince. Dagan stood and the Gardien Council followed his actions.

"Your Highness, good morning. Thank you for meeting with us. I hope your rest was comfortable," Dagan said.

"I have been extremely comfortable here." Nickson smiled then let it fade. "But I'm afraid what we have to discuss is less so. Please, let's sit."

Nickson didn't sit, and neither did anyone else.

"Samara, if you please." Nickson motioned to her chair.

She looked around the table in surprise. While her family had always shown her the utmost respect and courtesy, never did she think she should sit before royalty. She did sit, and only then did Nickson take his own seat. The rest of the council followed.

"Thank you," she said across the table to Nickson.

He smiled warmly at her and turned to Dagan. "Let's begin."

Samara's thoughts couldn't stop replaying what had just occurred. This was the second time the prince of Cascadia had placed her above himself, and it left her feeling positively elated. She was certain in that moment she had never met a kinder man. His humility in the face of his royal position elevated him in her eyes.

"My daughter has filled you in on the Hungau, I assume. I also assume my daughter has told you about our concerns."

"She has." Nickson's eyes wandered around the table. He took a deep breath. "I'm just not sure what to make of your report. The crown has investigated the rumors of the Hungau, and we have found nothing that supports your claim. And even if there is a threat against the crown, we have the royal guard."

Dagan pursed his lips and drummed a few fingers on the table. "I have a contact who confirmed a threat of attack against you. You do not want our assistance then?"

"I just don't see the need for all this action in response to a group that is no longer a threat," Nickson explained.

"As a witness, I tell you the Hungau remain a threat, and a strong one at that. With all due respect, Your Highness, you would be foolish to ignore the facts," Maddox cautioned. "Whether you want to believe it or not, the Hungau themselves have declared their intentions by branding themselves with the Red X. They have used this symbol for years to declare their state of war. We've seen it on them recently."

Nickson narrowed his eyes at Maddox. "I haven't seen anything concrete to support your claims."

"Support?" Maddox stood. "If you're looking for evidence, try visiting Samara's mother's grave and see if that will convince you."

Samara felt the blood drain from her face. Maddox was angry, and she understood his emotion all too well, but the Gardien Council never spoke openly of her mother like this. It was a private, solemn matter, and she refused to use it as a way to convince Prince Nickson to believe them.

Nickson's eyes widened, and he turned to Samara. "What does he mean?"

She looked at her father for strength, but she couldn't bring herself to discuss it. A moment of silent pleading passed from her to him.

"Maddox speaks out of turn." Dagan stared down at the table. "My wife was killed four years ago by the Hungau."

Nickson's eyes never strayed from Samara. When she felt

brave enough to look at him, she saw all the pity and confusion she hoped not to find. She did not want to play on his emotions like this for him to believe the truth. If he wanted evidence, she wanted to give him real evidence.

"Samara, I'm sorry," Nickson said as he turned to Dagan. "I don't want to pry, but can you give me the particulars of what happened?"

"Samara?" Dagan deflected his response.

She looked at her father in surprise. He wanted her to tell Nickson the awful story? How could she even get through it? She glared at Maddox. "Since Maddox has so gently reminded all of us of our pain, perhaps he should be the one to convey the details."

Maddox clenched his jaw, but he didn't meet her gaze.

"We will not speak of it until you are ready," Nickson suggested. "But if you could just clarify, she really was murdered by the Hungau?"

Maddox nodded. "Four years ago. That's when all of this started. We had a few casualties, Calida Wells being one of them, and it was then we realized the Hungau were rebuilding. That's all I'll say in front of Samara."

Nickson's eyes swept back to her, but they did not linger. He steepled his hands and brought them to his mouth, obviously unsure of what to do next. He turned back to Dagan. "I trust your legacy of military experience, Dagan; it has preceded you. I also trust your experience with the Hungau."

Samara saw in Nickson's eyes that something tugged at his mind, a piece of information he did not share. She also noticed a shift in his demeanor—where he used to be adamant on his stance toward the Hungau, he was now hesitant and uncertain.

"I wish to go home and address these issues with my father, but if I may return, I would like to come back in seven days' time," the prince said.

"Absolutely, Your Highness. We would be happy to host you for as long as you wish. Casimir will assist you on your journey and make sure your horse is prepared."

Nickson nodded once. "I appreciate the help. May we leave after breakfast?"

Casimir stepped forward. "I'll be sure to have the horses ready."

Nickson bade goodbye to Dagan with a bow of his head and turned to Samara. "My lady, it was a pleasure." His tone was formal, Samara thought, and very proper considering their little agreement. She did not know what to think of it, until he added, "Would you please visit with me before I leave?"

"Yes, Your Highness."

He smiled, but it did not reach his eyes. "Please, excuse me. It was a pleasure to meet all of you." Without another word, the prince left the room to prepare for his journey.

Samara turned to her father. "There is something he's not telling us," she mused.

"You saw that look on his face, too?" he asked. "I guess we shall find out when he returns."

Dagan adjourned the meeting. Samara hugged her father and made her way downstairs. She helped herself to some refreshments in the kitchen and after a short while headed outside to meet with the prince before he left. Once outside, she turned right and walked toward the gardens that graced the side and rear of the house. Her mother had had exclusive rights to the garden because of her talented green thumb. After she died, Dagan insisted the gardens remain healthy. So, they all took turns tending the garden, the most sacred part of the Forests, for it was also where her mother was buried. Instead of putting her body in the Gardien burial mounds, Dagan insisted she be placed as close to him as possible. The tombstone was elegant and hard to miss, and it was there she saw Prince Nickson standing alone, reading the words inscribed there.

"Your Highness," she said as she approached.

"I thought you were supposed to call me by my name?"

"My father would be outraged."

This brought a smile to his lips. "As your prince, I insist."

"Who can argue with that?" she teased. The garden was peaceful, despite the uncertainty of potential war hanging over them, and Nickson looked regal and comfortable. His presence filled her with awe and, surprisingly, shyness. She didn't know quite what to say, so she moved toward the tomb and silently read the words she had long ago memorized.

"Why didn't you tell me?"

The sympathy she heard in Nickson's voice almost brought her to tears. It never ceased to amaze her that even four years wasn't enough time to heal the sadness.

She closed her eyes and took a deep breath. "I did not want to convince you by manipulating your emotions." When he didn't respond, she opened her eyes and looked at him.

His eyes were fixed on her with an intensity that made her breathless.

"You are the most open and kind person I've ever met." He took a step toward her. "I would never think you capable of manipulation."

"I would hope not," she breathed. The green of his eyes deepened, if it were possible. She had to look away.

"I can see the hurt your people have been through. I cannot discount the reality of what I've been told, but I still need to get clarification and figure out the truth."

"There is something bothering you." She saw it in his eyes, just as she had in the council hall.

"Yes, there is something bothering me."

He looked worried, but Samara wouldn't push him. "Be safe on your journey. Casimir is a wonderful soldier."

"Thank you, Samara. May I call on you when I return?"

"Of course, Nickson. I look forward to it."

He bowed respectfully, gave her one last warm glance, and left her alone in the garden. Samara released a breath she didn't know she had been holding.

Nickson was confused and a little angry. As he entered the castle after his long journey, his thoughts continued to plague him. They rolled around and around in his head until he was sick of thinking, but still they came.

He had made it back to the castle in record time. Samara was correct about Casimir being a good soldier. If his short interaction with him was any indication, the Gardien warriors were disciplined and well trained. Up to this moment, he had nothing but praise for the Gardiens, and his trust in them was immediate. They were good, honest people. Rare qualities, it seemed, for even some people in this very castle could not live up to that standard.

Nickson could think of nothing but what Samara and Dagan had told him.

But no, he thought. *The Hungau are dormant and weakened—they couldn't possibly be active.*

They had been defeated long ago and his father, the king, had been sure to keep them that way.

The king. His father seemed to be the key to all of this, no matter how many ways he analyzed it. Dagan would have no reason to lie about the Hungau. By all accounts, including his own personal interaction with the man, Dagan was honest, full of integrity, and someone he could trust.

During his journey, and still in this moment, Samara's face haunted him. The moment Dagan's commander, Maddox, had spoken about Calida Wells' death, Samara's anguish was clear as day. He would never forget the expression that befell her features.

Like her father, Samara seemed to share a love of Cascadia. They would have no reason to fabricate their story. The only other possibility was they were uninformed and mistaken about the Hungau, but even that didn't sit right with him. His father, on the other hand, had assured him the Hungau were inactive, living quietly amongst themselves. Nickson had believed him.

Until now.

After Treewell and Bender Village had both burned, the king had sent a small guard to investigate. When they returned, the king reported the fires were due to disputes amongst the villagers and dry climate. The situation was now under control. A proclamation had been sent to the people with a warning about the dry conditions and the possibility of more fires, as well as a reminder to take advantage of the day to address their grievances with the crown. But Cascadia was rarely dry. She had always been a lush, moist environment with plenty of greenery. Despite the warnings, there had not been another fire, and those two towns seemed like isolated incidents.

It didn't take long before rumors about the Hungau began to circulate; they caused the fires, they killed those people, they were responsible. Nickson had largely ignored the rumors, but when he asked, his father simply laughed, claiming the group was disbanded. They could not be responsible for the death and destruction of those poor villages.

Now, the Hungau were in Nickson's path once more. He could not shake the idea this was more than a coincidence; however, he knew he did not have all the facts. He felt a surge of embarrassment for how unaware he must have seemed to the Gardien Council.

Nickson tore off his cloak and threw it into the library chair. The walls of books normally brought comfort to him, but as he stared at them, he could think of only one thing: *The worst enemy is the enemy you know nothing about.*

Samara was right. He did not know much about the Hungau. He searched through the books and pulled out every single tome on Cascadian history he could find. He opened a particularly promising volume and within a couple of pages the Hungau war symbol, the one Maddox had described, was right there on the page. He snapped the book shut.

After he did some research and spoke to his father, he would return to Dagan's home to do some more investigating and, hopefully, figure out a solution. If the Hungau were responsible for the attacks, and if what Samara and Dagan said about them was true, it meant the royal family had a responsibility to prevent the Hungau from killing more innocent villagers.

It also meant his father had lied.

CHAPTER SIX

"Get after it!"

"I'm trying," Samara moaned.

"You're not trying hard enough."

Samara had awakened early by Maddox's orders. Apparently, he still held it against her that she hadn't returned as quickly as possible after her excursion to collect the prince.

Well after sunrise, their training session had proved to be quite enough for her, but Maddox still pushed. They had already done their conditioning routine, twice, completed an obstacle course designed for bow and arrow, sparred hand to hand, and now sparred with quarterstaffs.

Maddox came down hard with a blow to her left shoulder. Thankfully, and mercifully, she had her stick in the right place and was able to block his strike. She pushed her staff up and around with her left hand, catching his staff as it came down. With her right hand, she lifted the opposite end of her staff and aimed right for his nose.

She barely missed.

Maddox turned smug at his successful block. "That's more like it. You fight better when you're feeling feisty."

Samara thought about striking him once again, but thought better of it. He was still her military commander. "Are we done yet?"

"Yes, for today."

She grabbed a towel and wiped her neck and shoulders. After taking a long drink from her goatskin flask, she handed it to Maddox. "Drink," she ordered.

He took it gratefully and finished off the water inside. "Thank you."

"I don't think I can train tomorrow."

"Why?"

"Because I'll be sleeping in."

Maddox laughed. "You never sleep in."

"I would if I could."

"I doubt it. Those little birdies in your window sing your tune every morning."

Samara smiled. The sound of birds in the morning were such a happy, welcoming sound. She couldn't help it; when she heard them long before the sunrise, she longed to be out with them. "Mother used to like the birds, too."

Maddox's smile disappeared. "Samara, I'm sorry about what I said during the meeting the other day. I didn't know you didn't want to tell the prince about your mother. I was just tired of him saying the Hungau were not a threat."

Samara forced the image that always plagued her out of her mind. "It doesn't matter. What's done is done, and I think he believes us now."

"Well, I didn't mean to be insensitive."

She sighed and leaned on her staff. "You weren't. Emotions are high when it comes to the Hungau. I know because I feel it too."

"The prince seems extremely unaware of what's going on," Maddox observed.

Samara nodded. She had a hunch about that—the something that had bothered the prince before he left was what he had gone to figure out. She was anxious for his return and to find out what he had learned. "The king told him this is all due to civil disputes."

Maddox looked at her intently. "He told Rawlins the fires were due to dry weather."

"I think we know what the prince went to figure out, then."

He raised his eyebrows. "Well, aren't you the little observer."

Samara shrugged. "I was surprised to find out how uninformed he was and just pieced a few things together."

"I would resent that," he said. "If Dagan kept me out of the loop and caused me to lose face in front of my soldiers, I would deeply resent that."

"We don't know if that occurred," she reminded him, "but I am anxious to know what the prince figured out."

"He'll be back in a few days."

Samara only nodded. She did not want any words to give away how she felt.

The prince would return soon. That thought alone was enough to propel her stomach into a flurry of anticipation. She admired him, despite their unconventional introduction a few mornings ago. Every time she thought about their initial interaction, it made her smile. Nickson made her smile.

Samara pulled out her dagger. "I'm going to go sharpen this."

"Sharpen my ax, too, would you?"

"You stole my entire morning. I don't think so."

He laughed. "I'll make it up to you."

"I'm not sharpening your ax, Maddox."

He laughed again.

Samara moved toward the gardens, where she found a quiet spot with a bench. She found a sharpening stone and quickly went to work.

Shing, shing. With each stroke, the gentle sound of her dagger against the stone helped to calm her excited heart.

Nickson would return soon.

Her heart leapt, and she nearly dropped her dagger.

"Father, do you have a moment?" Nickson asked the king.

The king was a regal man. His dignified air had always impressed Nickson, and he strived every day to be a leader like his father. Algernon Montcroix, king of Cascadia, was not a monarch to be trifled with. He was dignified, with a harsh, overly critical eye. He believed in efficiency and good use of time—it was never to be wasted.

"I have a moment," the king said with a wave of his resplendent purple-and-red robe. "I've been wanting to talk to you about your visit with the Gardiens."

"They are a marvelous people."

"Are they now?"

"Yes."

The king hooked a thumb under his graying, bearded chin. "Hmm."

"I want to talk to you about the report on Treewell and Bender Village."

"What about it?"

Nickson swallowed. "I do not believe it, Father."

Algernon narrowed his eyes. "Are you saying you don't believe me, the king? Your own father?"

"I didn't say that. I said I didn't believe the report."

"What do you believe, then?" he asked with impatience.

"The Gardiens had some interesting information to share, and I believe them."

"Do not trifle with me. Get on with it."

"The Hungau, Father."

The king froze. "The Hungau are not responsible for what happened in the villages."

"There have been eyewitnesses, Father. I met with Dagan Wells and his daughter, Samara. Samara's mother was killed by the Hungau four years ago. If the Hungau attacked the Gardiens, it's not unlikely they would attack Cascadian villagers."

"So, you're on a first-name basis with Dagan's daughter?"

Nickson clenched his jaw in frustration. Leave it to his father to pick up on minute details unrelated to the current conversation.

"Lady Wells," he corrected.

"She's a lady, then?"

"Father," Nickson warned. "I'm serious about this."

"So am I. Ladies don't live in the woods, and you would do well to remember your place in addressing your peers."

"What did the guard find when they went out to the villages?" Nickson tried again.

"It was as I told you. The villagers had attacked one another over well water."

"And set their whole town on fire? They killed their children and their wives over well water? Father, please. You can't believe that. No one believes that."

Algernon turned his critical gaze on Nickson and studied him for several uncomfortable moments. Nickson avoided the urge to shift under his father's trenchant eyes. When he finally spoke, his tone betrayed his vexation.

"The Gardiens seem to have convinced you. Show me their evidence."

Nickson's mind blanked. "Evidence?"

"They seem adamant to blame the Hungau for these village accidents; they must have some evidence."

Nickson's shoulders sagged. "They gave me their eyewitness accounts. Dagan's military commander, Maddox, was there in Treewell and Bender Village and—"

"I've met Maddox," Algernon said. "He's been here before during state business as a representative of the Gardiens. He's arrogant. I also met another man named Rawlins."

"When did you meet Rawlins?"

"He came to report Treewell."

Nickson did not know this. "What? What did he say?"

Algernon rolled his eyes. "He claimed the same as you. That Hungau had attacked the village."

"And you didn't believe him?"

The king smirked. "My son, you have a lot to learn about running a country."

Nickson clenched his teeth.

"If I believed every man who came through the gate, I'd be

playing judge for every petty dispute and disagreement between the citizens."

"I would hardly call Hungau involvement a petty dispute, Father." Nickson took a breath to calm himself. "You should have believed him and sent the guard."

"I did send the guard. We collected our own evidence, and nothing points to the Hungau as they—and *you*—claim."

"And what if you're wrong?"

The king eyed him suspiciously. "Are you saying I'm uninformed?"

Nickson looked his father square in the eye. "I would hope not, Your Majesty, but if you are wrong, we have a giant problem. Not only are they destroying our villages, but they are seeking to attack the crown."

The king smirked but didn't respond for a long moment. Nickson wondered if he had pushed his father too far.

"Well, then I'll tell you what you're going to do. You're going to return to the Forests of the North and you're going to get evidence."

"Why don't we just send the guard to investigate Eagle's Bay?"

"And waste manpower and resources? The Gardiens are already watching Eagle's Bay. You go back to them and ask them to produce proof that the Hungau are truly out for war. You bring that proof back to me, and we'll decide what to do."

"Father, with all due respect, we need to go to Eagle's Bay and send a message. The Hungau have already attacked two villages and killed over a hundred innocent people—"

"Proof, my son. Get proof they are at fault. I'm not going to start a war in my own country based on a few rumors."

Nickson flexed his jaw. "I'll get you your proof, Father. The Gardiens know what they are talking about."

"Prove it, then we'll talk."

Nickson turned on his heels and strode to the door in frustration.

"Oh, and Nickson?"

He paused at the door, tempered his emotions, and turned to face the king. "Yes, Father?"

"If the rumors about *Lady* Wells' beauty are true, be sure not to fall in love with her. We don't need a woodsmith for a princess."

Nickson's face flushed. "Lady Wells is more a lady than any of the women at court," he said through gritted teeth.

The king laughed. "You're obviously already attracted to her," he observed dryly. "Watch your feelings. You will one day rule this country, and it would behoove you to choose a princess from a neighboring country to be your bride."

"Father, I am not thinking about marriage at all. You and Mother have proved quite sufficiently how horrible marriage can be."

Algernon raised his eyebrows. "Marshal told me about your encounter with the Gardien princess."

Nickson mentally cursed his servant.

"He informed me how you behaved toward her."

"And how was that, Father?" Nickson asked, exasperated. "Please, do tell."

"It doesn't take much to see attraction, Nickson."

Nickson took a deep breath. "She is beautiful." Her face popped into his mind. "Any man would be blind not to see that. That doesn't mean I'm going to marry her."

"Good riddance. Now, off with you. I have work to do and you have evidence to collect."

Nickson happily accepted his father's dismissal. He slammed the door to his father's chamber harder than he had intended to, but his father had pushed him. It was always like that with his father lately—difficult and tiring.

It wasn't entirely unreasonable to ask for proof about the Hungau, but he would have handled the situation in a much different way. One day he would become king; that thought burdened and excited him all at the same time. But if there was one thing Nickson was absolutely sure of, it was that he was born to lead Cascadia. Right now, Cascadia needed him, and he would start by getting the evidence his father required. He would report back to the Forests of the North as quickly as possible so his father could do what Nickson knew deep down needed to be done. Putting the Hungau in Eagle's Bay was a temporary fix to a centuries-long problem. His reign would ensure that his people never had to deal with the Hungau again.

As he moved to his chambers to prepare for his return journey to Dagan's home, his head filled with thoughts of Samara.

Lady Wells, he corrected.

Except, she wasn't just Lady Wells to him. As anxious as he was to start working on the problem of the Hungau, he was equally anxious to see her again.

Samara, he thought, happy to ignore what his father had said.

Woodsmith or not, Samara was definitely worth getting to know, and his time spent in the Forests would give him ample time to do just that.

Samara burst into her father's council hall with a bang. "Our scouts have spotted Hungau on the northern outskirts of the Forests."

Maddox, who had been conversing with Dagan, stood quickly. "Scouts also reported movement from the castle yesterday. Prince Nickson is traveling today."

Dagan was already up and moving toward the door. "When did you receive this report?"

"Moments before I came to you. Danson sent his warriors north to head them off and meet with Uncle Tristan's warriors, who are near there."

"Will they engage?" Dagan asked Maddox as they strode down the hall.

"Yes, sir. I have them under command to kill any Hungau on sight."

Dagan shook his head, and for the first time in a long while Samara thought he looked genuinely concerned. "With the crown apprehensive to engage with the Hungau themselves, this could easily turn into our own war."

"What would you like me to do, sir?" Maddox asked.

"The prince is our first priority." Dagan turned to Maddox. "You are the best warrior we have; go and help him get here safely. Casimir will need to know what's going on if he and the prince are not to be caught in an ambush."

"You don't think the Hungau would cross the Forests' borders?" Maddox asked with concern.

"They have proven to be wary of the borders of our forests, but four years ago they crossed without a thought. I will not let that happen again."

"Should I send more warriors north?" Maddox asked.

Samara stepped forward. "I can go, Father. I can take additional soldiers."

Dagan did not even look at her. "Send Rawlins with a group."

Maddox bit his bottom lip. "Yes, sir." He mouthed "sorry" to Samara before he turned to fulfill his orders and get ready for his journey. Dagan did not stop to talk to Samara as he, too, went outside to help ready the warriors who would go with Rawlins.

Samara stood, alone, in the foyer of her home. She felt useless and mistrusted. She had once been a valuable member of the team, going on excursions with other warriors as they trained and practiced and watched the Hungau, but since her mother's death, she had been relegated to a domestic position that made her feel as if she were wasting her talent. Her father couldn't keep her locked up at home forever, simply because he was afraid of what the outside world could do to her. Could he? She promised herself she would address this issue with him soon. If things continued on their current path, every Gardien warrior would be needed, and Samara would not allow herself to be excluded no matter what her father said.

For today, however, she had been dealt her hand and had been effectively brushed off. She wouldn't be going anywhere with the warriors. She went outside to the courtyard and veered left toward the stables. Taiga needed a good brushing, and that was a task she could spend a good amount of time on. Between her anxiety for the warriors on the north border, and anticipation for the safe arrival of Prince Nickson, keeping her hands busy was the best thing she could do.

When her horse had been well brushed, she took to mucking his stall. She fussed over every detail and carefully arranged his straw. She gave him a fresh bucket of oats and moved to get her saddle. After she took nearly all afternoon shining it, she hung it carefully on the wall.

She looked at the results of all her hard work and walked outside. There was still no sign of anyone. Now that her work was finished, her mind grew impatient while she waited for some word of what was happening at the border. When she looked for something else to do, she spied Maddox's battle ax where he had left it earlier that morning. It was odd he hadn't taken it with him—it was his favorite weapon. She sighed and marched over to sharpen it for him after all. Just as she finished, the sound of hooves across the bridge caught her ear. She stood and looked in the direction of the noise.

Maddox and Nickson, followed by Casimir and two other Gardien warriors, had crossed the bridge and now trotted up to the courtyard. Samara's eyes first found Maddox and Casimir. They were safe. She glanced at the two other warriors—also safe—but her eyes landed and stayed on the prince.

Atop his white horse, he looked gallant and brave. Samara felt the butterflies in her stomach come to life as he approached. His eyes found hers and she offered a smile. When he smiled back, the butterflies went into a flurry.

"Have the others returned?" Maddox asked.

"They have not," she answered. "I'm glad you are all safe."

Nickson dismounted and handed his reins to a stable hand, who took the horse away to be fed. He removed his gloves and approached her. "Samara," he greeted her warmly. "You're a wonderful sight for sore eyes."

"Did you have a comfortable journey?"

"It was uneventful, thankfully. Maddox filled me in."

"I was surprised when he showed up," Casimir interjected. "Should we head to the border?"

Maddox, still atop his horse, flicked his eyes toward Samara. "No, we'll wait here."

"If Father needs us at the border, we need to leave now." Samara stepped toward the stables.

Maddox reined his horse in. "They are fine."

"They haven't sent word and you've only just returned. We should head out," she tried again.

"Samara, we're staying here," Maddox ordered. "If anyone has to go, we'll send Casimir."

"Casimir?" Samara started to shout. "We all should go. If there is a skirmish at the border, they'll need all the hands they can get."

"From what I understand, Samara, your father has insisted you stay here," Nickson explained.

Everyone went quiet.

"That's it, then, isn't it? You're not going to the border because Father asked you to stay here and keep me from going," Samara accused Maddox.

"I'm under orders, Samara," Maddox replied. "Take it up with your father when he returns."

"Believe me, I will." She turned to storm into the house—a grandiose exit seemed entirely necessary—but a gentle hand caught her by the wrist.

"Samara."

She turned toward Nickson, her hand still in his. Surprised by his action, she did not know what to say. Maddox eyed the prince with a curious expression, and Nickson seemed to remember himself. He released her arm.

"I apologize, my lady. I hate to see you upset."

Samara regained her composure. "I assure you, I'm fine. My father and I just disagree on a certain point."

Maddox dismounted and tapped her shoulder with his loose

fist. "Cut him some slack, Samara. He's not going to let you end up like your mother."

Everyone again fell silent.

Nickson looked at the ground. Casimir looked toward the stables.

Only Maddox continued to look at her. "Get mad at him for it," he encouraged. "Tell him how you feel, but don't do it at a time when everyone's emotions are high, and life-or-death decisions have to be made. He can't make sound decisions about others' lives if he has to constantly worry about yours."

Samara's anger deflated. Of course he was right. "Thank you, Maddox."

He gave her a small smile and put an arm around her shoulders. "I want you out there like all the other warriors, but you are valuable to your people. Never forget that, either."

She nodded. Her eyes inadvertently found Nickson and saw that he studied the arm Maddox had around her. Instantly worried he would misperceive their interaction, she grabbed Maddox's wrist and pushed it away.

"I sharpened your ax for you. You're welcome."

Maddox laughed. "I was in such a rush to get out of here I left it behind. Thank you, though. I'll give you the day off tomorrow."

Samara rolled her eyes and turned to Casimir. "Do you have any weapons that need sharpening? Maddox will do it; he owes me."

Casimir held his hands up. "I'm good," he said with a laugh. "Maddox, let's head toward the border and see if we can figure out where Danson and Rawlins are."

It was so quick Samara almost missed it. Maddox looked at Nickson, and Nickson gave a subtle nod in return. Maddox and Rawlins remounted their horses and took off.

"They have you in on it, don't they?" Samara said, though her anger was out of reach.

Nickson's smile was tinged with guilt. "Well, they just want you to stay here until they have a better idea about what's happening at the border."

"So they'll let me go as soon as they know?"

"You know, these forests are incredibly confusing. I can't believe how turned around I get in here. I need an escort wherever I go, and I requested you."

Samara laughed. "Oh, really?" Nickson was placating her; she could see right through him. She couldn't be mad, though. "Maybe you should visit more."

Nickson took a big drink from his water flask and eyed her with a playful gleam. "I could do that." He took a step closer and bowed his head. "It is good to see you again."

She smiled. "You as well, Nickson."

"May I?" he asked as he motioned for her hand.

She nodded her permission and he kissed the back of it. He did not let go right away. "If I may also say, you are more beautiful than the last time I saw you."

She blushed. "Thank you."

He reluctantly let go of her hand. "Your friend, Maddox, what is his story?"

Samara moved toward the stables and Nickson followed. "As you already know, he's the commander of my father's military. He showed great tactical skill from a young age and he oversees the training of all Gardien warriors. His family died when he was young, and he was an only child. My father and mother sort of adopted him as their own."

"Casimir, I got to know. He's very skilled."

They entered the stable and Samara grabbed a brush for Kalia. "That's Maddox's doing. He's an excellent trainer. Maddox personally spars with every warrior. No one has ever beaten him." She looked at the prince. "I'm sorry, I have gone on and on."

Nickson shook his head. "Don't apologize. I like hearing you talk of your home and the people in it. You do speak highly of Maddox," he hinted.

She shook her head. "Yes, but Maddox is my best friend. He's like my brother."

"I see."

Samara did not know why she felt the need to clarify her relationship with Maddox. Suddenly confused, she wondered if it were the best idea for her to be Nickson's escort.

"Perhaps one of the boys should be your guard," she suggested. She stroked the brush against Kalia's white coat.

The prince scooted beside her and took the brush out of her hand. "Everyone I've met has been welcoming, but I'd prefer you as my tour guide."

Afraid to look into his face, she kept her eyes on Kalia. "You are such a charmer."

Nickson laughed appreciatively. "Must be you. I never act this way with anyone else. Is it not working?"

Samara finally worked up the courage to look into his green eyes. "Oh, it's working," she assured him.

"Samara, would you—"

"They're here," Maddox's bass voice sounded from the stable door.

Samara looked up to see her friend in the doorway and was surprised to see he was angry. Nickson stepped away from her, and it was only then that she realized how close he had been.

"Dagan wants to see us," Maddox said.

"Tell Dagan we will be there shortly. I have one more question for Samara," Nickson said.

Maddox didn't move. "Dagan has summoned for his daughter. Surely your question can wait."

Nickson's eyes narrowed, but he took a few steps toward the house. When he stopped and turned, he looked Samara right in the eye as he spoke. "Would you like to sit with me at dinner?"

"I would love to. Thank you."

"It is good to see you again," he added. "I'm glad I could come."

Samara smiled and nodded.

Nickson brushed past Maddox and exited the stables. Maddox turned to watch him go, then whipped around and glared at Samara. "What's going on?"

Samara shrugged. "What do you mean?"

"You two looked awfully cozy."

"We were brushing Kalia."

He eyed her closely. "Perhaps you're not safe being left with the prince, either."

"Stop it, Maddox," she warned. "I am an adult, and everyone is treating me like a child. Everyone except Nickson."

Maddox's eyes widened. *"Nickson?"*

She hadn't meant to slip, but she had become comfortable addressing the prince by name. She grabbed his arm. "You'd better not tell Father."

He chuckled nervously. "What would I tell him? That you and the prince of Cascadia are on a first-name basis?"

Samara closed her eyes and shook her head against the embarrassment. "He insisted."

"I'm sure he did."

She exited the stables, but Maddox was close on her heels. She would discuss anything with him, but not this. "What happened at the border?"

"Nothing. By the time the warrior's got there, the Hungau had long since fled."

"What are they up to?"

Maddox shrugged. "Testing our borders for weak points, probably. The villages are more vulnerable and the Hungau know it would take the royal military a few days to march out. Which is why it's so foolish for the king not to be more proactive."

"Perhaps the prince can explain that this evening."

"It better be good. Rawlins' opinion of the crown is not high."

"I'm afraid a lot of people are beginning to feel the same way." She frowned. "King Montcroix's lack of action is drawing attention."

"It's a good thing we're not the conquering type," Maddox said. "Otherwise, we'd be in a prime position to lead the villagers in a revolt against the crown."

Samara looked up to see if he was teasing, but his expression was somber. It occurred to her in that moment what a precarious position the king was placing himself in. Hopefully, Nickson could explain, for the question in everybody's mind was, *Why?*

CHAPTER SEVEN

The atmosphere inside the council hall hummed with an eager current. After dinner, everyone assembled to discuss what Nickson had gleaned from his time at the palace. When Samara entered, Maddox, Danson, Casimir, Rawlins, Nickson, and her father were all seated and speaking amongst themselves. Her eyes sought out the prince. He must have been drawn to her, too, for he turned at the sound of the door and met her eyes with his.

Nickson stood. "My lady, welcome," he said.

The room quieted, and all eyes turned to Samara. She fought the rising blush in her cheeks and smiled at him. "Thank you, Your Highness."

Dagan also stood, as he always did for her, but her friends scurried to a stand in order to follow the prince's example. Traditionally, whatever royalty did was wise to follow. Samara suppressed a laugh.

As she reached her seat, Nickson pulled her chair out and tucked it in as she sat. He took the place next to hers; her father was at the head.

Suddenly, the door opened again. Samara turned to see a giant figure in the doorway. "Tristan!" She stood and crossed the room to give the man a hug.

Tristan, a big man like Dagan, shared some of Samara's features. He was her mother's brother and a crucial member of the

Gardien Council. Tristan always spoke his mind and rarely followed orders—unless he had been the one to give them. He was a ruthless fighter with an intellect that outdid them all and knew more about military tactics and training than Maddox. He was, in fact, Maddox's personal trainer and had been since Maddox was young.

Tristan scooped up his niece and spun her around. "Now that's a greeting one lives for," his deep voice bellowed.

"How was your time at the border?"

"Long and uneventful, until this morning. But even that turned out to be a waste of time."

Samara laughed. "I'm glad you're back," she said.

"I wouldn't miss this for the world." He turned to the prince. "Sire, a pleasure."

If Nickson seemed surprised, he hid it well. Tristan wasn't formal and never deemed it necessary.

"Thank you . . . Tristan?" Nickson asked. "Is that correct?"

"Aye."

Tristan turned to Maddox, greeted him, and shook hands with Casimir and Dagan.

Samara returned to her seat. "Tristan is my mother's brother and one of our more experienced military leaders," she explained to Nickson. "He has been gone the last three weeks overseeing the northern and eastern border with his soldiers."

"Your father certainly is covering his blind spots, isn't he?"

"Tristan is one of the best, and he hates being inside too long. He lives and breathes in the field. If there's one man you want with you when you're against the Hungau, it's Tristan. He knows them inside and out."

"I'll keep that in mind," Nickson said. "He looks like you."

"He and my mother were remarkably similar in appearances. They were very close."

"I can tell you're important to all of these men here," Nickson commented. "If I may say so."

"Of course, Your Highness."

"I hope my absence has not made you forget; you are to call me Nickson."

Samara leaned toward him. "I slipped and said your name in front of Maddox. I'm afraid he'll tell my father." She hid her mouth with her hand.

Nickson smiled wide, but before he could respond, Dagan cleared his throat and raised his hands to signal quiet.

"Your Highness, thank you for joining us during this pivotal time. The people you see before you make up the entirety of the Gardien Council: Tristan, who has just joined us, and the others, most of whom you have met, Maddox, Casimir, Danson, Rawlins, Samara, and myself."

Nickson stood. "I am honored to be in your company. I hope I can be of service to all of you."

Dagan nodded. "Thank you, Your Highness. Let's start with what happened at the border this afternoon."

"Hungau were spotted at the northern border," Tristan explained. "We quickly engaged, but the Hungau fled. This was their latest attempt getting across the border since four years ago, but they were not expecting to meet a whole slew of Gardien warriors." Tristan scoffed. "They scared off pretty quick."

"We cannot let them cross," Danson said. "The last time they breached our borders was tragic, as we all know."

Samara leaned over to Nickson. "We're referring to when my mother died. That was the last time they entered our forests."

"I am truly sorry," he said.

"Thank you."

"Why are the Hungau trying to breach the Forests?" Rawlins asked.

"I've been thinking about that," Maddox answered. "Treewell and Bender Village were easy targets. They've been spotted as far west as Poolside, and my guess is they've scouted out everything in between. If they are truly planning an attack on the crown, logically they must deal with us at some point along the way. They know we'd never sit by and watch them take the palace."

"This means we'll need permanent guards on the weakest parts of our borders," Tristan said to Dagan.

Dagan nodded. "Set up a rotation and make sure everyone takes a turn."

"Does that include me, Father?"

Dagan closed his eyes, and when he opened them, he stared at his hands. "Samara, my daughter, I will discuss this with you without the council."

Maddox nodded his encouragement to her, then looked at the prince. "Your Highness, you have seen firsthand what we're dealing with here. What are your thoughts?"

Nickson looked at every person in the room before he gave his answer. "The Hungau are indeed active. Your reports have proved correct. I think it's wise of you to defend your borders."

"When will you start to defend yours?" Rawlins scoffed.

Nickson pursed his lips. "You were the man who brought us the first report."

"That's me. The king did nothing."

"I can't answer for him. What I can tell you is that my father has done his own investigation, and his report does not match yours."

Rawlins shoved away from the table, knocking his chair over. "Are you calling me a liar?"

Samara carefully watched Nickson's response. He hadn't believed them before, but now he had acknowledged the Hungau's activity. He was the key to getting the villagers the aid and protection they so desperately needed. In her mind, only he could convince the king.

Nickson stood slowly. "I'm not. As I mentioned before I believe your reports. I am seeing what is going on here, and it is clear to me what Cascadia's next step should be."

Samara leaned forward in her chair, waiting for him to say the word. He had but to grant protection to the citizens of Cascadia and to the Gardiens by promising to send the royal cavalry to deal with the Hungau.

Nickson placed both hands on the table. An invisible burden seemed to settle on his shoulders and his head hung low. He took a deep breath, raised his eyes, and let them pass over every member of the council. A tense sigh escaped him. "The king is not convinced."

Samara's shock and disappointment were not exclusive to her; every man in the room stood and started to shout.

It was Tristan whose voice carried above the rest. "We don't have the manpower to defend ourselves and all the villages of Cascadia," he roared. "Add to that our duty to protect the crown should the Hungau attack, and we're done for."

Samara searched her father's face for an answer—any answer—as to why Nickson did not act as he should. Dagan met her eye, but all she saw was a quiet calm. Apparently, he felt it was good for Nickson to hear the complaints of his subjects.

"Your Highness, you have the biggest military force in these lands. Do your people mean nothing to you?" Danson asked. "Do you not care that women and children are being slaughtered before your very eyes?"

Nickson leaned on the table with his hands. "I do care," he said through gritted teeth. "The situation is not lost on me. Do not insult me by suggesting the crown is apathetic to the plights of its subjects."

"Plights," Rawlins guffawed. "This is bigger than some petty grievance. Your country is on the brink of war."

Nickson's green eyes flashed. "My presence here should speak for itself. Being an expert on the Hungau does not make you an expert on running a country. There is more here than what you care to think about."

"Your Highness, we see people in danger, and we answer their call," Maddox said. "As the protector of those same people, you should be first in line."

Nickson glared at him and pushed away from the table. "I don't disagree with you. But—"

Samara could take it no more. Though her father was calm,

inside she raged with confusion and frustration. She stood. "Nickson, what holds you back?"

Dagan's eyes widened. Danson, Rawlins, and Casimir looked at each other uncomfortably.

"Here we go," Maddox said.

Dagan eyed Samara apprehensively. "Daughter, your manners."

Samara realized she had slipped, and she glanced at Maddox. He lounged back in his chair and shook his head. She wanted to stick her tongue out at him.

"There is no need for formalities with me. I prefer to be called Nickson, if you please," the prince said.

Dagan shook his head at Samara. "Your Highness, my daughter needs to learn manners, as well as her place in this world."

"Her place, I assure you, is perfect where it is, as far as I'm concerned." Nickson met her eye.

Samara felt her cheeks blush. Her father's eyes landed on her face, a question clearly in them. She silently communicated to him that she would explain all after the formalities had ended and everyone had retired to their rooms for the night.

"Samara, you asked me a question. I will answer," Nickson continued. "But first, I need more information. Tell me more about your contact."

Everyone turned to Dagan, for no one else knew anything about the secret contact her father often utilized when word of Hungau movements came to the Gardiens.

"Our contact is a Hungau warrior."

Samara's jaw dropped. She had not expected her father to deal so closely with the Hungau. It didn't cause her trust in him to waver, but many questions filled her mind.

Nickson's eyes narrowed. "And you can trust this contact, even though he is Hungau?"

"Absolutely," Dagan said without hesitation. "I would trust him with my life."

"Who is it?" Maddox asked.

"I would rather not say just yet," Dagan replied carefully. "Keeping his identity secret is vital for his protection."

"So, all your information is being supplied to you by the enemy?" Nickson asked incredulously. "That does not bode well."

Samara made eye contact with Tristan. The Hungau were their enemies, it was true, but she knew of two who were not. She herself was a descendant of the enemy. Afraid to analyze what Nickson would think, she tucked the thought away.

"I need a name," Nickson demanded.

"I can't give it to you." Dagan shook his head.

"If I return this information to the king, your efforts, and your claims, will be immediately disregarded," Nickson shot back.

"I will deal with that if it comes," Dagan replied. "My contact's heritage does not negate the experiences we have had with the Hungau. Nor does it discredit what my commanders saw at Treewell and Bender."

"Dagan," Rawlins petitioned, "why would a Hungau work against their own? To help the Gardiens, no less?"

For a moment, Dagan didn't answer. "There are some on both sides of this struggle who know what is right. My contact is Hungau but does not endorse the Hungau ways."

Samara turned to Maddox. He shrugged. It seemed her father was going to keep his contact close. No one on the council knew anything about him, but if there was one person Dagan would tell, it was Tristan. She looked at her uncle. He stared at the table.

"Uncle Tristan, do you also trust this contact?"

"Without hesitation."

Everyone stared at Tristan.

He smiled at her. "How did you know?"

"I could see it on your face, and I know my father well." She turned to Nickson. "If my father and my Uncle Tristan say this contact can be trusted, then you should believe them. They are never wrong, and they would never put the Gardiens or the people of Cascadia in jeopardy."

Nickson took his seat and clasped his hands together. The men around the table fell silent as they watched their prince think through the next phases of their discussion.

"I will let this slide for now, but I expect more information later, Dagan."

Dagan bowed his head.

"Let's talk motive," Nickson said next. "I studied the history of the Hungau's conquests, but why these small raids? If they have come out of the woodwork after being in hiding for the last nine decades, surely they must have built themselves up enough to attack in full."

Dagan, having remained calm through the intensity of the discussion, spoke up. "His Highness asks a fair question. Maddox?"

"They've always been a violent people," Maddox faltered.

"That's not good enough for me," Nickson responded. "Obviously, the Hungau are bloodthirsty and violent, but I need more if I am to come up with a strategy that will save lives. I need a reason." He struck his pointer finger against the table.

"Actually, that is an idea," Danson said. "What is their reasoning behind raiding the castle? What gives them the confidence to attempt such an attack? Obviously the king's armies are strong and capable. There is no question of that."

Nobody had an answer.

"The Hungau don't do anything unless they are absolutely sure. Despite their violent nature and their need for blood, they are careful strategists," Tristan explained. "Sire, you said you studied their history, so you've seen how successful they've been as a people. The war against Volcania a hundred years ago would have been another victory had Cascadia not helped."

"They will see another victory if Cascadia does not once again step up," Dagan looked right at Nickson.

The prince shifted in his seat. "By any means possible, I hope to avoid war."

"War is a big word, that's true," Dagan agreed. "But that seems to be all the Hungau know. If and when it comes to that, Sire, you will have the support of our finest warriors and archers."

Nickson nodded. "I appreciate the offer, but our armies are capable. Let us be clear that I refuse to start a war in my own country."

"Sire, when a man as powerful as Dagan offers you his advice, and then backs it up with his help, you'd be a fool not to accept," Maddox said.

Nickson seemed to think about this for a moment. "One would be a fool to jump at the chance for war."

Maddox stood. "War is at your door, Sire, whether you like it or not."

For the first time since the meeting started, Nickson looked fidgety and uncomfortable. He stood slowly, his royal air bringing him to his full height. "I have spoken with the king regarding all of this. What he is demanding is proof that the Hungau are looking to attack the crown. Is this something that can be provided?" he asked, turning to Dagan. "If it can be provided," Nickson explained, "we can move forward."

Evidence? What kind of evidence could they possibly get other than what was happening right before the king's eyes? Samara looked to her father once more; his wise and calm demeanor brought her comfort. Dagan studied his daughter. He clasped his hands and thought about what the prince had said. Samara watched him anxiously, waiting to hear his reply. The room fell silent as Dagan considered his next move.

"My Hungau contact is the one who brought their plans to our attention. He said he has access to battle maps that outline the Hungau's attack plans," Dagan said.

"Can your contact bring those maps to you?" Nickson asked, his tone urgent.

Dagan shook his head. "I'm afraid not. It is too risky for my contact to acquire them without drawing attention to himself. It would put his life in danger, and then we'd lose him and our connection to the Hungau."

"How could we get it?" Nickson asked.

"I'm not sure yet, Your Highness. We will get the proof you require and go from there. We can get you your evidence."

"Father, he has all the evidence he needs!" Samara burst out and stood. "What he needs is to gather his armies and attack the Hungau." She turned to Nickson. "You need to send your armies," she said firmly. "Cascadia needs—"

"I believe it is my job to run Cascadia and not yours, Samara. You must understand where I come from."

His eyes pled with her for understanding, but nothing the crown decided made sense.

"If the king wants evidence," Dagan said, "then that's what we'll do. Getting more information will help us not to act rashly." His expression encouraged her to calm down.

She folded her arms. "I'm not rash," she muttered, "and I completely disagree. The Hungau have attacked, the Hungau will attack, and our next move is clear. We can't leave them to their own devices; they will continue to kill."

Nickson looked around the table at the council. "If I were king, I would act differently." He turned to her. "But I am subject to his decrees just as you are. I'm afraid to say this request for evidence comes directly from His Majesty. It must be acquired, and I'm sorry for that. If I am to send royal armies to war with the intention to attack the Hungau, then the king—and I—need proof that tells us we will not be the author of that war."

"So, the king wants us to collect evidence for his armies." Rawlins' lip curled with frustration. "Does he have any idea what he's asking?"

Nickson pointed eastward. "If the Hungau are out there planning more attacks on my villages, with or without intent to destroy the castle, then believe me, I will end them," he said through gritted teeth. "But I need to know how, I need to know why, I need to know when. I don't know what the king is thinking, but the sooner we get what he's asking for, the sooner we can take appropriate action."

Samara watched Nickson turn from calm and collected to ferocious and battle-ready. A tangible power exuded from him and for a moment she felt that if a war with the Hungau was on the horizon, they would win. With him behind the military, they could conquer anything. The realization came over her right then that Nickson was royal, not because of his bloodline, but because of his ability to lead and lead correctly. She felt safe with such a man on their side. Although she believed that fast action needed to be taken, she could understand his loyalty to his father.

"What are we going to do about the evidence, then?" Casimir asked.

"I think we've had enough for one night," Dagan said. "Sire, would you like a room to stay in? Otherwise we can arrange for your escort back to the castle."

"Staying here will be fine. I would not ask that we make that journey tonight. I was hoping I could stay until there is a plan in place that I can relay to my father."

"Of course you may. Samara," her father motioned for her, "would you show His Highness his room? Gentlemen, we shall continue this conversation tomorrow."

The men nodded and all of them stood. Samara led Nickson out of the room, but as she turned back, she saw Maddox's eyes on her. She smiled and closed the door.

When they entered the hallway, Nickson seemed to relax. She grabbed a torch from the wall and led him down a carpeted hallway to a staircase. As they ascended she spoke. "You look tired, but I thank you for working with us. I'm sorry you must stay here. Your castle is probably more comfortable."

"This will be perfect." he said. "It's good to get these issues on the table and work through them as a unified front."

"I agree."

Nickson glanced down at her. "You're not angry with me?"

"You are the leader of this country, not me. I may be too willing to rush off to war, but I understand your cautious approach is for the safety of all involved."

He raised his eyebrows, lost in thought. "Cautious approach? Yes, I suppose."

Samara stopped and put a hand on his arm. "Perhaps your caution is due to the king's restraint."

His features collapsed into a heap of worry. "I don't know what to think."

"The council didn't address this, but may I ask you what has been on my mind?"

Nickson let his breath out in a whoosh. "Ask me anything."

"Why did your father's report come out differently than ours?"

His shoulders sagged. "Nothing gets by you, does it?"

She smiled. "No, I would hope not."

"That's where I'm lost, Samara," he admitted. "It's obvious what's going on here, but my father denies it. He sends some knights out to gather information, but he's definitely not guarding the villages. The reports they bring back say nothing about the Hungau. I'm afraid to find out why, but I've been trying to get to the bottom of it."

"You will," she said. "And the Gardiens are here to help. You're a good man, Nickson. You're the right man for the job."

"I'm glad you understand. In order to get answers about my father's report, I must play along, for now."

They reached the top of the staircase and continued down another dark hallway. "I am curious as to why you didn't accept my father's help," she said.

"Ah," Nickson said slowly. "You are referring to why I did not accept the use of his armies."

Samara only nodded, feeling guilty about making him continue talk of war.

"I think that explanation can wait for another day," he said quietly as they approached his door.

Samara opened the door to Nickson's room. "You can stay here. It's one of our better rooms and should give you a good night's rest."

They entered and she put the torch on his wall. There were plenty of blankets on the bed, so she grabbed his washbasin from the table and carried it toward the door.

"I can take care of that, Samara," he offered.

"It will only take a moment," she assured him. Nickson jumped on his bed and put his hands behind his head. He laid back and closed his eyes. Samara watched him for a moment and then quickly left the room to fill his washbasin.

When she returned, she knocked quietly on the already open door. "Nickson?" she whispered. No answer came and she poked her head in. Nickson was in the position she had left him, and he was fast asleep. Samara smiled to herself and placed the water in its rightful place on the tall table in the corner. She crossed over to the bed and looked apprehensively at the prince's sleeping form.

"You're going to get cold," she whispered.

She loosened the lace of his right boot, untying the layers and layers of leather rope from his leg. She grabbed the bottom of the boot and pulled as gently as possible. The boot stuck for a moment and then came free, almost throwing her to the ground. Catching her balance, she held her breath and waited to see if he had awakened. He remained perfectly still, so she crossed to the other side of the bed to begin on the other boot.

Her fingers flew down the laces and soon she had the boot loose. She pulled at it, and just as it was about to come off, Nickson startled her.

"Undressing the prince? Surely you could have waited until I was awake. It would have been far more enjoyable."

The boot went flying out of her hands. "Nickson! I'm s-sorry," she stammered. She picked up the boot and paused. "Wait. What did you say?"

Nickson sat up with a laugh.

"I should have let you do it." She looked away, embarrassed. "I was just trying to make you more comfortable."

"Please, Samara, there is no need to apologize. I appreciate the care."

She retrieved the boot and held it out to him. "Your boot."

He raised his eyebrows at her and instantly she felt foolish. "I mean . . ." She took a deep breath. "Um, I'll just put it with the other one."

She placed the boots neatly at the foot of the bed and walked over to one of the chairs. She grabbed a blanket that was draped there, shook it out, and handed it to him. "I believe you can handle things from here."

He suppressed a laugh. "Thank you."

She let her eyes linger on his face for just a moment before she turned her back to him and walked for the door. In the hallway she exhaled and rested her back against the wall in relief. She felt so ridiculous thinking it would be okay to get a prince ready for bed! She shook her head at herself and quietly laughed. She made her way down the hallway to her own room and closed the door.

As she lay in bed, she pondered the events of the day. So much had changed in a short time. The royal family and the Gardiens were going to work together, she was coming to know the prince of Cascadia on a personal basis, and impending war with the Hungau was evident.

An uncomfortable pang of worry hit her. Thinking of her enemies always made her think of her mother, and not just because they murdered her. She had avoided dwelling on her ancestry since she met Nickson. It was no secret to the Gardiens, but Samara was also Hungau.

Her mother's voice filled her memory as she recalled the story: her mother was born in Eagle's Bay and trained in all the Hungau ways. Her Uncle Tristan was, too. When they left their people, they adopted the Gardien beliefs as their own. They were good people, despite their heritage.

Samara was a good person, too, but Nickson had promised he would end the Hungau, and he seemed to agree they were a terrible people. Would his opinion of her change when he found out the truth? She brushed these things from her mind. It didn't take long for the exciting turns of the day to put Samara into a deep sleep. She did not dream, she did not stir, and she could not wait for morning.

Chapter Eight

When Samara awoke, she immediately knew it was early. The sun's light had not yet pierced the forest canopy, and all was dark beyond the window. Sitting up and rubbing her eyes did little to relieve the tiredness that still hung over her. She stretched and yawned and swung her feet out of the bed and onto the floor.

A memory from the night before filled her mind. Nickson was still here. With a flutter of anticipation, she jumped out of bed and ran to the washbasin that sat chilled and waiting for her. The cool water doused all traces of sleepiness from her eyes as she cleaned herself up. Her hair took no time at all to style; the natural waves were easily managed with a quick brush. After donning a fresh pair of breeches and a clean tunic, she slid on her boots, attached her dagger to her waist, and then pinched her cheeks to get some blood flowing. She looked at herself in a small mirror and was grateful to see some color come to her cheeks. Her fair skin never held color for long.

She exited her bedchamber and made her way to Nickson's guest bedchamber. On her way, she ran into her father.

"Morning, Father." She hugged him.

"Where are you off to?"

"I thought I'd see if His Highness needs any help this morning."

Dagan pursed his lips. "That would be kind. I would like to

talk to you about what happened last night—addressing him by his given name."

"I know."

"We'll save that conversation for a quieter time, but know that I have not forgotten," he chastised.

"Of course, Father. We will talk when you are ready."

"We have a lot to discuss at the meeting today. Tell His Highness we'll be ready for him."

She nodded and watched her father walk back down the hall. Then, with more excitement than she could contain, she rushed in the opposite direction to Nickson's bedroom. She knocked and waited for his invitation to come in. When she opened the door, she poked only her head inside.

"Morning." She smiled.

Nickson was just buttoning up his tunic. "Morning, Samara."

"I had to come up to see if you were really here," she said playfully.

Nickson attached his sword to his waist as he approached her. "Thought I'd run away, did you?"

"No, but it's not every day one gets to have the company of the prince in her own home."

He shook his head. "I really wish you would stop seeing me that way."

"That would be difficult." She tapped the emblem on his tunic. "You are a prince. No one can ignore that."

He bent down so he was at eye level with her. "And no one could ignore you as the heir to the Forests of the North," he said, searching her face.

She did not know how to respond. His title would always loom over her. She wondered if she was being too friendly with him and not respectful enough. He didn't seem to mind, but deep down she knew it was probably wrong of her.

Nickson held out his arm. "Shall we head for the council hall?"

She hesitated only a moment before she threaded her arm through his. Her hand came to rest on his arm, and instantly she appreciated how strong he was. They walked the corridors of Dagan's home in companionable silence. When they reached the hall, Maddox and Danson waited just outside.

Maddox looked first at their entwined arms. He furrowed his eyebrows. "Dagan wants to see you, Samara. The rest of us are to wait here."

She unhooked herself from the prince and knocked on the door. She let herself in and found her father and Tristan already in the room.

"Father."

"Samara, thank you for talking with me."

"Your father wants to know what's going on with you and that prince," Tristan said easily.

"Perhaps I should have left you outside as well." Dagan pursed his lips.

Tristan waved a hand for him to continue.

"What is going on with you and His Highness?" Dagan asked.

Tristan chuckled quietly. Dagan ignored him.

"Nothing. When I first brought him here, he insisted I call him by his given name. I did not do it out of disrespect. Every time I tried to call him 'Your Highness,' he corrected me."

"Let the kids alone, Dagan," Tristan chimed in. "We have bigger problems. Like war."

Dagan ignored him again. "I guess if the prince has insisted, I can't change his mind."

"Probably not, Father."

"He's very attentive to you."

"I won't deny that," Samara said. "His courtesy toward me is unexpected, and I like it. You and the boys have always treated me with the utmost respect. For someone of royal blood to do it, well, it makes me feel even more valuable."

Dagan smiled. "I understand. He seems like a good man, but you had value long before he came along. Do not ever forget that."

"Thank you, Father." She smiled.

"Prince Nickson does seem honorable and morally sound. I do like that in an individual."

"And I don't," Tristan piped up again. "Can we get on with the meeting now?"

Samara laughed aloud, but covered her mouth when Dagan glared at her uncle. "I'll show the others in," she said.

"Wait just a moment," Dagan stopped her. "We have one more item to discuss, but bring Maddox in. He should be here for this."

She opened the door. "Maddox, Father wants you in here."

"Finally." Casimir started for the door.

"Ah," Samara put a hand on his chest. "Just Maddox."

Danson laughed. "Patience, Casimir."

Maddox entered past her and Samara closed the door.

"Thank you for joining us, Maddox," Dagan said. "You need to be here for this next discussion with Samara."

"What is it?" Maddox asked.

Dagan drummed his fingers on the table. "Samara has asked to be a part of the warrior rotation at the borders. How do you feel about her readiness?"

Maddox looked at her. "Honestly, Dagan, she's one of the best female warriors we have. Her skill surpasses that of many Gardiens."

"She gets that from her mother," Tristan said, and lifted his chin.

Samara smiled and looked at her father expectantly.

"Where is her time better served? At the borders? Here? Or in the villages of Cascadia?" Dagan asked.

"She would be an asset wherever she is placed," Maddox said with confidence.

"Does your glowing report have anything to do with the fact that you two have been best friends since you were kids?"

Maddox furrowed his brow. "You know me better than that, Dagan. If Samara weren't ready, I wouldn't recommend her."

"Father, you never questioned my ability to go out into the field before, but now I can hardly get your approval."

Dagan's eyes turned sad. "I don't question your abilities, Samara." He reached a hand out to her. "I'm so proud of the warrior you are and the woman you have become. But trust me when I say there are many reasons why I have kept you from going out into the field."

"And what are they?" Samara pleaded. She desperately wanted to know.

Dagan and Tristan exchanged a glance.

"It's because of how Mother died, isn't it?"

"That's part of it," Tristan confirmed. "But he's not keeping you locked up because he's afraid for your safety."

"That doesn't answer my question," Samara said.

"No, I suspect it doesn't," Dagan said, but he did not explain further. "I will think more on your position in the rotation. Please understand that you are the heir to these forests. If anything were to happen to you, where would we be?"

"Nickson is heir to Cascadia, but his father still lets him go out," she protested.

"His Highness shouldn't be going anywhere without his royal guard," Maddox contradicted. "We've been sending Casimir with him when he travels because he's an easy target with the Hungau out and about. He's foolish."

"Please trust my judgment, Samara," Dagan interjected. "The prince may do as he likes, but as my daughter you need to remain safe for your people."

It wasn't entirely a win, but at least he was considering it. "Yes, Father," she said.

"I'll fetch the others," Maddox said.

As the others filed in, Nickson found his way toward Dagan. He had a paper in his hand and spoke with a sense of urgency. Dagan listened to what he had to say, then nodded once.

Nickson stood tall and straight in the center of the room. "I am afraid I must leave immediately," he said to the council.

Samara bit the inside of her cheek while an unexpected knot began to form in her stomach. "Already? But what about gathering evidence?"

"I'm sorry, Samara. A messenger just arrived from the castle.

Dagan has assured me you will still move forward with a plan. I wish I could be of more help, but I must return today and attend to other business."

Samara sighed. "I will be sure to have your horse ready for you."

"Make it two," he requested.

"You take a party?" She wondered who it would be.

"Yes, hopefully," he stated, but said no more than that. "Dagan? May I speak with you about something in private?"

"Of course, Your Highness. Everyone, this meeting has been postponed. We'll reconvene later this afternoon."

Reluctantly, Samara left them to their business and went to prepare the prince's horses. Who would he be taking back to the castle? Maddox? Probably not. Her father? Most likely. She was thrilled that her father might be able to speak with the king. This was a rare chance her people took, and they needed it now more than ever.

As she prepped Kalia with a saddle and food bags, she heard someone enter the stable behind her. She turned and saw Danson. "Morning," she said.

"Good morning, Samara." He smiled back. "Need any help?"

"Sure, thank you."

"Who do you think will go with the prince today?" he asked.

Samara pulled the saddle strap taut. "I'm hoping it's Father, but Maddox said they made your brother the prince's guard."

"That would be good if it was Dagan," Danson agreed. "They could come to an agreement about what we discussed yesterday."

"I hope they do." She finished tying the bags on the horses just as Maddox, Casimir, and Rawlins entered the stable.

"There you are," Maddox said, throwing her an apple.

"Morning, Samara," Rawlins and Casimir said at the same time.

"Morning. Thank you for the apple." She took a bite.

"You're welcome. What's the plan for today now that His Highness has delayed our strategic meeting?" Maddox questioned.

Samara rolled her eyes at him, which earned her an annoyingly smug smile. "He is running a country, Maddox. Have some patience."

"He's sure convinced you," he returned with irritation.

"That's not fair," she shot back. She finished tying a bag onto Kalia and filled it with oats and carrots. "I'm almost done here, and then the prince can be on his way."

Maddox noted the horses that were prepped and ready. "Good," he muttered.

She was tired of his moodiness, whatever the cause, and she wanted it to end. She gave him a mischievous look. "Casimir, if you were to place a bet on a fight between Maddox and the prince, who would win?"

"Maddox," Danson and Rawlins said together.

"Hands down," Casimir agreed.

She looked at Maddox. "I'm not so sure about that."

Maddox looked at her with a smirk on his face. She was hiding her own smile. He was like her brother, but he had seemed edgy since the moment he caught her and Nickson in the stables.

"Rawlins," Maddox countered, "in a fight between Samara and me, who would win?"

Danson laughed.

"Samara. Hands down," Casimir exclaimed.

Samara laughed, not taking her eyes off Maddox. "Should we put it to a test?"

"I taught you everything you know," he boasted. He bent down so he was eye level with her. "Which means I'll be able to read you like a book."

"Not a chance," she laughed.

"Since we're not having a meeting, might as well train," he added.

All five of them stepped out of the stables and into the outer courtyard. There was enough space to hold a decent, but friendly, fight. Maddox raided the nearby collection of practice weapons and tossed her a stick roughly the size and shape of a small dagger. He grabbed a longer, wooden practice sword for himself. They stood about fifteen paces apart, and Maddox wore a huge grin on his face.

"You ready?" Samara taunted.

"Ready." He shook his shoulders loose. "But that little eating knife you've got there isn't going to hold up to my weapon."

"Never underestimate your opponent." Samara took a step toward him and he countered with a step to the side. They continued the footwork for a few moments before they realized neither of them would make the first move.

"Come on," she said to him.

"Ladies first."

She smiled and charged him. Her dagger struck his sword with a smack as he expertly blocked her first blow. She backed off slightly and charged him again with a stab at his midsection. He forced her to parry to the right, but she blocked his counter.

"She's got great footwork," Danson noticed.

"True," Rawlins agreed. "But his brute strength will pick her off shortly."

Casimir laughed. "I don't think you could get Maddox to go at her with full speed."

Samara could hear them as they fought, and this comment distracted her. In one move, Maddox successfully disarmed her. Her dagger flew across the court and landed at the feet of Nickson and her father, who had just exited the house.

Dagan laughed when he saw the scene before him. "Fifteen on Maddox," he shouted.

"Father!" Samara complained.

Maddox ditched his weapon and came at her with his fists. She ducked a blow from his punch, crossed her elbow over her body, and landed a strike straight into Maddox's jaw. She heard Nickson laugh; the sound brought a smile to her face.

Maddox retreated a few steps and then charged her. Samara knew that warding off his strength while he was coming at her full force would be impossible. She darted her eyes around the ground and saw her practice dagger lying at her father's feet.

"Father, the dagger!"

"You're on your own with this one," Dagan said.

"Slide me the dagger!" she said with more urgency as Maddox closed in. "Blast."

She turned to the side, catching Maddox in a spin, and threw him to the ground. She faced the small crowd and raised her arms in victory. The next thing she felt was her legs being kicked out from underneath her. She landed flat on her back; the ground knocked the wind out of her. She gasped for breath, rolled over onto her stomach and looked at Maddox. He was lying on his stomach across from her and rubbing his jaw with his fingers.

"You've definitely gotten stronger," he praised her.

Dagan and the other men laughed, and Casimir helped her up.

"That was excellent form, Samara," Nickson said with admiration.

Samara bowed her head slightly. "Thank you."

"Your Highness?" Rawlins asked.

"Yes?" Nickson turned.

"If you don't mind my asking, what kind of combat training have you had?"

Nickson took the challenge willingly. "As head of the military, I have taken it upon myself to learn as much about fighting as possible. I cannot, in good conscience, send my men out without knowing how to support them and fight alongside them if necessary."

Maddox rolled his eyes and harrumphed.

Nickson didn't acknowledge the insult and turned to address everyone else. "I'd be happy to show you some of the things I've learned at another time, if you are interested."

Danson and Casimir hollered in agreement. Rawlins seemed intrigued, but his irritation with the royal family was still evident.

Maddox looked ready to fight the prince himself. "I'm sure there isn't much left you could teach them," he said. "They've all been well-trained."

The men looked from Nickson to Maddox and back again. The undercurrent of tension between them was palpable.

"Your Highness," Dagan interrupted, "going to your castle will take at least a two-day ride. You had better be on your way."

Nickson looked up at the sun. "You're probably right. Samara, you'd better go pack your things."

"Pack?"

"My daughter," Dagan responded, "His Highness needs a guard for the journey, and we need someone to go to the castle to speak with the king. Prince Nickson has convinced me that you would be good for the job."

Maddox's mouth dropped open and everyone looked at Dagan in surprise.

Immediate excitement filled Samara. This would be her first time going to the castle. A personal invitation from the prince himself made her feel particularly important, and she couldn't help but feel curious about what would happen there.

"Sir, wouldn't it be better for one of us to go? Surely one of your warriors would be better suited to protect the prince," Maddox objected.

Dagan eyed him curiously. "Samara is one of our warriors and is more than capable of protecting the prince. Your training has ensured that possibility. Now that the opportunity has arisen, I don't see any reason why she can't accompany him." Dagan turned to reenter the house.

"But, Dagan," Maddox continued with a huff. "She's never been to the castle. Casimir has and knows the route well."

"It would be beneficial for Samara to learn the route, too, though I'm sure she knows the way. His Highness has convinced me she would be of use at the castle."

Danson cleared his throat. "Sir, I must agree with Maddox on this one. What could she possibly do that one of us cannot?"

"Danson!" Samara felt offended.

"Boys," Dagan said firmly, "Samara has as much knowledge as any of us about the Hungau. I insist the prince take a guard for the journey, and Samara is quite capable of his protection. It will also be good for her to get a feel for nobility and learn about that world and what it would take to serve as a representative in court." He turned to Maddox. "You yourself said she would be an asset no matter where she was placed. My decision is final." He turned, and with Nickson at his side they reentered the house.

Samara turned to Maddox. Trying to hide her excitement, she asked, "Why does this concern you?"

Maddox looked angrier than she had seen him in a long time. "Do you see what is happening here, Samara? Because I do."

Samara shook her head. "What are you talking about?"

"Nickson claims that you will be of use in the castle. Do you know what he means?"

Rawlins shook his head. "Maddox—"

"Hush, Rawlins," Maddox said through gritted teeth. "All he wants from you he can get from his mistresses."

His face had turned red with anger, while Samara's flushed with embarrassment.

"Maddox, you're crossing a line," Casimir warned.

"It's true!" he shouted. He put his hands on his hips and looked at the ground.

Samara was embarrassed at the direction the accusations had taken. It was one thing to assume a man would be better for a job she was perfectly capable of doing, but it was an entirely different matter to accuse a person of immoral intentions.

"Maddox," Samara snapped, "do you think if that were the case, I would feel comfortable going? I trust him and do not think he is capable of such awful things. You don't even know if he has mistresses."

"Maddox, let it go," Rawlins said, annoyed.

Maddox ignored his friend and threw his hands up in the air. "All royalty has mistresses, Samara. That's what they do. I've seen the way you look at him, so maybe it's not a problem for you."

Before Samara knew what she was doing, she reached up and slapped Maddox. "You have offended me in every possible way."

She clenched her jaw. "Do not make the mistake of coming to see me when I return home."

Filled with both surprise and anger, she stared at Maddox for a moment longer. Then she turned on her heels and ran up the steps to the front door. She went inside, shaken by what had occurred with her best friend.

Surely Nickson doesn't have mistresses. The thought alone made her uncomfortable. Maddox's accusation shocked her, but it explained the moodiness he had exhibited the past few days.

Certain he was wrong, she made it to her room and packed some things that would last her a couple of days. She went to her closet and pulled out a fresh pair of breeches. Her eyes caught sight of something hanging inside, and she reached up to touch the soft fabric.

Her mother's dress had gone untouched for months. It was the only dress she owned, but simple and attractive as it was, she didn't think it would fit well within the prince's world. Most of the women at the castle would have dresses much more embellished than this. She decided not to take it. The king and his court would have to get used to a woman who wore breeches. She made her way to the stables to attach her bag to her horse. When she arrived, she found Rawlins pouring water into canteens for the journey.

"Thank you for the water, Rawlins," she said to him.

"My pleasure, Samara."

She tied her bag onto Taiga and turned to Rawlins expectantly. "Tell me what's on your mind."

He looked toward the door of the stable and back at Samara. "He's really struggling with this, Samara."

"That's not my problem."

"Samara, I'm serious," he urged her. "You're like his sister. He's worried about Nickson's true intentions with you."

"I've been around men before, Rawlins."

"None of them have stared at you the way the prince does."

This comment made her pause. Nickson stared at her? She

swallowed. "He's the prince, Rawlins. I'm sure he looks at a lot of people. If Maddox is upset about that, he should take it up with the prince instead of fighting with me."

"The man is royalty, Samara. This little friendship you have with him is not normal behavior between a Gardien and a prince."

"What would you consider normal behavior?"

The voice interrupted them from behind. Rawlins looked over Samara's shoulder, his eyes wide. Samara turned quickly. Nickson stood in the doorway, his expression one of impatience.

"Your Highness." Rawlins bowed.

It occurred to Samara right then that she did not feel the need to bow when Nickson walked into a room. Awkwardly, she bent to the ground as well.

Nickson watched her closely. "Please stand," he said to both of them. "What behavior would you consider normal for the prince of Cascadia?" Nickson asked Rawlins. His green eyes flashed with annoyance.

Rawlins averted his eyes, as was customary, but Samara knew her friend—he was trying hard to control his own emotions.

"Whatever you think, Your Highness," Rawlins answered. "I think I'm finished here. Excuse me."

Rawlins slipped out of the stables and Samara and Nickson were alone. At first, neither of them spoke. Samara didn't know what to say.

"Samara," Nickson finally said, "I would very much like your company today, but I seem to have caused a rift between you and your friends."

She didn't respond. Nothing Maddox had said changed her mind, but the prince had overheard a potentially embarrassing conversation for both of them. If she went with him, Maddox might stop speaking to her, and Rawlins, Danson, and Casimir too. Samara pursed her lips. If she did go, she would get to see inside the castle, spend more time with Nickson—which she didn't mind doing—and learn about diplomatic procedures like her father mentioned. Couldn't Maddox see that this was a big opportunity for her? Her father had given her a chance to go out into the field; Maddox used to be supportive of that.

Nickson took a step toward her. "I assure you that you will not be used as my mistress," he said with a serious expression.

Samara blushed. "You heard that?"

"Every word."

She tilted her head back and looked at the ceiling. She clutched at her neck as if that would ease the stress she felt.

Nickson took another step toward her. "I also assure you that I will treat you with the utmost respect a man, and a prince, can offer."

Samara studied this dignified and respectable man. As soon as he said the words, she knew they were true. He had already demonstrated on more than one occasion that he was a man who would respect those around him—especially women and, in particular, herself.

"I will go," she said with excitement. "I'm ready when you are. How did you ever convince my father to let me go?"

Nickson smiled. "It took some careful persuading, but in the end, he couldn't argue with the fact that you are an excellent warrior. Your fight with Maddox this morning proved that. I also assured him you would be safe in the castle. The royal guard lets no one through."

"I guess that's the secret to his permission," Samara sighed. "My safety."

"Perhaps. Let's go say goodbye to your father, then." He motioned toward the door and then followed her outside.

Dagan stood at the entrance to his home. "My daughter, are you ready?"

"Absolutely, Father." She hugged him. "Thank you for letting me go."

He hugged her tightly. "I trust you and I trust His Highness. Keep him safe and be on your guard."

"I will, Father. I love you."

"I love you, Samara."

He squeezed her tightly once more and then released her. As

she mounted Taiga, she spotted Maddox standing near the gate. Casimir, Danson, and Rawlins were not far from him. They looked worried. She trotted Taiga over the bridge and stopped where Maddox was. Nickson followed.

"I wanted to say goodbye," he said only to her.

"It will be fine, Maddox," she assured him.

Maddox turned to Nickson. "If anything happens to her, I will hold you personally responsible."

"Maddox," Samara chastised.

"Why do you feel the need to protect her from me? Why the need to protect the lady at all? She's more than capable of defending herself."

"I have my reasons," Maddox spat. "She is like family to me, and I will do anything to protect her from harm."

"Perhaps you should ask her permission first," Nickson ventured.

"Perhaps you should be sure to give her plenty of space," Maddox growled.

Nickson eyed Maddox coldly. A silent conversation that Samara could not even begin to understand passed between them. The look of disdain Maddox had for Nickson, and the look of hatred that passed over Nickson's features, made Samara realize how heated things had become.

"Boys," she called out, "enough is enough." She looked at Maddox. "I will see you when I get back. Nickson, let's ride. It will be dark before we make it out of the Forests. Yah!"

Her horse surged forward and Nickson trailed behind her. She left the perimeter of her home and made her way through the brush. Nickson would have to catch up. He did after a short time, and Samara slowed their horses to a light trot. She guided Nickson through the forest, aiming for the river they had crossed on their way in. There, they would rest for a few moments and allow the horses to have some water.

Riding under the forest canopy turned the already hot day into a hotter and more humid one. Insect activity was alive and well, and after a while Samara got tired of having to swipe at all the bugs. They had been on the trail for half a day. She pulled to a stop at the bottom of the steep incline that led to the top of the shelf where the river was. The waterfall was to their right, and the trees swayed in the cooling wind.

"Let's pull our horses up to where the water is." She climbed off her horse. "And maybe I can take a bath," she muttered to herself.

They guided their horses through the rock and grass and after a decent climb they made it to the top. Samara cupped at the water in the river and splashed it on her face. She pulled off her boots and soaked her feet in the cool stream.

"It is blistering today," Nickson commented.

Samara only nodded. She let her feet dangle in the water and lay back on the grass to rest. She closed her eyes and let her face soak up the warmth of the sun. The caressing rays helped her feel focused and relaxed, and soon she found that she could think of nothing else but the feel of the grass beneath her arms and legs. When she opened her eyes, she viewed the fluffy clouds that floated above her; the brilliant blue sky was the perfect backdrop for the pure-white wisps. She glanced over at Nickson to see if he was as relaxed as she was. It surprised her to find he knelt on one knee, his sword drawn.

"Nickson? What are you doing?"

His eyes grazed the forest's edge before he stood and sheathed his sword. "I thought I heard something."

From her reclined position she raked her eyes along the treeline. "I'm sure it was an animal or something."

Nickson chuckled. "You're probably right, but with my bodyguard lying down on the job, I figured someone should keep watch."

Samara sat up and threw a pinecone at him. "I know these woods. I feel comfortable here. You're as safe as you'll ever be. No one knows you're here." She brought her feet out of the crystal water and dried them on the grass. She put her boots back on and approached Taiga.

Nickson picked up the pinecone and when Samara's back was turned, he threw it at her. When she turned around, he was smiling. His green eyes sparkled and glistened.

"You would throw a pinecone at a woman?" she teased.

"You would throw a pinecone at a prince?"

"Are you going to arrest me for treason?" she said with a hint of a challenge.

Nickson stepped toward her. "Can I ask you a question?"

"Of course."

"You don't think—" He paused.

"Do I think what?"

"You don't think that I—" He moved his hands as though he was trying to pull the words from his mouth. "That I—"

Samara fixed her gaze on him. "That you what?"

"You don't think that I have mistresses, do you?"

Suddenly the air felt much too warm. "Um, no. I guess not. Do you?" she asked.

"No! Of course not," he said quickly. "I would never—"

"Of course not," Samara agreed.

Full of awkwardness they both turned to their horses to prep for their ride. Samara tried hard not to be angry at Maddox for his role in initiating this conversation. She was glad, however, to clear the air with Nickson. Her initial impressions of him continued to prove true, and her respect for him deepened. She hooked her foot in the stirrup and hoisted herself onto Taiga's back.

"You didn't have to ask me that," she said.

"I think it's obvious why I did."

Samara waited.

"I do not want you to have the wrong impression of me," he explained.

Samara pulled on the reins and thought about what her response should be. "Well," she considered, "I don't."

Nickson studied her closely. "What *do* you think of me?" he ventured.

Samara smiled. "I think that explanation can wait until tomorrow."

This reminded her of the explanation he owed her. "My turn to ask a question."

"Yes?"

"Why wouldn't you accept help from my father's armies?"

Nickson nodded in remembrance. "I want to see if the Hungau are a people my armies can take care of."

He averted his eyes and pretended to be preoccupied with his boot in his stirrup. Samara couldn't shake the feeling that he wasn't being completely honest with her, but didn't see any other reason why he should lie.

As they galloped off, she pondered Nickson and his life. She wondered what his life would show her and what things she would learn at the castle. She was excited to see the inside of the place he called home and was anxious to see how he looked in it.

She looked over her shoulder and noticed how deep in thought he was. She wondered what he was thinking—she was fascinated by the way his mind worked. He always seemed to say the right things and he always had command over a room full of men. She was interested to see how he worked among his court and other leaders.

Suddenly, she felt nervous. Though she stood to possess a large portion of her own land and had just as much right to be present at court, the thought of meeting with other land-owning nobles filled her with uncertainty. Her father had rights to a regular seat in the royal court, but rarely attended. The Gardiens had always been a loyal, but solitary, group of citizens within the Cascadian realm—long before Nickson's family line had come to power. The treaty signed between her forebears and the Montcroix line had only served to solidify their secluded way of life. The Gardiens kept to themselves, living in Cascadia but not necessarily being *of* Cascadia. They were always ready to fight on behalf of the crown, but equally willing to withdraw into the shadows of the Forests when their military expertise was no longer needed. Because of this, the Gardiens were often seen as an enigma to the regular citizens of Cascadia.

The noblemen of Cascadia, on the other hand, dealt with the king on a regular basis, and Samara was fairly certain none of them were women. Of the women who did flit around court, they would be beautifully dressed and decorated. She glanced down at her own attire. Surely they would view her as a vile creature from the woods.

Samara shook her head to rid her mind of these thoughts. She squared her shoulders and determined she would not care what they thought. Their lifestyles were completely different. She had need of muscles and skill in the woods. At court, the women never had to shoot an arrow at a bird for dinner. They never had to live off the land, and they certainly never felt what it was like to hunt in a dress. Samara chuckled at the preposterousness of such a situation.

She focused again on the ride, and after they had ridden for a short while to the border of the forest, they popped out on the trail where she first encountered Nickson. Determined to protect the prince at all costs, she put herself on full alert. Though she was positive he could defend himself in a fight, she had been tasked to protect him, and this required every ounce of her concentration.

After setting up camp for a night on the road to rest, and long after the sun had sunk below the horizon on their second day, they made it to the castle. Samara was grateful they had made it without incident, but as they approached the giant gates, she felt butterflies in her stomach. She sized up the magnificent walls and studied the tremendous flags that waved the crest of the king.

Nickson reared up alongside her with a smile. "Are you ready?"

She looked up at the white stone walls once more and took a deep breath. With a steady and confident voice, she answered.

"I'm ready."

Chapter Nine

The outer wall of the castle was built of white stone that was as thick as a man was tall.

The interior of the castle was an exquisite combination of creams, golds, blues, and greens. Everything seemed bigger, grander, and more beautiful than Samara could have ever imagined. Flowers arranged in various bunches brought a floral smell to the entire palace and was a surprisingly feminine touch.

While Nickson checked in with the king, she explored the bedroom where she would be staying. Her room housed an ornate four-poster bed, cream-and-blue silk curtains, and a giant area rug made of intricately woven sheep wool. The brilliant colors reminded Samara of home, while the golden hues reminded her of yellow Cascadian roses.

Servants were strategically stationed at various locations in the corridors. Many, many servants. If she needed anything, all she had to do was ask.

When Nickson finally summoned her, she was guided to a quaint parlor on the third floor. Its color scheme was a brilliant red, and she intuitively knew this room belonged to Nickson. The servant left her at the door, and she turned to the prince with a smile on her face.

"Your home is beautiful."

"I'm glad you like it." He smiled back.

"The sheer number of servants is quite a marvel."

"We have a lot of work to do, and their help is always appreciated. For tonight," he changed the subject, "dinner will be ready soon. I have arranged for us to eat in the dining hall. I'm afraid my father is taking care of some business and will not be joining us. He did insist we meet over breakfast tomorrow. Lunch will be served midday and for dinner tomorrow—" Nickson's eyes sparkled—"we will be fed at the banquet."

Samara blinked. "Banquet?"

"Don't worry." He shook his head. "You'll be fine. I must attend the banquets because most of the people at court will be there. As my father puts it—" he raised his finger and quoted verbatim—"'It is a time for me to appear interested in their lives and the lives of my subjects.' I insist that you attend with me as my special guest." He bowed.

Samara was torn. The idea of court made her nervous, but at the same time she wanted to see what it was like. She had the feeling she would do well if she got an opportunity to speak to the courtiers. "If you insist I be there, then I will not decline."

"Excellent," Nickson said. "Having you there will make court more bearable."

"You dislike it?"

"Tremendously," he confessed. "Being at court is nothing more than showing off the latest fashions and being seen. It is all about publicity."

"That is unfortunate," she deemed. "Being at court should be about getting work done. Not about showing oneself."

"Ah, my lady." He looked at her. "If members at court felt as you did, then they would not be at court."

Samara laughed. She liked understanding Nickson more. She also liked being prepared about what to expect with the people at the banquet tomorrow evening.

For a moment she thought about Maddox. She wished he and the boys could be there, to see what it was like, but she had a feeling that anything she had to say about her stay would not be welcomed. Before Maddox got frustrated, they would have been able to discuss it. Nickson, unintentionally, had changed all of that.

A servant came from out of nowhere and pulled Samara from her thoughts. "Dinner is served, Sire."

"Excellent. Samara?" He raised his arm, offering it for her to take.

She graciously accepted and side by side they walked into the dining hall. To the right of the table, against a wall, were two washbasins. There they cleaned their hands and faces. The towel Samara was given to dry her skin was soft and luscious. She felt the fabric and pleasantly rubbed it against her hands and cheeks.

Another servant joined the first and helped them into their chairs. Samara thought this was rather unnecessary—she was perfectly capable of pulling herself up to the table—but Nickson had treated her the same way at her home. It wasn't as much of a surprise now.

Despite her best efforts to fit in, Nickson caught her amusement and winked at her. Samara smiled while the servants brought in two covered trays and placed one in front of her and the other in front of the prince. The cloches were removed, and the sweet, succulent smell of duck met her nose.

"This looks wonderful." She closed her eyes and inhaled again.

"Thank you," the servant returned with a head bow. "I will give your compliments to the cook."

Served with the roasted duck came a side of wild grain that had been planted on the castle grounds. Nickson informed Samara that the king planted much of his own food on several acres of land that lay a mile to the rear of the castle. Samara was then served a goblet of red wine. The prince readily drank, but she hesitated.

"Is something the matter?" he asked.

"I would just like water, please." She was parched, and water was what she craved.

The servant looked confused at her choice and she felt she had to explain.

"When you live in the woods and travel the distances we do,

water is an important commodity. We do not have drink at home. I'm afraid my body would react badly," she confessed.

Nickson nodded in understanding. "Water for the lady," he spoke to the servant, who nodded and left. "Have you ever had a strong drink before?"

"Yes, Maddox and the boys sometimes acquire it from nearby towns. I do not like the way it makes them unalert and crude." She furrowed her brow.

Nickson stared at her. "You have convinced me," he declared. "Servant, I would like water also. I would not want to offend the lady."

"Thank you, Sire," she said, and bowed her head to him.

"I'm amazed by your ready opinions and your honesty," he said. "It's refreshing."

His green eyes confirmed his sincerity, she decided. With a smile she raised the water that had been placed in front of her and Nickson answered it with a raise of his own. Together they both drank. Samara then turned to her duck. She picked up the knife to her right and began to cut out bite-sized pieces.

"You needn't do that," Nickson stopped her. "The servant can take care of that."

"The servant cuts your meat for you?" she asked, bewildered. The servant approached her and motioned for her knife.

"Yes, such a menial task can be accomplished by the servant." He tilted his head and glanced at the knife in his hand.

Samara let out a small laugh, and the servant stood waiting. She composed herself. "It's all right. I can do it myself."

The servant looked helplessly at the prince for instruction.

A big smile crossed Nickson's face. "Thank you, you are not needed."

The servant nodded once and turned and left.

"I hope I did not offend him."

"Not at all. They are just not used to not being needed," he said with a wide grin.

"They do so much for you. Are you not capable of doing those things yourself?"

Nickson took a bite of duck. "I guess I never thought about it. You grew up in a world that required you to do everything yourself. I was taught that servants take care of the mundane chores and tasks. The king and I never cut our own meat," he pondered.

"What of your mother? Does she not prepare the food?"

Nickson's eyes opened wide. "No, she doesn't. My mother has been unwell as of late. I can't imagine her being in the kitchens. I'm afraid you might not have the chance to meet her while you're here."

"When my mother was alive, she participated on the Gardien Council and prepared almost all of our meals."

"Really?"

Samara nodded and almost laughed at his disbelieving expression. "She was very involved, but I understand that illness can effect a person enough that they stay confined to their rooms."

Samara and Nickson stared at each other as they let these lifestyle differences sink in. She was amazed he was not allowed to do much for himself, and he must have been just as amazed that she would dream of doing so much at all.

"I must confess that staying with your father in your home was enlightening. I mean, I know the country folk have worked a lot harder for food and living than I have. But you must understand, the tradition of having servants was established so we could run the country, without having to worry about lesser tasks."

She thought about this. "I see what you mean, and it makes sense. My family is well off, but not in terms of money. The Gardiens believe we should share all we have with one another. Together we work, together we reap the benefits."

"I have been impressed that you work as hard as you do. Your people are self-sufficient and capable. My responsibilities just take a different form, usually at court," he said with a smirk.

"Well, I have been impressed we can come from two different lifestyles and still understand one another."

Nickson bore his intense eyes into her own. "My lady, you have no idea how happy I am we agree."

Maddox sat at the giant conference table in Dagan's home and looked at his fellow military men—his friends. Rawlins and Casimir chatted amongst themselves while Danson read a book. Dagan shuffled a few papers until Tristan took his seat next to him. Maddox admired the powerful men of the Gardien Council, and he loved them, and Samara, as family. As they managed the affairs of the Forests of the North together, he felt a strong sense of purpose. He wished Samara could be here for this meeting too.

Samara.

That girl had frustrated him more in the last two days than she ever had before. Where he was normally calm, cool, and collected, he had been only irritable and angry with her. The last few days had proven exceedingly difficult—ever since he saw Samara with Nickson in the stables. Nickson looked a little too comfortable with her. Maddox wondered why he was being so protective of her.

If Prince Nickson assumed he could stroll in here and charm their Gardien women, Maddox would thoroughly educate him on the matter. He supposed he was angry Samara would break the social rules and return the prince's attentions—she barely knew him and was normally more careful—but this felt like only part of the reason.

Finally, Dagan cleared his throat and Maddox shifted his focus.

"You all know why we're here today," Dagan began. "With Samara at the castle speaking to the king, I felt it best to keep things rolling here. The prince has required that we obtain evidence against the Hungau. I agree with this foresight and have gathered you all here to discuss how that can be accomplished." Dagan eyed the council. "Be it known by all of you—if we find no such evidence, the prince will relax his position even further on the matter, and we will be forced to comply with any terms he declares. Our actions against the Hungau are tied to this evidence."

"Even though I do not agree with the prince at all on his approach, the role we play is understood," Maddox offered. "What kind of evidence is he looking for?"

Dagan pursed his lips. "He is requiring current evidence that the Hungau intend to attack Cascadia in full."

"You mean all or nothing," Rawlins countered. "Evidence they are planning on openly coming to war?"

"That is correct," Dagan confirmed.

Maddox and his friends looked at one another. Their role was much more dangerous than they had supposed.

"Is there another way?" Danson asked.

"If there is, I'd like it mentioned quickly. I do not embrace the fact that our sons must put themselves in danger," Dagan said, and looked at each one of them.

Maddox looked at the man who had become his father figure. "Nor would we wish to put such strain on our fathers."

Dagan smiled. "A simple scouting party would do no good in this case, I'm afraid. Our word is not enough for His Majesty the king."

Casimir harrumphed. "So, he needs actual papers," he muttered. "Why doesn't he send his own soldiers?"

"In my meeting with the prince, he acknowledged we have the most experience and knowledge when it comes to the Hungau. He respects and trusts our warriors enough to do the job and to do it safely," Dagan explained.

"How many are we sending?" Rawlins asked.

The full weight of their task settled upon Maddox. To get evidence, they had to go to Eagle's Bay. Sending anyone so deep into the Hungau territory would be dangerous. He thought of the warriors he had served with his entire life. He couldn't sentence them to death.

"We are sending one," Maddox explained. "Unless we have volunteers, I will go alone. I cannot ask my brothers to put their life on the line for so little as information."

"What?" Danson and Casimir said together.

Rawlins clenched his jaw.

Dagan looked worried. "I cannot ask you to go alone, Maddox."

"We can set up a relay," Maddox pursued. "Once I've acquired the information, I'll make for a certain checkpoint. Once that checkpoint is reached, the information will be passed on to subsequent checkpoints. That will ensure that if any of us get killed, someone will have the information and it will get passed on. It will also ensure that only one has to enter the heart of the Hungau."

"Absolutely not," Rawlins argued. "We're with you all the way. What if you never make it to the first checkpoint?"

"We're not staying behind to watch you die, and Rawlins is right. We'd inevitably come in after you," Danson said without hesitation.

"You have to let me go," Maddox asserted. "A team of four would be too noticeable. It would mean certain death for all of us."

As Maddox's friends objected, Tristan spoke loudly. "You men speak of death as if it's at the door. The Hungau do not know we are coming."

"We will have a team of five go into the heart of Hungau territory. You will acquire papers and plans that prove they are engaging in war with Cascadia," Dagan decided.

"Five?" Danson asked. Dagan's main scout team—Danson, Rawlins, Maddox, and Casimir—made only four.

"Five," Dagan confirmed. "Tristan will go with you."

The next day at the castle proved to be an exciting one. Samara woke early to get ready to have breakfast with the king. This meeting was imperative to their civil relationship and how the next several months would pan out concerning their actions against the Hungau. As she washed her face, she heard a knock on the door.

"Come in," she called.

A servant entered with a gown and Samara gasped.

"His Highness has insisted that you have full access to a wardrobe during your visit," the handmaiden explained.

Samara stared at the silky fabric. The dress was a soft green with swirling patterns marked by gold thread throughout the body. The sleeves went to the elbows, where they flared outward. From the waist down, the dress spread to the floor.

Samara couldn't stop staring. "I can't wear that."

The servant hung the dress from the changing screen. "You can, and you must. The prince has insisted."

Samara pursed her lips. Nickson knew she didn't wear dresses, but she was about to meet King Montcroix. She had to take a few moments to think about it, but in the end, logic won out over social expectations.

Nickson looked surprised when he saw Samara enter the parlor. "You're in breeches."

"I saw the dress and it is beautiful, but I couldn't wear it. I need the king to see me as I am, and I need to be me when I talk to him about the Hungau."

Nickson smiled. "I figured as much. Might I convince you to wear a gown to the banquet tonight?"

Samara laughed, but hesitated. "I guess that is unavoidable, right?"

"You will be beautiful no matter what you choose to wear."

She met his gaze. "You think so?"

He nodded purposefully. "I don't put you in a dress to change who you are or to compare you to women at court."

"I know. The banquet is a formal event and I should dress for the occasion."

Nickson closed the distance and Samara's heart fluttered in response.

"May I be so bold as to claim the first two dances?" The green of his eyes intensified.

Samara couldn't speak. The very presence of the prince, standing close to her in this way, made her lose her breath. All she could do was nod.

He bowed to her. "I look forward to being your dance partner."

"And I yours, Sire."

She evenly met his gaze. He took another step toward her.

A knock sounded at the door and a servant entered abruptly. "Your Highness, the king is ready for you."

Nickson moved away from her, and Samara, suddenly embarrassed, cast her eyes to the floor.

"Thank you," Nickson said to the servant. He turned to her. "Are you ready to meet my father?"

Still breathless, words continued to escape her.

He held up his arm for her to take and she willingly did so. They walked through the hallways in companionable silence until Nickson stopped.

"My father is not easy to deal with," he said with concern in his eyes.

"I'm sure it will be fine," she tried.

He looked in the direction they were headed. "Don't be offended if he is sharp with you. He will be respectful, but he's not always kind."

She put a hand on his arm. "Don't worry about me. I can handle whatever comes."

He nodded, but his expression was still uncertain.

The dining hall was as Samara remembered. The only difference was the king's presence—which seemed to fill the entirety of the room. Beside him at the table were several other men who looked rather important.

When she entered, King Algernon did not stand the way Samara knew Nickson would have. Nickson led her to the table where he sat. When he bowed to his father, Samara also bowed. She averted her gaze to the ground and bent her head. She could feel the king's eyes on her, but she didn't dare look up until she was invited to.

"Please, rise."

Samara lifted her head. Her eyes found the king first—he was hard to miss. His light, graying hair fell to his shoulders, and his graying beard made him look both regal and formidable. His gaze was harsh, judgmental. When he finally stood to greet her, she watched the rest of the guests stand in mimic of their king. The king's eyes fell to her breeches, and their eyes followed. The hush of whispered voices sounded from the other guests.

"Welcome, Samara Wells, from the Forests of the North," the king said.

"Thank you, Your Majesty."

"Please sit and join me for breakfast."

Nickson led her to a chair at the table. After she was seated, by Nickson himself, the others also sat. It may have been her imagination, but when Nickson tucked in her chair, Algernon Montcroix set his jaw in what looked like annoyance. It was so fleeting, she decided she was just being self-conscious.

"Let me introduce you to some of the most important men in Cascadia," King Algernon said. "This is my chancellor, William Forde."

An older man stood. He smiled easily and had a kindness about his face that Samara immediately found pleasing.

"Lady Wells, a pleasure."

"Chancellor," she nodded to him.

"These two men are my most trusted lawyers: Jensen Scrivens and Theodore Dempster."

They nodded to her but did not speak. Each wore a giant ribbon around their neck. Attached to the ribbon was a giant medal emblazoned with a symbol of a scroll with a crown. These medals showed who practiced law on the king's legal counsel. Samara could tell they wore them proudly.

"We are missing my cavalry commander, but I'm afraid he had some business with the troops this morning."

"Carson Ryker," Nickson supplied. "He's very dedicated to his cavalrymen. You'll meet him tonight."

"Thank you for having me, Your Majesty," Samara said.

"We appreciate your father in lending you to us," the king said. "Though I must say I am surprised."

"Surprised?" Samara asked.

"It has been quite some time since we've had the honor of

having a Gardien here at court, and usually the affairs of the kingdom are reserved for the men. Not the ladies," he hinted.

Samara caught on at once. "Please do not be offended by my father's absence. He is currently taking care of some other business regarding what I am here to discuss. I don't doubt he sent me here in his place not only because I am capable of relaying the information but also to teach me a thing or two about how these games work."

A smile crossed the king's face and the lawyers chuckled. Samara knew she had said the right thing. Nickson unexpectedly reached under the table and grabbed her hand. He reassured her with a quick squeeze and then released it.

His gesture had distracted her, but it had served its purpose and she felt more at ease. She turned and smiled at him.

"Tell us, then, Lady Wells, what your father sent you here to discuss," the chancellor prompted.

"My father is genuinely concerned about the Hungau. Eyewitnesses have seen firsthand that the tragic events at Bender Village and Treewell were not the cause of civil disputes. Hungau were spotted at each site; they started the fires and massacred the villagers. I am here to testify to the truthfulness of these accounts."

"Your father sent Rawlins here the night it happened," the king stated carefully.

Samara nodded. "Rawlins was present at both scenes."

"Dagan is a powerful man," the king considered. "I suppose the entire Gardien nation believes as you and Rawlins do."

"Our experience with the Hungau will not allow us to ignore the truth of what is happening in Cascadia."

"Your truth? Or mine?"

Samara hesitated. How could she refute the king's claims without calling him a liar? She could not accuse the king of dishonesty straight to his face. She had to choose her words carefully, for what she said next could either help or hinder their progress. Her eyes wandered to William's face, and his expression was encouraging. Nickson again reached under the table and grabbed her hand. This time, she did not let go.

She swallowed and looked the king right in the eye. "You know about everything going on in Cascadia, I have no doubt. As my family is uniquely close to the problems concerning the Hungau, my role in coming here is to convey the intimate details about the circumstances."

Nickson squeezed her hand again and she released a silent breath. King Algernon lifted his chin ever so slightly, and his eyes narrowed marginally. He did not move his critical gaze from her face, and she fought the urge to squirm underneath it. With Nickson's grip in her own she held her ground, though the silence grew uncomfortable. After a breath too many, the king finally spoke.

"I am not unaware of the history you share. There have been battles between the Gardiens and the Hungau before. How do I know this isn't some ploy to get my armies to protect you? If this is some territorial dispute, then you may fight amongst yourselves."

"It is a territorial dispute," Samara countered, "but it's a dispute with the crown. Bender and Treewell are not under Gardien control; they fall under your protection."

"We cannot afford small skirmishes within the country," Nickson added. "We cannot allow groups that provoke our citizens to go at each other like chickens in a cockfight. We run things with law and order."

Again, the king was silent. Samara knew her answer had left him in a precarious position. If he acknowledged the Hungau attacks, he would have no choice but to act accordingly. If he didn't, then Samara was in a prime position to educate him on what he did not know. The king did not strike her as a man who liked to be educated by the people beneath him.

She waited. Whatever the king did next would speak volumes to her and her people. If he alienated the Gardiens now, the king risked weakening a major defense on the northeastern side of his country and abandoning the treaty that secured Gardien loyalty. If that happened, life would get harder for Algernon Montcroix. In order to keep the Gardiens on his side, he had to address the falsities of his reports. Samara genuinely wondered if he was capable of such humility.

"And what if these were Hungau attacks?" the king asked.

"Then you have a problem," Samara said bluntly.

The king brought a finger to his lips. "And what problem would that be?"

"My father has contacts all throughout the region. One of those contacts has informed him that the Hungau are looking to invade Cascadia in full. Treewell and Bender were but a taste of what is to come."

"That's impossible." The king stood. "The Hungau would not dare to attack me."

"They already have, and I'm inclined to believe Dagan's contact," Nickson said. "The report seems valid."

"You're asking us to trust a report from a person we've never met," Jensen said. "That's hardly wise, Your Majesty."

"I'm asking you to trust my father," Samara countered. "He would not have sent me here with false information."

Algernon turned to his son. "You seem to be in line with the Gardiens."

Nickson nodded. "Spending time with them has allowed me to see firsthand how they operate. Dagan's reputation speaks for itself, and he is more convincing in person. I do not believe he would lie."

The king's eyes swept back to Samara. She had the distinct impression he, too, would not call Dagan a liar. He sank back into his chair and clenched his jaw.

"Dagan is prepared to offer his finest warriors to aid you in this fight," Samara said.

"Use of the Gardien warriors does not need to be decided now," Nickson said quickly. "We can address that later."

Samara took note that this was the second time Nickson had

refused the use of her father's armies. She put it in the back of her mind for now but determined she would speak to him later and get an explanation.

The king looked between them. "You both think I should go to war?"

"I think the Hungau should be stopped. What form that takes is your decision alone," Samara said.

He laughed. "It's clear you think my decision should be to attack them. To what end? Am I to obliterate an entire nation of people?"

"They have murdered your own people." Samara raised her voice. "And they have vowed to do it again. I am not alone in wondering why the rest of Cascadia has been left unprotected."

Algernon's piercing eyes locked on hers and a shudder threatened to crawl up her spine. His face flushed in annoyance. "You speak out of turn."

"My apologies—"

"Silence!"

Samara flinched at the king's outburst. She was about to reach for Nickson's hand, when she realized they had been holding hands throughout the discussion. He had never let it go. He stroked the back of her hand with this thumb, and the action soothed her anxious heart.

"Father, did you or did you not know about the Hungau attacking those villages?" Nickson asked.

The king blinked. Samara kept her eyes on Nickson, grateful he had asked the question that had been on her mind since this discussion had started.

"You do not need to answer that question," Theodore said quickly.

"Lady Wells," the king hissed, "leave here immediately. We are finished."

Surprised by the turn their meeting had taken, Samara moved to stand, but Nickson stopped her.

"Samara, stay right where you are," he said. "Father, let's speak in private."

The chancellor stood and pushed the two lawyers out of their seats.

"Your Majesty, we should be present for this conversation," Jensen said.

Nickson's hand slipped out of Samara's and he stood. An angry expression fell upon his features. "You are dismissed, gentlemen."

Of all the reactions today, it was Nickson's that took Samara most by surprise. His tone, though calm and controlled, seethed with an undercurrent of authority. The anger thickened and deepened his voice, but his careful governance of his temper made him more commanding than anyone else in the room.

The lawyers, aware of what they had released in their prince, wisely departed. William followed. Soon, the king, Nickson, and Samara were alone in the room.

"Answer the question," Nickson demanded. "Did you know about the attacks?"

Algernon took a deep breath. "One of my first duties as king is to protect the people. That also means I must protect them from themselves. If I acknowledged the attacks, there would have been panic."

Nickson's eyes widened in shock.

Samara felt her jaw drop.

"You lied to me," Nickson said through clenched teeth. "You lied to your own son!"

"Waging war would be a waste of lives and resources. They only attacked the small villages, and by the time I received word, it was too late anyway."

"You murdered those people," Nickson accused.

The king's eyes flickered to Samara. "I did not, son."

"You left them to die. What's the difference?" Nickson inhaled, an action clearly intended to calm himself. "Our job for the past century has been to watch the Hungau. Do you see the danger you have brought upon your country? The rebel group attacked your eastern side. By not responding truthfully from the beginning, you have allowed them to continue to grow, and now we're dealing with the possibility of war. If you aren't going to stop them, it's the same as siding with the enemy."

An awkward feeling sprung up inside Samara's chest. Why was it, whenever she was with Nickson, she was reminded of the Hungau blood coursing through her body? It suddenly felt like a shameful secret. She was here to declare that the Hungau were enemies to the country, but was her mother not a Hungau? Her uncle? She felt a potent desire to let Nickson know the truth, but fear of his response halted her from doing so. She bit her bottom lip in silence.

"Then what do you suggest?" the king asked with a dismissive wave of his hand.

"Me?" Nickson bellowed. "You're the king. You figure it out."

"Nickson, this country is as much yours as it is mine, and you will do as I say," the king hissed.

"You told me to ignore the Hungau—to ignore the people who are dying because of your lack of protection. I will not follow you in this way."

The king froze.

"You will leave it to me to figure things out, Father. You have let this go for far too long. I will head this campaign against the Hungau."

Nickson took Samara's arm, helped her stand, and brought her closer to him.

"Samara will be my contact with the Gardiens, and she will be allowed inside the castle whenever I see fit."

The king's eyes were ablaze. "Do not forget that I am still the king. I will not sanction the military to follow any of your orders until you get the proof we discussed."

"You still need evidence the Hungau are looking to attack you?"

"I demand it, my *son*."

The way the king addressed Nickson reminded Samara of a snakebite, venomous and deadly. The king did not acknowledge her again before he strode out of the room. He slammed the door behind him.

She closed her eyes against the problems she had just caused between Nickson and his father. She had not meant to be a wedge in their relationship.

Nickson's anger was palpable, though his efforts to remain calm were paying off. Samara didn't speak; she wanted to give him as much time to compose himself as necessary, but mostly she didn't know what to say. The king's confession spoke volumes about the situation with the Hungau.

Finally, Nickson turned to her. "I am sorry you had to see that," he said in a low, tense voice, "but I wanted you to get your answer."

"I am sorry."

He took both of her hands in his. "Please do not tell Dagan or the council about my father's lies. Not yet. There are still pieces I need to figure out."

"I will need to return tomorrow morning," she said. "I will keep things to myself until after we get the evidence, but then my father should be filled in."

He nodded curtly. "If you'll excuse me, I need to get some air."

"If it's easier for you, I can leave today."

"I do not want you to leave."

Samara took a deep breath. "I caused a rift between you and your father. I am sorry. I don't know if he likes me much."

"If you want to go, I won't stop you, but I'm asking you to stay. Do not worry about him."

Samara stared at the man who desired her company. "Nickson, I have caused you much grief in the short time I've known you."

"You are not to blame for what is happening here. Things have been strained for quite some time; today was the pivotal point."

She nodded. "If you're sure, I'll stay."

"I'm more sure about you than anything else," he said, looking relieved. "So far, you're one of the few people who hasn't lied to me. Now if you'll excuse me, I do need to get some air." He bowed and left the room.

Samara also departed and went straight to a place that reminded her of home. She found refuge outside in the royal gardens, away from the king's wrath and away from the prince's false notion that she was honest. Cursing her Hungau heritage, she took a deep breath. She needed fresh air too.

CHAPTER TEN

The sun dipped in the sky before Samara saw Nickson again, but she figured it was for the best. She spent her time out in the gardens, sitting on the cool grass reading a book from one of the castle's libraries. No one bothered her there, except for the gardener, but he was busy working. He clipped away at some flowers and put them in a basket. Samara recalled the several vases of flowers throughout the castle and assumed the gardener was charged with beautifying the indoors as well as the out. It wasn't until the sun had started to set that Nickson found her outside.

"How are you feeling?" he asked her.

"I'm fine," she said with a yawn. "I'm more worried about you." She eyed him curiously.

"I'm much better." He kicked at a rock with his boot. "I apologize for my temper."

"You don't have a temper, Nickson."

He cracked a smile, and the sight was a relief.

"I came to tell you the banquet is starting soon. The servants have been asking where you are, so I told them I would come find you."

"Do they need something?" Samara gathered her book and stood.

"They need you." He smiled. "They seem anxious to get you ready."

"Get me ready?" She looked in the direction of her bedroom.

"Yes, they insisted upon it. Come, let's indulge them this once." He held out his arm and she took it, as was becoming their routine.

He led her inside and left her to her room so he, too, could get ready. Samara opened the door to find that a bath had been drawn. The scent of lavender and honey drifted to her nose.

"There you are, miss." It was the same handmaiden who had helped her before. She practically danced with excitement.

"What is all this?"

"We are going to get you ready for your first banquet!" she cried.

A second handmaiden came out of the bathroom with a towel. "Get undressed. These scents will make you smell divine."

Samara did as she was told. These girls seemed so excited to attend to her needs that she didn't want to dash their hopes. Once she was in the tub, she let the soap envelop her. She took a deep breath and let the herbs they had added clear her mind. She was so relaxed, and the water felt so good against her shoulders, she barely noticed the handmaidens as they roughly scrubbed and washed her hair.

They chatted excitedly about the dress Samara would wear. Samara mostly tuned them out, but heard enough to catch their names. The girl who had been helping her was Mary. The other was Constance.

"Just wait until you see the dress!" Mary sang.

"I can't believe he picked it out himself," Constance piped in.

This broke through Samara's reverie. "Wait, what?"

Mary smiled. "The prince, he picked the dress out himself. Just for you!"

"He said, and I'm quoting this exactly, 'This one. It will look great with the dark shade of her hair,'" Constance chimed.

"Why would he pick out my dress?" Samara asked, confused.

Mary and Constance exchanged a loaded glance. "I can think of a few reasons," they giggled together.

Samara tried to sink low into the water.

"Oh, no you don't. It's time to get out! We need to dry your hair and brush it out."

Samara wanted to complain but decided it wouldn't do her any good. She climbed out of the tub and Constance placed the warmest, coziest robe around her.

They sat her down in a cushioned seat in front of a large mirror. The mirror was part of a larger vanity set of drawers and cupboards. After drying her hair they combed it. Samara's hair was already thick and naturally wavy, and the girls adorned it with a wreath of small white flowers.

"Flowers in my hair?"

"Of course," Mary said, her tone suggesting that to wear no flowers would be a sin. "Normally the ladies at court wear their hair up, but we decided yours should be worn down."

Samara nodded, not really understanding what they were talking about. With careful patience, her hair was soon beautifully arranged. The wavy locks cascaded to the middle of her back. They applied a little face powder and some lemon oil to her lips, giving her cheeks a nice rosy glow and her lips a nice shine.

"Do you like it?" Mary asked as Samara eyed the stranger in the mirror.

"I do!" Samara said. "I mean, it's different."

"You look gorgeous!" Constance beamed.

"Come look at the dress." Mary bounded over to the closet. Samara couldn't help but smile as she realized she would fit in at court after all.

Mary yanked open the doors and stepped aside so Samara could see. Hanging in the closet was a beautiful, scarlet dress. Unlike the green dress, the sleeves hugged her arm just past the elbow. The neckline swooped slightly off the shoulders. The bodice, covered in red lace and floral appliques, fit snugly at the waist. The dress flowed to the floor with a red train following close behind. Sections of material had been gathered and pinned throughout the bottom of the dress, creating a fountain effect. On the shelf next to the dress was a small box with a white pearl bracelet.

"This is for me?" Samara couldn't believe her eyes.

"All for you," Constance crooned.

"Quick, let's get it on!" Mary begged.

Samara laughed and agreed.

In no time, the dress had been put on and the bracelet clasped to her wrist. A pair of red shoes completed the look.

"All set." Mary bounced up and down.

Samara looked in the full-length mirror and couldn't help but admire the beauty of the gown. She loved how she looked in it and was grateful to Nickson for taking care of her.

"You need to go. The banquet has already started!" Constance wailed.

Samara gathered her dress and made her way to the ballroom. She had not seen this part of the castle yet, but when she reached the huge oak doors, she realized she was nervous. The guards at the door opened them up for her, and a person standing at the top of the stairs asked for her name.

"Samara Wells of the Forests of the North," she said. She wrung her hands when a nervous energy flushed her face.

The person loudly announced her entry. She focused on keeping her hands still and began the long descent down the grand staircase to the dance floor. She looked for Nickson and saw him approach the bottom of the stairs. For a moment, their eyes met, and Samara wondered what he thought of her dress. He had picked it out for her, after all. Nickson never took his eyes away from hers as she made her descent. When they finally came together, he took her hand and kissed it.

"You are beautiful," he said.

She smiled. "Thank you. You picked a wonderful dress."

"Ah, but you were the inspiration." He took her hand and led her to the middle of the floor, all the while not taking his eyes off of her.

He turned to face her. "Would you please dance with me?"

She smiled. "You sound as if it is an urgent matter."

He put his arm around her lower back and pulled her closer. "I've got to claim my dances before others swoop in."

Before she could respond, he had her twirling across the floor. With one hand on his shoulder and the other held tightly in his, he led her to the upbeat tune coming from the small group of minstrels.

Samara noticed for the first time what Nickson wore. He had on a navy-blue coat with gold buttons and a thin gold border. A white, button-down tunic, under a blue overcoat, also with gold buttons, completed his top. He wore white breeches with a navy-blue stripe down each leg, and black shoes. To complete his ensemble, a decorative dress sword hung from a sturdy, black belt fastened around his waist.

"Your Highness, you look very handsome this evening," she complimented.

"Thank you." He smiled. "*You* are absolutely stunning." His eyes ran over the length of her dress.

Samara blushed. "Thank you. I love the dress."

"Do you?" he urged. "I wanted to get it right, and after seeing you, I believe it suits you perfectly."

"I do love it. I have never worn anything this fancy." She couldn't suppress a giggle.

He laughed. "I'm glad you're having fun," he mused.

They both fell quiet for a moment. Samara, suddenly aware of Nickson's proximity, looked up at him. "I'm having fun with you," she clarified.

Before he could respond, the song had ended and everyone around them lightly clapped. They both followed suit and turned back to each other.

He leaned down and whispered in her ear. "I would like to introduce you to some of the people at court."

"People don't care about me," she countered.

"On the contrary." He smiled. "Everyone was looking at you when you entered."

Samara eyed everyone suspiciously. "Why?"

"There are two reasons I can guess. First, you are part of the Forests of the North. They all know who you are though they've never seen you. Second, because you're breathtaking."

Samara laughed. "Now you're just trying to make me feel better."

She stopped laughing when she realized he was being serious. "You are so breathtaking; I can't keep my eyes off you."

Her heart beat wildly as she realized what Nickson was saying. His intense green eyes searched her face, her eyes, her cheeks, her nose. They lingered on her lips.

For a moment the crowd around them disappeared. The music faded into the background and all she could see was Nickson. He looked so handsome with his brown hair, green eyes, and olive-toned skin. His strong shoulders and strong hands that had held her while they danced left a lingering feeling on her back. For a moment she longed for them to hold her again.

"Nickson. Introduce me to your friend."

Samara turned to see who had spoken. A tall, dark-haired man, well-built with observant eyes, smiled at her.

Nickson subtly rolled his eyes. "Commander Carson Ryker, this is Lady Wells of the Forests of the North. Carson is one of my friends here at court and the king's cavalry commander."

He took her hand and kissed it; his lips lingered a little too long. "My Lady," his bass voice sounded. "I would love to have the next dance, if you are not otherwise engaged."

Nickson shook his head behind his friend's back and Samara pursed her lips to keep from laughing.

"Actually," she replied, "I am taken for at least the next two dances."

Nickson visibly relaxed.

"As I suspected," Carson said. He pulled her a little closer. "But save one for me." With a wink in her direction, he turned. "Good to see you, Nickson." He strode off.

Nickson grabbed Samara's arm and pulled her to him. "Of all the vultures here at court, you do not want to mess with that one."

"I thought you said he was your friend?"

"Friend *at court*," he emphasized. "It's code for 'not my friend at all but I have to pretend for the sake of my father.'"

Samara laughed. "I'll be sure to steer clear of him."

"I have a feeling he won't be the only one," Nickson muttered.

She put a finger to his lips to quiet him. "You still have two dances, and you never know when I'll have to rest my feet."

He laughed loudly and pulled her in for another dance. She was able to ward off two other "vultures," as Nickson called them, before the music stopped, and dinner was announced.

A meal of salmon, vegetables, bread, and wine had been spread before the guests. Nickson had reserved a seat for Samara near the head of the table where he sat, and the king sat at the other end of the long table. She was dismayed to find that Carson was seated directly across from her. She did not like the forward and presumptuous way he had treated her before—as if she ought to save him anything, let alone a dance—but it wasn't long before he engaged her in conversation.

"So, tell me, Lady Wells. I hear you have experience with the Hungau."

Several other people tuned in to listen to the conversation, including the chancellor, two other men Samara did not recognize, and Nickson. She thought carefully before she spoke. "I do. What else have you heard?"

Carson's eyes glistened. "I have heard you are in favor of war and are here to persuade the king."

Samara finished chewing a piece of roll. "If I may ask you, Commander, how would you feel if a group of men approached you with fire and arrows? How would you feel if they slaughtered your family and your loved ones? How would you feel if you heard they were coming back?"

Carson didn't miss a beat. "I would kill them, of course."

Samara had a feeling he was just saying what she wanted to hear. "And what if the king deemed that against the law?"

More people stopped to hear their conversation. Carson hesitated. "Of course, I would do what is right."

"And what would that be? In your eyes, of course," she asked him.

Carson twirled his dinner knife. "Of course, there is no way to gauge without being in that situation," he said with a laugh, while others joined in with him.

Samara nodded in understanding; he would not put himself in a compromising situation that affected his status with the king.

"What would you do?" he asked her. A manipulative gleam filled his eyes.

Samara met his gaze, unafraid. "I would not let innocent people die, regardless of what any king had ordered."

Carson's lips twitched. "You would then be hanged for treason, Lady Wells."

"But at least my conscience would be clear," she retorted.

The people around her fell silent as she took a bite of her fish.

Carson's smile widened. "Of course, you speak theoretically." He took a longer than necessary sip from his wine glass.

Samara didn't reply. She only smiled at him.

Carson pursed his lips. "Nickson! You can't sit over there and listen to this woman speak treason." Then he laughed as if this were all playful banter.

All eyes fell on Nickson. He looked at everyone around him. "I expect people I know, especially those in my court, to do the morally correct thing. Man is not perfect; therefore, laws are not perfect." His gaze fell on Samara. "Is Lady Wells speaking treason? Or is she merely defining the boundaries of her moral character?"

Small chatter played around the table, and Carson frowned.

"Carson, you are the one who sparked this conversation," Nickson said. "If you do not like its outcome, then next time I suggest you think before you speak."

Everyone laughed, and Carson turned a light shade of blush and took another drink. Samara suppressed a laugh and smiled gratefully in Nickson's direction. He nodded once, and they all continued eating as if nothing had happened. Carson didn't say one more word during dinner, and for that Samara was grateful. When she felt full, she waited, as everyone did, for Nickson's actions to excuse everyone else from dinner. At his signal, the dinner plates were cleared, and the dancing resumed. Dessert tables lining the dance floor were filled with sweets of every kind. Samara sampled a few before meeting Nickson on the dance floor.

"Colorful people, don't you think?" Nickson rolled his eyes.

Samara shook her head. "I do not like Carson. He seems half a man as any I've seen."

Nickson laughed appreciatively. "I wish he could hear you say that."

They had only spoken for a few moments when Carson approached them. Samara groaned quietly.

"My lady, to show no ill will, I would be honored by a dance."

Nickson tensed beside her, but she felt that in good grace she could not decline Carson's invitation again. She accepted. The music began, and they went twirling away, leaving an irritated Nickson behind them.

Carson wasted no time cutting to the chase. "I did not appreciate your little stunt back at the dinner table," he jeered politely. As if jeering politely were possible.

"I only told you what I thought. I cannot help other people's comments," Samara said calmly.

Carson smirked. "Don't play naïve, Lady Wells. You seem to have the prince wrapped around your pretty little finger."

She glanced across the room toward Nickson, who watched them with a sour expression. "I do not know what you are talking about."

"Of course you don't," he taunted her. He pulled her closer. "You would be wise to stay out of the king's way, as well as Nickson's. They do not need your Gardien assertions any more than they need a peasant at court."

Samara tried to pull away from him, but he held her fast. "You're threatened by me," she stated.

Carson laughed. "Not in the least."

"Then why the warnings? The prince obviously disagrees with you, and values my opinion and my expertise."

Carson stared at her. They had stopped dancing, yet he grabbed her arms and pulled her closer still. His fingers dug into her arms and the smell of wine on his breath was unmistakable.

"Let me go," she hissed. She could easily free herself from him, but she did not want to cause a scene, and she especially did not want to rip her dress.

He leaned down and whispered fiercely in her ear. "Lady Wells, heed my warnings. All this talk about disobeying the crown will only get you and your forest-dwelling father a charge of sedition. You cannot afford to get on the king's bad side."

Something in Carson's eyes told Samara he was serious. In them she could see something deeper, deeper than the charming, popular jester she had met at dinner, but it was a puzzle she couldn't figure out. What she did know was that another moment spent in his company was a moment too long. She recoiled from him but wasn't able to go far. Carson, the same height and build as Nickson, was deceptively strong. She glanced at the spot where she had last seen the prince, but he no longer stood there.

Suddenly, Nickson's voice came out of nowhere. "Let her go, Carson," he said calmly, though there was an edge to it.

Carson's grip tightened and he didn't say anything.

Nickson gripped Carson's arm. "You've had one drink too many, my friend. Let go."

Carson kept his narrowed eyes on Samara's for another moment before a haughty smirk lifted the corner of his mouth. His chin jutted out and his stance relaxed, giving the appearance he didn't care about what had happened. His face was the picture of charm. He finally let go.

"You be careful with this one," Carson hissed. "She has no place in the castle."

Nickson moved closer to Samara and instinctively put her behind him. Carson's face flushed.

"You choose her over your trusted friends, then?"

"You're making a big deal out of nothing, Carson. Go to bed, now."

Carson released a short, nervous laugh. He glared at Samara. "You remember what I said, sweet." He tucked his hair back into place and sauntered off.

Nickson let out his breath. Samara hadn't realized it, but she had been holding hers as well. No one else in the ballroom seemed to have noticed the exchange.

She looked at Nickson. "I am causing so much trouble being here."

"I've always had trouble with Carson, but never, admittedly, like that." Nickson looked worried.

"I do need to leave tomorrow morning and return home," she said. "Things need to be finalized."

Nickson nodded in understanding. "Do you have it in you for one more dance?"

Samara looked at the dance floor where couples were still twirling. "If you promise it's with you."

Nickson smiled, though his face was still tense. "I wouldn't dream of it any other way, Samara. You are not leaving my side for the rest of the night."

Chapter Eleven

The next morning, Samara arose early to prepare for her journey. After her adventures last night, she felt it best to get away from the castle as soon as possible. She wanted to say goodbye to Nickson, but he was nowhere in sight as she finished packing her horse. The stable hand filled flasks with her in the stable.

"Excuse me," Samara asked him. "Have you seen the prince?"

"I haven't, my lady," he said. "I'm sorry."

Samara looked back at the castle before she returned her focus to Taiga. Her hands adjusted and tightened her pack with ease, then she led her horse out of the stable where she put her foot in the stirrup and mounted. A longing to see Nickson one more time drew her gaze back to the castle, but she would have to live with her disappointment. The young man handed her the water, she double-checked that her dagger was at her waist, then she turned her horse toward the gate.

"Samara!"

She turned toward the familiar voice and smiled. She gave the stable hand the reins and jumped down, meeting Nickson on the ground.

"I was worried I missed you," he explained.

"Still here for now." She smiled.

"Thank you for dancing with me last night. I enjoyed your company. I enjoyed your company over the last few days, in fact."

Samara felt a tiny blush rise to her cheeks. "And I yours, Sire."

"Samara, I hate to see you leave. I understand it has to be done, but you will be missed."

She nodded. "It was a different experience staying here," she admitted. "But thank you for taking care of me."

"I apologize for Carson," he said.

Samara held up her hand to stop him. "You never apologize for him," she demanded. "Ever. You are not the same."

"I want to see you again."

"I would like that very much," she agreed.

She turned and climbed on her horse. Nickson took her hand and kissed the top of it. He didn't let it go right away, and Samara didn't want him to. His hand was warm and comfortable.

She looked up toward the sky, mostly out of habit.

"You need to go," he said with a hint of regret, and released her hand.

"I do."

She grabbed the reins. "We'll send word of our progress. I'm sure much was decided in my absence."

"Of course. I'll be waiting."

Samara gave him one last smile and took off with a bolt. Nickson watched her until she was out of sight. She didn't realize the stifling effect of the castle until she was riding free under the gray morning sky. The clouds rolled overhead and a cool breeze whipped past as her horse sped toward the Forests. Soon, the sun was rising, and the birds began their songs.

During her ride she mused over her stay at the castle. It would be quite a story to tell. Of course, she would leave out some of the details—all the compliments Nickson had given her, how he picked out her dress, and her run-in with Carson. She did not want to worry her father, and she did not want to anger Maddox. She did wonder when she would see Nickson again. A few days without him wouldn't hurt. It should also make Maddox happy.

It took her two days to make it back to her father's home, but as she rode up to the gate everyone scurried about. Her father was discussing something with Maddox and the other men. Tristan was among them, and for a moment, Samara was worried. What had they decided while she was gone?

"Father?" she called out.

Dagan turned. "Samara! It is wonderful to see you." He gave her a hug. "Was your stay enjoyable? I wasn't expecting you back so soon."

"It was great, but it's good to be home."

"Welcome back, Samara," Danson called. Rawlins and Casimir followed with Maddox at their heels. Samara studied her friend's face and could see she was not forgiven yet.

She noticed their packs and weapons. "What are you packing for?"

"Just getting ready for our trip," Rawlins said casually.

None of them made eye contact with her.

"What is going on?" she demanded.

Dagan spoke first. "Maddox can catch you up. We will finish packing."

Maddox reluctantly stepped forward while the others disappeared. "Come help me in the stables."

As Samara helped him prepare the horses, she asked, "Maddox, what is going on?"

He looked uncomfortable. "Samara, there is something you must know." He took a deep breath. "Your father is sending a party to collect the evidence."

Samara felt the blood drain from her face as his meaning sank in. She knew her father's tactics: a small team would slip into Eagle's Bay unnoticed, spy for an indeterminable amount of time, recover the evidence, and slip out. If all went well, they would return with the strategies and directions and anything else that would reveal the Hungau's plans. If it failed, as parties had before them, they would be killed on the spot. She also knew the team would be volunteers—and Maddox always volunteered.

Her eyes welled with tears, but she succeeded in holding them back. "This means you're going."

Maddox nodded. She wanted to ask him why, but already knew his answer: he fought for the weak and believed himself to be one of the most able-bodied members of their people. He would go and he would fight, and he would do all he could to bring down the enemy, even if that meant giving his life. She wished she could be as strong as he was.

"We are going into the heart of the Hungau," he said. "We have decided we will not get the evidence we need by talking to our contact alone. He doesn't want to risk exposure by handing it over."

"And the king demands it."

Maddox nodded. "We have our route all planned out, and the five of us will make contact when we can."

Samara nodded. "Who is the fifth?"

"Tristan," he said with admiration.

"He's former Hungau," she said. "He will be a great asset to you. He knows their land well."

Maddox crossed his arms. "Not everyone knows he's former Hungau."

"I haven't told the prince," she said. "There is no reason for the crown to know; it's not important."

"It might be important to him," he countered. "And what if he finds out? What would he do if he found out your mother was former Hungau too?"

"Family sticks together, Maddox. That's what we do. If he has a problem with it, then that is his alone." Samara sighed. "Why are we even discussing Nickson? You're leaving—that's more important right now."

Maddox had been on several missions, but his experience never lessened Samara's worry for her family. Dagan believed in an active military that understood their enemies' goings-on. They had always kept watch, especially on the Hungau, but going this far into Hungau territory was a rare thing. Few ever returned from such a dangerous journey. And whatever missions Maddox went on, Danson, Rawlins, and Casimir would be there too. They always stuck together and were one of the best teams the Forests of the North had to offer. Samara snatched her head up as an idea occurred to her.

"I'll be right back," she yelled to Maddox as she scurried out of the stables.

"Samara, wait!"

She ran to her father's chambers with Maddox right behind her. She fell against the door and thrust it open. "Father."

"Yes, dear?" Concern creased the edges of his forehead. "Are you all right?"

"I'm concerned."

"What about?" he said, and pat a chair for her to sit in.

"Maddox."

"Samara, what are you doing?" Maddox asked impatiently.

Her father pursed his lips. "Both of you sit down."

"I don't want him to go," she confessed.

"Samara, he is one of the best I have."

"Father, I know," she said briskly, "but he's one of the best *I* have."

Maddox looked at Samara in surprise.

"These men are my family," she said. "I can't let them go out alone while I sit here and worry."

"What do you propose I do? I can't ask him to stay, can I, Maddox?"

Maddox shook his head. "I'm going, Samara."

"You see?" Her father pointed at Maddox. "Asking him to stay would insult him. He wouldn't stay even if I did ask."

"I know." Samara's shoulders slumped. She needed to work up the courage to ask what she really came for. She knew before she even said it that her father would not take to this option well. "Let me go with them."

The idea caught Dagan by surprise. "No. End of discussion."

"Absolutely not," Maddox sternly agreed.

Samara's excitement died. "Father, it would be of use to you and the people. You forget that I am also one of the best you have."

"And the most stubborn." A smile threatened his lips, and she couldn't help but smile in return. "You have already served your people, by going to the castle to take care of matters there."

Maddox spoke. "Sir, please do not let her go."

Dagan nodded. "Samara, you are my only child. Your mother would have my head if I were to send you on a dangerous mission like this. There are things I need you here for." He put his hand on her cheek. "*I* need you here. You give me a strength only your mother could provide. Now I get that strength from you."

She felt tears, but was able to hold them back. "I understand, Father. I just feel ill thinking of the possibility they could never return."

Her father took her face in both of his hands. "It is scary. Death is all around us and is a threat to all that is living, but we must not run from it."

Samara nodded, knowing her father was right. "You always told me there are things in this world that will require great sacrifice and courage, and that we must always accept what we are able to give. To back down would be to give in to a foolish—"

"—and cowardly life," her father finished for her. "So, you see? Maddox will perform well; he will ensure the safety of all those men even if it means giving his life first."

Samara nodded and turned to Maddox. "I guess I can't ask you to stay, either?"

"I'm sorry, Samara, but I need to go. I cannot ask another to go in my place."

She sighed loudly and Dagan hugged her again.

"I admire your courage," he said. "But I cannot let you go." He turned and grabbed Maddox's arm. "Samara, I see Maddox as a son. He also lies close to my heart. I love you both. I am sorry that hard things must be done in your time."

"Some of us wouldn't have it any other way," Maddox muttered, and Samara laughed. Of course Danson and Casimir would have a field day with this assignment. They were brothers, and similar in the fact they never saw the dark side of things.

Samara put on her brave face, and she smiled at her father. "Come on, Maddox. I'll help you finish packing."

The party was sure to leave tomorrow morning, and Maddox would be the first awake, ready to go and conquer. They left Dagan's chambers and Maddox took the opportunity, away from Dagan's presence, to scold Samara.

"You didn't actually think he'd let you go?" He put his arm around her.

Samara clutched his hand. "I had to try. Having me on your team would be beneficial."

He pondered that. "Perhaps," he relented. "But every one of us would be beside ourselves with worry with the constant need to protect you."

She laughed. "That's only because I'm female."

"No offense," he offered, "but exactly. The Hungau do not like Gardien females. If they saw you or ever got close enough to—to—" He stammered over the rest of his sentence.

She squeezed his hand. "Maddox, it's okay. I'm not going. I'm staying here, under house arrest."

He laughed. "As it should be."

They made their way back to the stables so Maddox could finish packing. They worked in silence for a few moments.

"Um, how was your stay at the castle?"

Samara turned to study his features. He looked genuinely interested, but she decided to put him to the test.

"You wouldn't believe it." She began to recount the story of her stay. The magnificent meals and the servants doing everything for her were the pinnacle of her tales. She did not dare mention Nickson's friendly nature, but she did share the king's anger and what she had said.

"You called out the king?" he laughed. "What did he say about the raids?"

Samara busied herself with a saddle. She had promised Nickson she wouldn't say anything until after the evidence had been collected, and she debated now what she should do.

"He didn't say."

Maddox rolled his eyes. "The coward. He'll have to acknowledge it sooner or later."

She nodded. "Yes, he will."

She felt guilty about lying, but Nickson would tell the rest of the Gardien Council when the time was right. She decided she felt safe telling Maddox about Carson and jumped into that story.

"Is this Commander Carson Ryker? I've never met him, but his reputation precedes him. I imagine his objections were because you're female. Were there any other women talking about the Hungau?"

Samara thought for a moment. "Not that I remember. Probably not. They were more interested in other things."

"What did you wear?" Maddox asked curiously.

"A dress."

"What did it look like?"

"Well," she hesitated. "It was scarlet, with flowers. It was huge! But gorgeous. I loved wearing it."

"I bet you looked nice."

She shrugged. "I doubt it." She rubbed the spots on her arms where Carson had bruised them. "But Carson thought so," she muttered.

"What?" Maddox demanded. "What do you mean?"

Samara regretted her words and bit her lip. "He just—" She tucked her hair behind her ears. "It's not important. I'll never see him again."

"Tell me. What happened with the cavalry commander?"

"He asked for a dance and warned me about meeting with the king and Nickson about the Hungau. While we danced, he grabbed my arms. He seemed angry with me." She felt uneasy sharing this with Maddox.

"He did what?" he shouted. The vein in his neck throbbed. "Where was the prince during this?"

"He got Carson to let go of me. It all happened so fast, and Carson had had too much to drink," she tried to explain.

"You are not going back there without me, or some type of guard," he ordered.

"Maddox, stop. I'm probably not going back there ever."

"You can't be sure," he challenged, staring her in the eye.

She stared back. "Well, it's over now."

"I want to have a chat with Carson," he said, still angry.

"Maddox, he really rubbed me the wrong way. I don't like him."

"Understandably. Of all the trouble you get in," he muttered as he raked up more hay.

Samara was grateful their companionship was back, but her mind would not let her forget about the dangerous mission before them.

"Be careful out there."

"I will, Samara. Don't worry."

She dropped her rake. "I will worry, about all of you." Her voice broke.

Maddox stepped toward her and put his hand on her shoulder. "We'll be back," he said, and attempted a smile.

She nodded, but wouldn't believe it until they all returned. She looked at Maddox, taking in his features and the kindness of his brown eyes. They had been friends for years and endured so much together. All her best memories centered on her father and mother, Maddox, Danson, Rawlins, and Casimir. They were her family.

And family sticks together, she thought.

Without making a conscious decision, Samara knew she would be going on that mission. No matter what her father said, she had to help protect Maddox and the rest of the team. It would be a tactic the Hungau would not expect—a Gardien woman in their territory. As long as she could keep her presence hidden, even from Maddox, she could assist them unnoticed. She would stick to the high ridges and act as lookout.

Maddox put his arms around her and gave her a tight squeeze. "You just stay out of trouble while we're gone. We'll all do something fun when we get back. Okay?"

"Okay." She turned away, not wanting to betray her plans. "I'll stay out of trouble."

Maddox eyed her suspiciously. Samara felt she revealed her calmness too quickly, but she did feel calm. The moment she confirmed she would be going, it had felt right. She released Maddox and handed him his pack. Tonight, she would pack her own gear.

Her mind was alive with her plans all through dinner and she barely spoke. When she finally got to go to her room, she assembled her equipment, being sure to keep it light. If she was going to keep up with Maddox and the team, she had to pack as little as possible. She collected her bow and arrows and sharpened each tip, and then prepped her black leather boots. She reinforced them with more leather and put some fustian fabric in the soles to help protect her feet. She could go for days with these boots. She filled her canteens and attached them to her pack, then got dressed in her nightclothes.

That night, she tossed and turned with horrible dreams of Maddox being burned or stabbed by the Hungau. She even dreamed of Nickson's palace getting attacked and destroyed, and she awoke in the middle of the night with a start. Sitting up, she grabbed the dagger hidden under her pillow and held it out to the darkness.

She looked into the room around her and squinted her eyes. She sensed there was someone there. "Hello?"

"Relax, Samara," a gentle but deep voice called out.

She looked harder. "Maddox? What are you doing here?"

"I needed to see you before I left. Your father is not the only one who draws strength from you."

She put the dagger back under her pillow and sat straighter. "Come sit," she said.

She heard movement and Maddox was quickly by her side, letting his legs hang off the bed. He looked at her.

"Are you okay?" she asked.

"I'm not sure."

"Well, this is something that has the whole forest on edge. I don't blame you."

"It's not that," he responded.

She waited for him to continue, but he didn't. "What, Maddox?" she urged gently. "Usually you sleep like a rock."

A smile crossed his face, but disappeared. "I was just thinking about how your mother died."

Samara didn't answer, and didn't know if she wanted to. Her mother's death had been horrible. Despite the years that had passed, she could never erase from her mind the images of that day.

"I know you don't want to talk about it, but I think it would help," he continued.

"Maddox, I haven't talked about her in a long time."

"I know, and I am worried for you. I can only imagine what you might be thinking, and I don't want you to worry."

"Not worry? Maddox, every day I will worry. Until you all return, I will not sleep."

Maddox scooted closer. "Tell me you're not thinking of your mother's mission."

Samara caught her breath in her throat and coughed. "I can't," she confessed.

"I thought so. You know why your father doesn't want you to go."

She glared at him, though she knew in the darkness he couldn't see her face. It was as if he were reading her thoughts. "I know."

Maddox didn't say anything more, and they spent the rest of the early morning sitting side by side. As the darkness whisked by, the solemnity of their mission settled over them, making her uneasy. Samara let this feeling engulf her, as if facing her fears would allow her to handle them better. She succumbed to sleep and closed her eyes.

Long before the sun rose, Samara was awakened by movement. She didn't even realize she had fallen asleep. She reached next to her and found the space empty. Concern filled her before she even opened her eyes, and she bolted upright. "Maddox!"

"Shh," he whispered as he laughed. "I haven't left yet."

She threw the blankets off her. "I'm sorry; I thought I had missed all of you. When do you leave?"

"Soon. All my stuff is downstairs, and the crew is gathering." He motioned to the window and she looked out to see the shadows of the four other men with their horses and packs.

"I can't believe you're all going. Although I can't say it isn't expected."

Maddox nodded. "My friends never leave my side. We trust each other."

As Samara watched the team assemble, it dawned on her that a group of five would be easily noticeable. "I know father usually sends four to five warriors, but why this time, to Eagle's Bay, when the risk of being spotted is much greater?"

"They volunteered when they found I was going. I trust them with my life, more than anyone, and they wouldn't settle for waiting for me to return." He turned to Samara. "I have to go," he stated, and squared his shoulders.

Samara sensed his eagerness. It usually hit at the beginning of a mission then tapered off later, only to spike again if they faced any action. Already prepared for battle, he exited her room. She dressed and met everyone downstairs.

Dagan and what looked like the entire nation of Gardiens had gathered with the team to see them off. Danson, Rawlins, and Casimir brought their horses out of the stables and proceeded to say goodbye to their families. Maddox finished tying his pack to his horse. He glanced at Samara and Dagan, and a grim, cautious expression fell upon his features. Samara wondered what he saw in her face that made him cautious. She hoped he hadn't sensed what she was about to do.

Samara looked at her father, and he nodded in approval. With a few quick steps she approached the men who had become her brothers. She hugged and gave each of them a kiss on the cheek. "Be careful," she pleaded. "Come home soon."

She hugged Maddox last, and his grip suggested that he never wanted to let go. "I will miss you," he whispered.

She nodded. "I will miss you. I will miss all of you."

This seemed to fill Maddox with a surge of confidence. He released her from his hug, lowered his eyes to her face, and spoke in a slow and intentional tone. "Do not get into any trouble. I mean it."

For a moment it seemed he understood her plan. His eyes bore deeply into hers, and she looked away in fear he would see right through her. She backed away when he mounted his horse and reared it up on its hind legs. He circled his horse around, all the while keeping his studious gaze on Samara. Rawlins, who rode in the front of the party, let out a grunt and his horse took off. Danson's horse followed, then Tristan's, and Casimir's and Maddox's.

"They'll be fine," her father assured her.

Samara only nodded, knowing that as soon as her father was back inside, she would be riding toward Eagle's Bay as well. She would be an outlook for the team—their guardian and defender—as she watched over them through every ridge and crest line to be sure they got out safely.

When her father turned and entered the house, Samara wasted no time. She attached her pack to Taiga and mounted the strong horse. She dug her heels into the horse's side and took off through the forest after the team.

CHAPTER TWELVE

Samara knew the route the team would take up to a certain point, so it would be easy to track them for now. She was only a few miles behind them, and she kept Taiga at a slightly faster pace. She would catch up in no time. Of course, once she got closer, she would have to keep her distance to ensure they did not spot her.

Eager to be of use, energy pumped through her veins as she raced on to meet the team. Her father would be furious when he discovered she had gone missing, and she was sure he would form the right conclusion about her absence. But he had to understand—everyone had to—that she needed to be on the team. She could not sit and wait. The mere thought caused her muscles to ache and her head to explode with worry.

She turned her thoughts to something else. She needed to stay focused and alert. She thought of the Hungau and her mother. Her mother had died on a mission to Eagle's Bay and she understood why her father worried, but her mother had been capable and so was she.

An image of her mother's dead face as she last saw her blinded her vision.

A shudder went through her as she recalled those memories. She could not think of them now. A small tear escaped her eye, and she caught it with her gloved finger. She could not afford to lose focus or courage.

With her hand, she gave Taiga a loving pat on the side of his head, grateful for his company. He was truly a gift and had been since the day her mother gave him to her.

She looked ahead of her and realized she had been traveling for half a day. She was still in the safety of the Forests of the North and would be approaching a traveler's cache. Provisions were kept there along with fresh water from a stream.

Soon she approached and cautiously looked around. No one was in sight, but the marks in the dirt were plain to see. Maddox and the boys had stopped only briefly and moved on.

Samara put her hand to her forehead and wiped the sweat there. As she followed their trail, it suddenly disappeared. Forced to stop and analyze the ground more closely, she tried to put herself in Maddox's mind to determine what she should do next. It occurred to her that he would make his trail harder to find. There was no way he would allow anyone to track him beyond this point.

What would Maddox do? She closed her eyes. Up to this point she had been sticking to the trails. Maddox and the team had stopped at the cache for a moment, probably to pick up some spare food, and moved on. If it were Samara, she would leave the trails and make the journey through the forest brush. The trail would be more concealed, although it would take longer.

She circled Taiga around the prints in the dirt and restudied them. For several quiet moments she circled and studied until she found what she was looking for. A smile crossed her lips and she guided her horse in the direction of the team. Leaving the trail meant slower progress for her and Taiga, but meant the same for Maddox and his team of four. She should catch up to them soon.

By the time the sun was high in the sky, she began to think she had tracked them incorrectly. Then she heard voices. She stopped to listen and knew she was on the right track. She slowed even more; if she could hear them, then they could hear her, too, if they were listening.

"Be quiet now, Taiga. We can't afford to be seen." Taiga nodded his head and Samara was confident he understood her.

For a whole day she tracked them patiently, keeping to the cover of the trees as much as possible. A couple of times she saw them ahead of her, and she stopped to allow more distance between them.

At this rate, one day's ride to the east from Dagan's manor brought a rider to the edge of the Forests of the North. Beyond that spanned Cascadia country—an expanse of grassy hills and rivers. Half a day from the edge of the Forests, continuing east, led a rider to the coast. However, the easier route to Eagle's Bay—the Hungau stronghold—was to follow Cascadia country to the north for an extra half day. At this point, a turn to the east put them into the dense forest that surrounded Eagle's Bay. Eagle's Bay was a vast expanse of woodland that led from the coastal cliffs inland for miles. Once they reached the woodland, it would be another day's journey into the heart of Hungau territory. At least, that was the assumption; no one from the outside world had entered Eagle's Bay since Calida's death.

The trip, from Dagan's home to the heart of Hungau lands, could take about three days. The return trip to home was another three. With six to seven days on the road, Samara was glad she had planned her gear accordingly.

During the ride through Cascadia country, Samara kept even more distance between her and the team. Through open country it was easier to see if someone was following, and she was intent on keeping her presence unknown.

The ride up the coast was more challenging. The team was sleeping for short periods at night, each taking watch in their turn. Samara was growing tired and wondered if she could spare a few moments of rest. She would have to catch up with them and perhaps retrace some steps, but she was confident in her abilities to do so. Just as she considered stopping, she saw the team had stopped up ahead.

She brought Taiga to a halt. It was late in the afternoon of their second day, and they were still a few miles from the edge of Eagle's Bay. She wondered what they were doing, but her questions were answered when she saw Maddox remove his pack from his horse.

They were resting!

Samara was ecstatic, and she backed Taiga up to keep a safe distance between them. A nearby stream provided a clean water source, and while Taiga drank, she unloaded her supplies from her pack. Ready for nourishment herself, she pulled out some food and made dinner. During an earlier rest she had shot a rabbit with her bow; it would be her meal. She started a small fire, ensured she was downwind from her unknowing companions, and roasted her rabbit the way she liked it. With a few dried fruit squares and some vegetables from her father's garden, she felt like a queen back in Nickson's castle.

Her thoughts wandered to Nickson, and she wondered what he was doing. He was probably getting ready to eat dinner himself. She chuckled as she remembered how the servants cut his meat. She was fond of him, and for a moment a dull ache hit her chest. She missed him. She admired his kindness, his goodness, and his strength. She admired the way he had treated her during her stay in his castle, but all of this could not erase the fact that they came from two different worlds.

Samara looked at her surroundings. Here she was, near coastal rock faces, alone, with only Taiga as her companion, eating a rabbit she had shot and killed herself. She compared this to Nickson's world, the world of which she had had but a taste. There was no way these two worlds could ever exist simultaneously. It occurred to her that if she pursued her growing feelings toward Nickson, she would have to give up one of these worlds. She liked them both, but loved only one.

Her place was with her people.

Her thoughts became gloomy and she pursed her lips. "Of course, it would never work out between Nickson and me," she said to Taiga. "I am only a peasant." She laughed to herself as she rolled over next to the warm fire to sleep.

Samara woke up well rested the next morning. The sun was

not yet up, and she crept to her perch to check on Maddox's team. They still slept while Danson kept watch. She smiled at her boys and moved off to collect her bow.

This morning's catch was fish. Samara used her arrows as a fishing pole and collected two fish from one of the many streams that ran down the coast and into the nearby ocean. As she roasted her fish, she ate a few more fruit squares. She also pulled out a couple of nuts she had brought with her and washed them down with a nice, long drink from her water flask. She fed Taiga some carrots and encouraged him to eat the grass that surrounded them and to stock up on the plethora of nutrients they provided. She even picked some handfuls and put them in her bag. They wouldn't last long, but they would be a good snack for him once the sun had risen.

She returned to her perch and looked down at the team. They were up and getting ready to move. Samara prepped in response.

They were about two miles from the edge of Eagle's Bay Forest. The daylong ride that came after would be the slowest part of the journey—and the most dangerous. Hungau could be anywhere within the forest, and it was imperative they all kept watch.

They started their journey and made it to the forest's edge in good time. Samara stayed behind and noticed they left their horses at the entrance, tied up for their return. This signaled they had a timeline. The horses would be fine while they fulfilled their mission. Whatever happened after two days, those who remained would rendezvous at the horses, with or without information, and head home.

She waited a few moments after they entered the forest before she tied Taiga beside the small herd. Once the mission was over, she would tell them of her involvement. She hesitated at the boundary before she crossed. With a deep breath, she summoned her courage and took her first step into enemy territory. An eerie feeling pressed in around her as she realized that somewhere in these woods were people who had known her mother. The uncomfortable connection raised a shudder up her spine, but she made her way on foot in pursuit of the team, an arrow nocked in her bow, ready at all times.

The first couple of miles were uneventful. Eagle's Bay was an unfamiliar place, and Samara felt as if every step were being watched. The dark shadows of the dense trees and shrubs diminished her ability to tell what time of day it was. She fought the feeling of being trapped and pushed on, keeping her bow loaded and eyes up.

The team finally came to a stop and Samara found a ridge to stay hidden on. Looking down, she could see the movement of the team as well as the surrounding land and was grateful for the small clearing the trees had provided. She looked up at the sky, grateful she could still see it. The ocean stretched to her left. After briefly appreciating its beauty, she returned her focus to the team to resume her watch.

They rested without incident and took a few more moments to discuss their approach. Samara watched them huddle and wished she could hear what they were saying. She would be better able to protect them if she knew their plan.

The team started making their way into the more dangerous parts of the forest. Rawlins slipped and fell from the top of a ridge, and slid to a stop on the edge of a cliff face. They helped him up and kept going. Danson found what he thought was a mudhole—the situation turned sticky when he realized it was a tar pit. For the most part, Tristan's guidance and knowledge of the land kept them safer than Samara would have dreamed. She was grateful he had been so willing to come on the mission.

The team stopped again after a long while. The rocky slope of the terrain made it difficult to maneuver, but the ground had started to level out. They were on the edge of a small clearing. Samara kept her position high above them on the ridge, again grateful for the view this afforded her. She did not like where the boys were, however. If anyone came down her side of the ridge, they could be ambushed. Should that happen, Samara determined she would lead the Hungau away from the team to give them time to get away. If the Hungau came down her ridge, she was as good as dead anyway.

She remained hidden, but sensed something was not right when Danson and Casimir loaded their bows and aimed all around them. Samara listened for the sound that had startled them, but she could hear nothing. She swept her gaze down the left side of the clearing, far past the team at the edge, and up the right side. It was there she noticed a figure.

Hungau! She caught her breath.

She wanted to yell its location down to the team, but that would reveal her presence. Instead, she watched the Hungau watch the team. From where she was, she could assist by picking off any other Hungau warriors one by one, depending on how many there were. She looked at her quiver of arrows. She only had twenty.

She watched for Maddox's position and realized he knew which direction the Hungau was in, though he could not see him. The rest of the team didn't move; apparently, they were waiting for the attack that was to come. Since their vision was limited, it would be foolish to rush into the trees looking for the Hungau.

Samara pulled the arrow back in her bow and aimed it at the enemy warrior. Without warning, Maddox turned his back on the Hungau and faced the opposite direction. Samara immediately knew what was happening; Maddox had heard another sound.

It was an ambush.

Seeing Maddox's back turned, the Hungau decided to lead the attack. He rushed toward him with his seax raised. He made no sound of attack, and if it hadn't been for Samara's arrow, the Hungau would have killed him. Her arrow pierced him in the heart. With a groan he fell back, blood pooling around his body. She grabbed another arrow and loaded her bow. By this point, the team's position was known and other Hungau began to flood the area.

Maddox shouted, "Who shot that Hungau?"

Danson, Rawlins, Casimir, and Tristan all denied it. Maddox scanned the ridgeline.

"Stay focused, Maddox," Samara said under her breath. As if he had heard her, he returned his attention to the defense of his team. Three more Hungau entered the field; one engaged Tristan in hand-to-hand combat, Danson shot the second with his bow as he approached, and the third stood twenty paces away. He held a dart gun, which he aimed at Tristan's fighting figure. Samara pulled her bow taut and released the arrow. With a whistle it landed through the neck of the Hungau, causing him to fall back. Maddox went to Tristan's aid and ended the fight. Samara scanned the field and the surrounding trees. She didn't see any Hungau, but she could sense them. She kept her bow at the ready.

Maddox looked around him. "They know we're here. We've got to get their plans."

The men gathered their packs and weapons and took off on foot. Samara stayed low, keeping an eye out for any more Hungau in the clearing. Maddox was the last to leave the field. He took one more look toward Samara's ridge, then sprinted after his team.

Samara made sure they were clear before she went down to the clearing. She grabbed her arrows from the Hungau bodies and thrust them over her shoulder into her quiver. She ran after the team, keeping her eyes focused on the trees around her in case any more Hungau were prepared to ambush.

After a long while of constant moving, Samara calculated they had covered about four miles. Over the stretch of land that was Eagle's Bay, this was a difficult task. The forested terrain was rocky as well as muddy, making speed almost impossible. If previous scouting missions were correct, they were another six miles from the center—where the Hungau thrived and lived, planned and prepared.

Samara kept pace with the swift team, though it wasn't easy. After an intense push to the heart of Hungau territory, the team stopped, and she chose another ridge high to the team's left. She took this opportunity to hydrate and nourish herself. A few handfuls of nuts and dried fruit lifted her spirits immediately.

After her quick snack, she loaded her bow and scanned the

land below her, keeping an eye out for enemy warriors. The team had stopped in a more forested area than last time, forcing Samara to stay closer than she would have liked. Trees protected men, but could also blind them in combat. With the dense forest cover, she wouldn't be able to climb to a higher ridge, but being this close limited her range of vision anyway—fifteen, twenty paces tops.

It was better than nothing. She scanned the direction from which the team had come, then scanned the path in which they were headed. All seemed clear, but Samara knew better. She sensed, rather than heard, the presence that approached the team from behind. Instinctively, she pointed her bow and searched the shadows of the trees.

Without warning, a Hungau launched himself from his hiding place. Casimir didn't see him coming, and before Samara could release an arrow, they had both moved behind a tree. She heard Casimir cry out.

"No!" she shouted.

She ran to her left to get a better view. As soon as her target was in sight, she aimed and released her arrow. It sunk into the Hungau's abdomen and he collapsed.

Maddox and Danson rushed to Casimir's aid, but the fight was far from over. Four more Hungau appeared. With half of their team distracted, Rawlins and Tristan were left to fend for themselves. The odds were against them.

Samara reached over her shoulder and grabbed an arrow. Loading it on her bow, she aimed for one of the Hungau, shot, and missed. She grabbed another arrow and shot again, this time catching the Hungau in the thigh.

Tristan had killed one of them and Rawlins was fighting the final two at the same time. Samara successfully shot one, and Rawlins finished the other as three more Hungau attacked.

Samara glanced at Casimir's form lying on the ground and watched as Maddox and Danson treated his wounds. From her position, she could not tell how bad it was. She loaded her bow and fired at another Hungau coming up behind Rawlins.

Tristan and Rawlins handled the other two. Samara wiped sweat from her face once the battle was over. She debated whether she should make her presence known to check Casimir's condition, or keep herself hidden. No one seemed to know she was there so far. She decided the element of surprise would be more beneficial for the team. She would stay put.

Just then, she heard the snap of a twig behind her. She whipped around, keeping her arrow tight against her bow. She aimed into the treeline behind her, but saw nothing.

Then, to her left and upon the same ridge, heading straight for the team, was a Hungau warrior. He had a bow drawn and pointed at Maddox, who had his back turned. If Samara wanted to save his life, she had to make this shot.

She pulled her arrow taut and released it a breath before the Hungau released his. Samara could not even watch to see if her arrow had struck her target. She turned her head and rushed forward, almost crying out Maddox's name for fear he would be killed. She was relieved when the arrow sailed past him and landed in the trunk of a tree.

She turned to see whether her arrow had found its mark and was thankful to find it had made a deadly connection. The timing of her shot had knocked the warrior's off course, missing Maddox enough to save his life. With that taken care of, she looked back to Casimir.

"How's he doing?" Tristan's voice boomed.

"He's alive," was all Danson said.

"What do we do now?" Rawlins asked. "Do we take him? He'll slow our progress. But if we don't, he's as good as dead."

Samara knew she could take care of him until they returned, but that would leave them without protection. So far, her decision to stay on the ridgeline had proven wise.

"I'll stay with him," Danson answered. "You three go ahead and get the evidence. I'll try to take him as far out of here as I can before you *all* return."

Maddox put his hand on Danson's shoulder. "You're good

with wounds," he assured him. "Casimir will be fine. If it's too much for him, don't move him and we'll help you when we get back. Stay concealed as much as possible. Hopefully, the Hungau will be racing toward us, giving you plenty of time to head out."

They all nodded, knowing the situation looked bleak. The sound of moving brush behind them alerted them all, including Samara.

"Go!" Danson urged them.

Maddox hesitated to leave his fallen comrade but gave the order for Tristan and Rawlins to follow him. They took off through the woods. Samara watched them go, but also watched as Danson moved Casimir under the brush for cover. Casimir groaned but remained unconscious. Danson reached into his quiver to load an arrow, and Samara noticed he had none.

She scanned the trees for the source of the sound. A Hungau, apparently not expecting to find Danson there, was caught off guard when he saw Danson crouched protectively over his brother. The Hungau raised his seax and rushed forward.

Samara charged from her position and landed an arrow square in the Hungau's chest just as he raised his arm to strike. She reloaded her bow and moved in to cover her two friends.

Danson looked at her in surprise. *"Samara?"* he said in disbelief.

She kept her eyes on the trees a moment longer. Then, relaxing her bow ever so slightly, she turned to Casimir's body. "How does it look?"

Danson, still recovering from Samara's sudden appearance, stammered over his response. "Uh, he's breathing—"

"Danson!" Samara shouted, impatient. "Focus. How does the wound look? Is blood still flowing?"

This snapped him back to reality. "Yes, but barely. They got a nice shot in his side and he fell, but I've stopped the blood for the time being and will move him in a little while. Just moving him to the brush caused the wound to pulse."

Samara looked at the blood that trailed to their hiding spot. She stood and kicked the dirt around to cover the evidence. "That should help you." She pulled a handful of arrows from her quiver and a pouch of dried fruit from her pack. "Here, you'll need these."

Danson accepted them gratefully.

"Listen, Danson." She looked in the direction the team had gone. "I've got to follow Maddox and the others."

He nodded in understanding. "Go, we'll be fine."

Samara put a hand on his shoulder. "Stay hidden." Her eyes fell on Casimir, unwilling to leave him behind.

"Go, Samara! They need your arrows."

Danson smiled, and Samara couldn't help but smile in return. She ran toward the team, grabbing arrows from bodies as she went, and left Danson and Casimir on their own. A part of her hated to do it, but for the sake of the mission it was imperative that she maintain her focus and make the best decisions for the team as a whole.

It didn't take her long to catch up to Maddox, and again she kept to the ridges. She remained above them, moving silently but as fast as her legs could carry her, and keeping her eye out for the enemy. She counted down the miles methodically in her head: *six miles, five miles, four miles.* She felt her legs growing weak, but the energy pumping through her body gave her the strength she needed to continue. As they approached the center of Eagle's Bay, her heartbeat surged. Each step brought them closer and closer to the most dangerous part of the forest.

And with one man down, Samara thought.

Three miles, two miles.

As the sun prepared to set, she pondered the distance they'd travelled. She felt tired but still fully alert and ready to fight. If, with luck on their side, they made it to the center of Eagle's Bay and got the evidence they needed, they would still have to travel the ten miles back out. Round trip, that made a grueling twenty miles. Samara began to wonder if they would all make it out alive.

And we have a man down, she reminded herself.

She changed her mindset and began to count again.

One mile to go.

The team stopped just shy of the center of Eagle's Bay to rest and make plans as the sun retreated from the sky. Samara kept to the ridge and listened to their conversation as closely as possible.

"Do you think they're okay?" she heard Rawlins ask.

"Focus, Rawlins," Maddox commanded. Then, in a kinder tone, he said, "I'm sure they are fine. Tristan?"

"We aren't far from the heart," Tristan replied. "It's dark now and we have several options." Rawlins handed him some water and he took a quick drink. "We can work under the cover of darkness, but in this unknown territory it's more dangerous. If we choose to rest tonight, our extended stay obviously presents its own set of risks."

"And if we travel by day, then we may have more encounters with the Hungau," Maddox added. "Tristan, do you know your way well enough to lead us through the dark?"

Tristan hesitated. "It's been many years since I've been here. Already there are some segments I do not remember at all. But this close to the heart, I feel the Hungau spreading in my blood. I think I can safely lead you."

"You think, or you know?"

Tristan looked toward the heart of the forest and fixated on something there. He straightened his shoulders. "I know."

Maddox gave a curt nod. "What do you guys think? Can we work tonight with a short rest?"

Rawlins yawned. "I'll admit I'm tired, but I also don't want to sit around waiting for the Hungau to find us. Not when we're this close."

Maddox looked up at the darkening sky. "Then we'll go in tonight," he concluded.

They passed around food and water and got off their feet. None of them let go of their weapons, and they kept a constant eye out on their surroundings.

"I give us until the moon is high, men," Maddox began. "I do not want to extend my stay here any longer than necessary. Meet back here if we get separated, and if any of us do not show up by the time the moon is at its peak," he sucked in a quick breath, "leave anyway. The information needs to get passed on, and the rest of us need to make it out alive. If we all make it back, then we'll head out of the forest together. We'll pick up Danson and Casimir on our way out. Any questions?"

Rawlins flinched. "Every man on his own? Really?"

Maddox's face fell. "Normally, no, but we're not safe anywhere in this forest, and I don't want any of you coming back for me if I'm lost. It would be a waste of time and energy. Let's face it, if any one of us is taken by the Hungau, we can assume we're dead."

"I agree, Rawlins. Maddox is making a tough call, but I believe it is the right one," Tristan said.

Though Samara shared Rawlins' concern, she, too, knew Maddox was making the right choice. She only hoped they could get in and out before anyone noticed they were there. After two ambushes, the Hungau would be on the lookout.

Samara debated what she should do at this point. Entering the heart of Hungau territory could mean her use as a markswoman was over. If she made herself known, she could only imagine the stress that would put on the boys. She considered the trees; they were close together and covered in vines. She could shoot from the treetops and use the vines to get from tree to tree. It had been a while since she had played monkey, but she could learn again. It was her only option.

She checked her boots to see if they were secure and, reluctantly, removed the string from her bow. It had been under tension for a couple of days now and needed to rest. Otherwise, her bow would be useless. Once she was settled, she took the short time they had to rest. She was sure she would remain unseen in the cranny where she had chosen to hide. She covered herself with leaves and grass and closed her eyes.

Samara woke a long while later. Her body ached, and she was slightly cold. She listened for a moment and sat up, being careful to stay close to the ground. It was still dark out, which meant the sun had finally gone down. She looked to where Maddox was and saw them all sleeping soundly. She realized they had all been asleep during the moon's ascent. The sound of music and laughter reached her ears.

They were way behind their deadline.

Just as she was about to throw a rock in their direction, she saw Maddox stir. She watched him get up and come to the same conclusions she did. She almost laughed when she saw him scurry to pack things up, except nothing was funny about being in Eagle's Bay.

"Rawlins!" he whispered. "Wake up."

Rawlins rolled over and looked at the sky. "How long have we been asleep?"

"I'm not sure, but I would say the sun has already been down for quite a while," Maddox said, and rubbed a hand through his hair.

Rawlins cussed, stood up, and started to gather his things. "Tristan!" he whispered. "Time to go."

Tristan got up and together they finalized their plans. They decided to fan out, each taking a separate entrance. They would meet in the main campground, where most of the Hungau lived, and search the tents if they were unoccupied. Samara didn't like the idea of them splitting up, but was in no position to say so. She would have to be doubly on her guard for their plan to work. She collected her things and followed them into the forest. She would keep to the ground for now and ascend into the trees as they approached the camp.

They all moved carefully. Though Samara wasn't sure where the others were, she trusted they were all moving toward their goal, and she trusted her instincts to take her to the trees to give them the best protection.

When they reached the camp, she saw no movement. The forest was dark, and the only light came from the campfires dotted throughout the camp. Now would be her best chance to get in position, so she climbed the nearest tree and used the vines to swing toward the camp. She noticed movement to her left and watched Maddox sneak his way toward one of the larger tents. He was encased in shadow as he moved stealthily toward the entrance.

Samara caught her breath as he went inside. She heard nothing and concluded the tent either held a sleeping occupant or was empty. She watched him slip out again with nothing in his hands. Her heart sank.

She tried to find Rawlins and Tristan. Now that she knew where Maddox was, it would be easier to keep him safe. She saw Rawlins to her right, with Tristan close by. She breathed a small sigh of relief and continued to watch the grounds.

Rawlins and Tristan finished checking several tents, as did Maddox. At first Samara thought luck was on their side, but it took her a moment to realize none of the tents were occupied. Earlier she had heard music and talking, but that all seemed distant now. Samara scanned the campsite again—there was absolutely *no one.*

Where is everyone? she thought. A chill went up her spine. *It's a trap. They knew we were coming. Otherwise, they wouldn't leave their camps unprotected, knowing we were on the loose.* Samara's heart beat faster as the realization struck her. For a moment she couldn't breathe.

From her perch on the tree, she could see it all come together. The small attacks had ensured their arrival to this campsite, the unprotected living quarters of the Hungau. It all centered on one fact . . .

"They wanted us to come here," she whispered out loud.

Chapter Thirteen

Nickson paced back and forth in Dagan's council chamber. He had arrived earlier that day to see if any progress had been made on collecting the evidence. Now that he was here, all his thoughts were on Samara. He couldn't believe she had taken off by herself. It made him nervous that Dagan believed she had gone with the scout team.

If everything had gone according to plan, the team would already be in Eagle's Bay—and hopefully on their way out. This gave him some reassurance, but not much. He continued to pace, wondering when they would hear from the team, if at all. At last Dagan entered the chamber.

"Any word?" Nickson ceased his pacing and brought a fist to his mouth. His eyes were fixed on Dagan.

"Sire, we are still waiting."

"How long have they been out?"

"Three days."

"Has *anyone* heard from them?" Nickson asked.

"I'm afraid not, Your Highness," Dagan said. "It takes two days to get to Eagle's Bay. The plan was not to make contact until after they got the information."

"Maybe I should go after them." Nickson looked toward the window.

"Your Highness, now is not the time to make rash decisions. I am upset with my daughter for going, but she is skilled and I trust her judgment. Panicking will get us nowhere." Dagan took a deep breath.

Nickson stared at the floor. Panic? He never *panicked,* but the thought of Samara in Hungau territory unsettled him, and it made him experience an anxiety he hadn't felt to this degree in some time.

"What do you expect to find?" he continued, returning his gaze to Dagan.

"Plans for future attack. The men who were sent out are experts on military tactics and movement, and they are resourceful."

"But?"

Dagan lowered his voice. "I know for a fact the team will take the most risks in order to succeed. I wouldn't go so far as to say they are reckless, but their fearlessness can take them too far."

Nickson gave him a long look. "Is that supposed to make us feel better?" he asked. He felt his jaw clench.

"I don't know what Samara's role is in all this, running off the way she did makes it impossible to tell, but Maddox and Samara make a great team. They read each other well."

"What route did they take?" Nickson turned to the map on the table.

"As far as I know, they made for the coast and turned north, following it straight to the bay. Once they got there, only they would know the best way to proceed to the main camping ground."

Nickson eyed the map and pointed to the main camp. "How far is it to the center?"

"Ten miles," Dagan responded.

Nickson closed his eyes and calculated. Ten miles on horseback would be half a day's ride, but if they chose to go on foot, it could easily add an extra day before they made contact. His breath escaped in a whoosh and he sat down, exhausted.

Silence enveloped the room.

"This plan was foolish," he finally said.

Dagan stared at him. "The proof you required of us meant a

dangerous mission. This is why I told Samara she could not go."

Nickson inwardly beat himself for what he had suggested. The Gardiens' safety had always been in his hands. When he decided to ask for proof based on his father's initial command, he had still clung to the hope that the Hungau were not as active as Dagan and Samara had claimed. That his father had been right all along. He had hoped the mission would prove that, but because of his reluctance, he had put Samara in danger. He hated himself for it in this moment.

In the giant hall, the two of them sat in utter silence. Everything surrounding Dagan's loved ones was out of their hands.

Samara had to warn Maddox about the trap. She landed on the ground with a light thud, pausing to make sure no one had heard her, and headed in the direction of the closest team member. Within moments she ran into Tristan.

"Tristan!" she whispered.

Tristan spun and held out his seax.

"It's me, Samara," she whispered again.

"Samara? What are you doing here?" he asked, shocked.

"No time to explain," she said. "This is a trap! You need to get Maddox and Rawlins out of here, *quickly*!"

Tristan looked around the completely empty campsite and let loose a string of curses. "You're right."

Samara's voice shook. "Go and find the others. I'll check a few more tents for the evidence, then bring up the rear and cover your escape. Be careful and expect an ambush at any time."

She turned toward the closest tent to begin her search, but her uncle grabbed her arm. "You can't stay behind and search by yourself! We have to go."

"But, what about the evidence?"

He shook his head in anxious frustration. "I have it already. Let's move."

As they moved between the shadows back through the camp, Samara clutched her uncle's arm with excitement. "You got the evidence?"

Tristan looked back toward the tents. "Yes. Now, please hurry. If we don't leave now, we'll be caught."

They moved swiftly around some tents and stopped near a stack of cut logs.

"I'll get the team out," Tristan said. "Do you want Maddox to know about you?"

Samara bit the inside of her cheek. "Don't tell him I'm here. It would just make him worry."

Tristan nodded once and put a hand on her shoulder. "Be careful."

She watched him disappear then headed back toward the entrance of the camp. She would climb a tree and cover the team's escape and then run for her life toward the exit of Eagle's Bay Forest.

Her heart racing, she scanned the campsite and the trees for any movement. She could no longer see Rawlins or Maddox, but she trusted Tristan to get them out as they had planned.

Where are you? she thought. *Come out, come out, wherever you are.* She used her bow to scan the ground around her, and finally, as if on cue, the deadly Hungau began to flood the campsite.

She watched their movement as they headed through the campsite and back out again—directly for Maddox and the others.

Inwardly, Samara rejoiced. *They must have made it out!* she thought. A small handful rushed to the exit of the site and she picked them off one by one. Then, flinging herself down from the tree, she ran.

And she ran hard.

She kept to the left of the mass of running Hungau and used the trees and surrounding darkness as cover. A mile out of the center and to her left, a ridge appeared and she climbed the steep slope so she could run along the top. She would protect her team if it killed her.

She was only fifteen paces above the maddening scene below, but it gave her a huge vantage point. She was also surprised to find that the sun was already rising. The trees had done an excellent job of blocking all light.

Looking down into the small valley of forest, Samara saw the angry mob of Hungau hunting for her team. Just ahead of the Hungau, Maddox, Rawlins, and Tristan were running for their lives.

She picked up her pace, trying to keep ahead of the rushing sea of Hungau warriors. Several of them would get ahead of her and she would pierce them with an arrow from her high spot on the ridge. They would fall and give the team more distance until the next warrior started to catch up. She aimed and struck over and over again.

Samara knew she could not keep this up forever. Eventually she would have to get ahead of the Hungau to give her enough time to mount Taiga. The Hungau would not stop just because the forest did.

She kept her eye on her team and suddenly three Hungau warriors approached them from the front. She took a knee to the ground and steadied her bow. This slowed the team, but for a moment, her arrows flew true and she killed one Hungau after the other. Maddox killed the third as he ran by, thrusting his ax fatally into his neck.

She stood and continued running. If they could stay ahead of the Hungau, they could escape! She felt more optimistic about their circumstances, and this helped her to continue her consistent pace.

Samara looked ahead of her and saw the ridge coming to an end. In the spot where the ridge stopped, however, were the random dirt mounds where she had taken cover before. It was also where they had left Danson and Casimir.

Once the ridge ended, she would be on the same field as the Hungau, level with and only thirty paces ahead. She ran faster still and slid down the ridge's slope. As soon as she felt the ground under her feet, she sprang and ran.

Her eyes focused on where she had last seen Danson, but there was no sign of him. By this point, Maddox and the others had advanced well ahead of the Hungau. She could only hope they had found the others and were successful in getting them out.

She continued to run and kept her eyes open for any sign of Danson or a wounded Casimir. At one point, she spotted a small trail of blood leading to some underbrush. Barely slowing, she used her bow to lift the branches. Seeing no one, she picked up her pace and continued to run. She could hear the Hungau behind her but had since lost sight of Maddox.

For a small stretch, the land leveled out, and for this Samara was grateful. Her legs were beginning to cramp and her lungs felt as if they would burst. The Hungau had grown quieter in their pursuit and she still had seen no sign of Maddox or Danson.

Samara did not slow down.

She ran, hoping Maddox and the others were closer to the exit. One thing she did not want to do was spend the night in this forest. If after this great race the team did not make it out, the Hungau would be sweeping the forests until they were found. Death would be their fate.

Whenever a ridge emerged, Samara took to it. The higher and wider range of view helped settle her nerves. A little ways ahead, she finally saw the team, still running. For a moment she was happy.

They were going to make it!

She squinted and counted the running figures. There were only three. Fear flooded her chest and she scanned the woods, looking for any sign of Danson and Casimir. Mentally, she prepared herself for the reality that awaited them if Danson and Casimir had not made it out. A sob threatened to escape her and she bit her lip. Crying would not help her run.

Step, step, step, Samara thought. *Six miles down and four to go, keep going!*

Slowing her pace, she listened closely for the sound of pursuit behind her. She heard the Hungau moving, but they were not moving as fast as they had been before. She wondered why, but focused on the trail ahead. She was only a few yards from Maddox and the others. They had stopped, and Samara stopped to listen.

"Did you see them anywhere?" Tristan glanced all around.

"Not at all," Maddox said between deep breaths. "There was blood back there, but it was dried. Who knows how long it has been sitting there?"

During this conversation, Samara climbed another ridge and moved closer to the team. Kneeling directly to their left, but staying within earshot, she kept a lookout for the Hungau. She collected as much information from their conversation as possible.

"We have no choice but to go," Rawlins stated. "The Hungau are not far behind us."

Maddox looked toward the center of Eagle's Bay and back toward the exit. "I can't leave them." He clenched his fist.

Tristan put his hand on Maddox's shoulder. "We have not seen any sign of them. Perhaps they made it out last night while we slept."

"There is no way to know for certain," Rawlins countered. "We have to make our choice, and now." The sound of Hungau voices reached them, emphasizing the urgency to decide.

Maddox looked back toward the Hungau. "We go to the entrance. If they're not there, we are no longer a spy team. We are a rescue team."

Rawlins smiled and Tristan laughed. "Let's move!" Tristan boomed.

Just as they started to move forward, two Hungau warriors charged the team from behind. If Samara stood the team would clearly see her, but with the Hungau closing in, she had no choice. She stood, grabbed an arrow from her back, and fired. Instantaneously, she grabbed another arrow and shot the second warrior.

The team spotted her; shock filled their faces.

"Samara!" Maddox feigned anger. "I knew it was you!"

"Like I would miss all of this fun." She tossed her hair.

Maddox smiled. "Keep it up, Samara. Let's move!"

She ran along the ridge while the team moved parallel to her below. Samara counted down the miles in her head, and after they had made it two miles without any interference from their enemy, she started to feel hopeful.

Occasionally, Maddox looked up at her to be sure she was safe. She was sure, though, that her presence had remained largely unknown to the Hungau.

They had two miles to go until the end of the Eagle's Bay Forest.

So focused was she on these happy thoughts that she didn't see the Hungau warrior coming for her. Her breath escaped her as she was knocked to the ground. She gasped for a moment before she could stand, but finally, on shaky knees, she regained her footing and unsheathed her dagger.

She looked toward the team, but they kept going. Maddox had not seen her go down, and they rounded a bend out of sight. She eyed her surroundings but saw no one. She felt like she was being hunted—she was the prey and her enemy was the hunter. She did not like the feeling.

Her breathing was heavy and labored as she tried to find her attacker. She imagined the Hungau approaching, and she hated wasting this valuable time. She sheathed her dagger and picked up her fallen bow and began to move in the direction of her team. She took one step before a Hungau warrior stepped out in front of her.

It was a man. His eyes narrowed as he studied her. Dressed like the others, his tunic was sleeveless and around his forearms were leather armguards. The muscles in his arms flexed in anticipation, and he reached his hand behind his back. Slowly, he pulled his seax from its sheath. The corner of his mouth raised slightly as he positioned the deadly knife in front of him.

Samara clutched the hilt of her dagger, instantly aware that her weapon was no match for his. She adjusted her position, keeping light on her toes, and raised her dagger to prepare for his strike.

He lunged without warning. With what felt like sheer luck, she blocked his strong blow, then turned and prepared to face him again. He struck, and she dodged and turned. Her small dagger would not protect her for long. She thought ahead and worked out a countermove that would instantly disarm him.

When he lunged a third time, she blocked and spun into him, moving closer than she would ever want to be to a Hungau, and connected her elbow to his face. Before he could recover, she reached around his neck with both hands and shoved his face into her knee. He dropped his seax and fell over.

She scooped up her bow and flung it over her shoulders, then took off running in hopes she could catch up to her team. She would never hear the end of it if she were the reason for their delay. The thought made her smile. A surge of energy filled her body and she raced the last two miles to the exit.

The team was well ahead of her. She pumped her arms and kicked her legs into the ground as hard as possible. She wanted to collapse but could not give up.

Two miles. One mile. She counted each step. A short distance from the exit and her team was nowhere in sight. She prayed they did not return to the forest to look for her. This worry alone helped carry her to the exit despite her fatigue.

"Where is Samara?" she heard Maddox yell.

Tristan looked worried but could not answer. Maddox sat on top of his horse at the edge of the forest. He scanned the opening for any sign of her. Samara came bursting through the trees just as Maddox jumped off his horse.

"Go!" she yelled. "They're on my heels!" She grabbed Taiga's reins from Tristan's hands and flung herself up.

She quickly counted the party. She smiled when she saw Danson on his horse with a wounded, but conscious, Casimir draped over his lap.

"You have no idea how happy I am to see you two!" she said with relief.

Danson smiled. "You and me both."

"We've got the evidence," Rawlins shouted. "Let's get out of here."

A series of "yas" escaped their lips and the party of six raced down the coast and headed for home. Not out of danger yet, they moved swiftly away from Eagle's Bay, anxious to get as far away as possible.

After riding for the better part of the day, the team, exhausted from their mission, stopped to rest. Tristan lit a fire and Danson made Casimir a comfortable bed nearby. Casimir's condition was stable, but weak. His face was pale and his mouth was constantly dry. They had picked a spot right by a fresh river, so water was plentiful. They all drank their fill.

"Can you believe it?" Rawlins laughed. "Samara was our secret weapon this whole time."

Maddox smiled at her. "She turned out to be a great asset. I think I would have died a couple of times if it hadn't been for her."

"We're all daft," Casimir whispered from his bed and everyone laughed.

"Tristan," Maddox said, "we're another day from home; let's see those papers! I want to see what I almost gave my life to get."

Her uncle looked uncomfortable. He rubbed the nape of his neck in silence.

"Tristan?" Maddox reached his hand out expectantly. "The papers."

Tristan shook his head. "I don't have them, son."

Maddox dropped his hand and stared hard at Tristan. "You don't have them? You told me back in Eagle's Bay that you—" He turned his back to the rest of the team.

Samara could see he was trying hard not to say something incredibly rude. She stared at her uncle, shocked he had lied, but she understood why. He would never have let her stay behind to search the tents alone. Her happiness at their success instantly died.

"Why did you lie?" Rawlins demanded. "We risked our lives and we walk out with nothing?"

Maddox turned. His jaw was tight and the anger on his face silenced everyone. "You lied to your team!" he shouted at Tristan.

"We should be able to trust the members of our team." He took an angry step toward her uncle.

Samara stepped in front of him, halting his advance, and placed a steady hand on his chest. "We had to get out of there," she explained. "Entering the camp was a mistake, and they were ready to ambush. We would have been killed had we stayed."

Maddox's eyes lost focus as he thought about her words. "Then we failed."

A tense silence engulfed them. Samara herself felt guilty for her role in forcing them out of Eagle's Bay, but the Hungau would never have let them succeed. Maddox wouldn't have left without the papers and Tristan knew it. The lives of her friends were far more important than their mission, and she stood by that.

"King Montcroix will never help us now." Danson sat on a log, his shoulders slumped. "We needed that evidence to convince him."

Maddox cursed and rubbed his face with both hands. "This was a complete waste." Without another word, he grabbed his battle ax and marched off. Samara watched him go, debating whether she should follow. After a quick decision, she grabbed her bow and followed him.

When they had walked some distance from the others, she called after him. She was surprised when he stopped.

"I'm angry right now, Samara," he warned. "I can't believe Tristan—" He couldn't finish his sentence.

"I know," She turned her face away. "It's my fault, and I take full blame."

He shook his head. "No, it's not your fault. You were right; it was an ambush and you saved our lives." He met her gaze. "I don't want to tell Dagan we failed. We needed those papers."

"What should we do next?"

Maddox shrugged, still angry. "We'll have to counsel with Dagan."

"Let's focus on Casimir now," she gently reminded him. "He's wounded and we need to get him home."

Maddox agreed, but before they returned to camp, he stopped her. "You really did save my life back there. I owe you one."

"You're my family, Maddox. You don't owe me a thing."

He smiled, but it didn't reach his eyes. They turned back to camp and together prepared dinner for everyone.

Conversation between the team members was nonexistent; worry over Casimir's wounds made all of them tense. Samara and Maddox helped keep it clean until it was time for bed. When Samara fell asleep, Danson was still awake with Casimir.

Sometime later, Samara awoke with a start. It was dark and the fire next to her had dwindled to nothing.

Looking around her, she saw Rawlins, Tristan, and Maddox sleeping soundly. Casimir was also sleeping but Danson was wide awake, still sitting by his brother's side.

She went to him. "Danson." She put a hand on his shoulder. "Have you been awake long?"

"Define long," he said with a tired smile.

She sat next to him and handed him her blanket. "You haven't slept?"

Danson got a sheepish grin. "Not yet," he confessed.

"You should sleep," she suggested. "I'll keep an eye on him. How's he doing?"

Danson's demeanor changed and Samara could see he was worried. "He's been slipping in and out of consciousness more frequently and saying strange things. He's delirious."

Samara put a hand to Casimir's forehead. He was breaking out in a cold sweat, and concern draped her. "How does his wound look?"

"Not good," Danson replied, peeling back a layer of clothing so Samara could see.

Underneath his bloodstained tunic lay a horrible wound. Danson's rough stitching had closed it up, but infection was evident. The smell was even worse. For a moment Samara was appalled. The horror of her friend's condition threatened to creep over her. She quickly covered the wound, fighting to keep her terror in check.

"Danson, it's infected."

Danson's jaw clenched. "What can we do?" He tried to sound brave.

"You go to sleep. I will take care of him." Danson shook his head and Samara gently grabbed his face to hold it still. "You are exhausted and need to sleep. You will be no good to any of us, especially Casimir, if you aren't well rested."

Danson's eyes betrayed his worry. "Wake me if his condition . . . changes."

Samara nodded and watched Danson take his place in his makeshift bed. She then prepared herself for what she had to do next and moved toward Tristan's bed to wake him up.

He rolled over, still groggy from sleep. "What is it, Samara?"

"I need you to come look at Casimir's wound. It doesn't look right to me," she whispered.

Her uncle didn't hesitate. He sat up quickly and followed her to where Casimir lay. With a deep breath, she removed Casimir's tunic. "It's terribly infected."

Tristan's eyes remained riveted on the festering wound. He knelt closer to analyze it, then swallowed hard and faced her. "That's not infection. It's Hungau poison."

"Poison? But he wasn't hit with a dart."

"We used to line our sheaths with it, sometimes even soaking the tips of our weapons in it before we went off to fight. Poisons are an old Hungau tradition." Tristan put a hand to his head and cast his eyes downward.

Samara felt the blood drain from her face. "His attacker must have lined his seax with it."

She dug out a small knife from her wound kit and Tristan helped her pull out the crude stitches from Casimir's body. A fresh pulse of blood freed itself from the wound. Samara ignored the pus that also escaped.

Using her flask, she poured fresh stream water into the wound and dabbed at the torn flesh with a clean rag. From her wound kit she pulled a carefully folded strip of linen. Coated on the inside of the cloth was a specially made balm from the juice of the tersusa plant that was abundant in the Forests of the North. The juice was good for cleaning away infection, and she applied a liberal amount to Casimir's side.

"Samara, all of the Hungau poisons have a specific antidote," Tristan said. "The balm may help, but I don't think—"

Her uncle was too emotional to continue, but Samara refused to give up hope. "We will get him home," she assured him, though she needed to hear the words herself. "We'll get him home, and then we'll get him a cure."

With a fresh needle she sewed up the wound, dabbing here and there for any spilled blood. Once the wound was stitched up as cleanly as possible, she covered it with cloth folded into thick squares. She then tied larger strips around Casimir's midsection, covering the wound and binding it tight.

She and Tristan kept anxious watch through the rest of night until morning, when the team finally began to stir.

Chapter Fourteen

Maddox approached Samara. "How are you feeling?"

"Don't worry about me," she said, honestly. "I'm worried about Casimir."

"How's he doing?"

For the first time since she had learned about the poison, tears filled her eyes. "He's been poisoned, Maddox."

Maddox's eyes widened. "Are you sure?"

"I had Tristan look at it last night. He's certain."

Maddox muttered a series of curses. "We need to ride fast today." He turned to the team and gathered them together. "Casimir's wound has Hungau poison in it and we need to get him home. Danson, can you carry him?"

"Of course," Danson said. His eyes met Samara's gaze. "Is it really poison?"

She nodded. "Tristan looked at it last night."

"What's the cure?" Danson demanded.

"We have to identify which poison was used," Tristan said. "I have a few guesses, but I can't be certain. Calida kept a record of all the poisons favored by the Hungau. The cure will be in her garden, as she saw it fit to continue her practice of cultivating the traditional Hungau plants."

"Let's move out," Rawlins said. "We can't waste any more time."

The team agreed, and soon they were on the road. They moved at a brisk pace, but with Danson carrying Casimir, it slowed their progress. Worry for Casimir battled with Samara's disappointment as to how the entire mission had gone. She replayed over and over the moment he had been hit. If only she could have made the shot or moved faster to get in a better position.

Suddenly, everything seemed her fault. She couldn't protect Casimir, and she had created the situation that resulted in her team's failure.

So the journey continued, with worry and failure as her constant companions. They stopped only if necessary, and one time to transition Casimir to Tristan's horse so Danson could have a respite. Still the journey felt slower than it should have.

Just outside the border of their homeland, a cry came from behind and broke Samara from her gloomy thoughts. Commanding Taiga to stop, she turned her horse and raced back toward the sound.

Tristan was holding a convulsing Casimir. "He's seizing! Help me get him down."

Samara jumped from her horse and with Danson's assistance they lowered Casimir's violently shaking body. Once they laid him on the ground, Samara cupped her hands under his head to prevent him from slamming it against the ground. His eyes rolled to the back of his head and Samara's heart beat frantically. She could not stop thinking this could be the end for Casimir.

"How long has he been seizing?" Maddox demanded as he rode up.

"Not long," Samara said with a shaky voice.

Time slowed to a crawl, and each whip of Casimir's body caused Samara to lose hope. But in time, as quickly as it had happened, the seizing stopped. She felt Casimir's forehead. "He's burning up."

"I know what poison they used," Tristan said. "*Slifiwa*. That would explain the convulsions."

"Are you sure?" Maddox asked.

"Certain. The cure is derived from a combination of two different plants: the yellow honey oat flower, and the white sand-slip flower. Both grow in Calida's garden."

Maddox looked back toward where they had come, and then toward home. "We're half a day from home," he stated solemnly.

Samara racked her mind for a solution. They were half a day's ride from her home, but Casimir was getting worse every moment. He needed the cure and he needed it fast.

"We have to push on or he'll never make it," she said.

"The going is slow," Tristan countered. "It will take us longer to get home if we're carrying Casimir like this."

"We can't stop!" Danson shouted. "Sitting here making a decision is wasting valuable time."

"We're trying to make the best decision to help Casimir. We're not the enemy here," Samara countered.

"Samara, how fast would it take you to ride home yourself?" Maddox asked, breaking up the escalating fight.

She looked at him. "Without stopping?" she asked quietly.

Maddox nodded. Samara felt a pain in her chest and she looked at her horse. Taiga knew every part of this country and was the fastest horse of the herd. He had done extraordinary things before, but a journey like this would kill him.

"If I push Taiga as hard as he can go and we rest for short bursts," she answered hesitantly, "we could be back to you by nightfall."

Maddox looked at Casimir's still form. "Do we stop and let Casimir rest, or do we keep moving?" he asked the team.

Nobody answered. If the team kept moving, it could be a great risk for Casimir. If they stopped to rest and Samara rode home on her own, they would add another day to their journey and help for Casimir would be delayed.

Until she brought back the cure. Ultimately, it seemed the wiser choice; Casimir could have medicine that night.

But it would cost one horse.

She walked over to Taiga and rubbed his head. Leaning her cheek against his nose, she quietly asked, "Can you race through the Forests, boy?"

He neighed in response and Samara felt a weight rest on her

shoulders. Saving Casimir wasn't something anyone would have to ask her to do, but she wasn't ready to lose Taiga. He was a dear companion and had been a gift from her mother before she died. She turned to Maddox.

"Casimir could have medicine tonight if I leave right now," she said. She wanted to take back the words so she wouldn't have to make the sacrifice, but it had to be Taiga. He was the fastest horse.

Maddox looked to Danson. "It's your call."

Danson looked at Casimir's still form and then back at Maddox. "Ride to the garden," he said. "We'll set up a place to rest for now, but will move in your direction as we can."

Samara removed his saddle and her pack.

"What are you doing?" Rawlins asked.

"She's making the horse lighter," Tristan answered, "so he can run faster."

Samara felt tears sting her eyes, but held them despite her grief.

"I will go with you," Maddox offered.

She shook her head and moved her hands to the horse's hind legs to rub his muscles. "Taiga will outrun your horse. You'd be left behind, anyway."

"Could he carry us both?"

"Yes, but it would slow him down."

"I don't want you going alone." Maddox grabbed her elbow and turned her toward him.

"We don't have much of a choice," she shot back.

Tristan stepped forward. "Samara you forget that my horse and Taiga are brothers. They are almost a match for speed and endurance."

Samara looked at her uncle. "I'll be faster by myself, and there is no point in losing two horses." Her words hung heavy. "I couldn't make you do that."

"No one is making you, either," he pointed out. "I'm deciding for myself. Take him. Casimir needs those medicines and Taiga will need a companion to encourage him."

He handed his horse's reins to Maddox. Tristan gave his

horse one final pat and whispered something to him. Samara could not watch.

Once the horses were stripped of anything that would slow them down, Maddox and Samara jumped on, without saddles, and prepared to ride.

"If you feel you can move him, do it," he told Danson.

"Clean his wound again," Samara added. Even though it wouldn't stop the poison from spreading, it could stave off any infection that would make Casimir's condition worse. Danson nodded and turned to make a resting place for Casimir.

Maddox and Samara took off at full speed. Samara became one with her horse, tucking low and meshing to the beast. Taiga, sure-footed and nimble, leapt easily over fallen trees and around the brush. She felt his rippling muscles beneath her and tried hard not to think that this would be the last time she would ride him.

Samara had always pushed Taiga in training, and she knew he could run flat out for two miles before he had to stop. But to endure for the length of a day? A wave of sadness engulfed her knowing he could not survive such a strenuous run. Even if they stopped for short breaks, it wouldn't do their horses much good. She felt a sudden sadness for Tristan's sacrifice. He didn't have to do it. As the horses raced, their brotherly connection seemed to keep them together, and Tristan's suggestion had proven to be a wise one. Taiga would finish his mission, he always did, but having a friend always seemed to make things easier.

After pushing for a long time Maddox suggested they stop. They pulled up to a stream and let their horses drink. Taiga breathed heavily; mucous and liquid escaped his nostrils. She had to keep him hydrated if they were to make it back.

"I'm sorry, Taiga," she choked. "It's going to be hard, but we can do it." She tried to sound optimistic, but she sounded unconvinced, even to herself.

They ran on. Tristan's horse kept up with Taiga, and even though Samara and Maddox didn't talk much, she was glad for her friend's company, as well. They kept up their pattern, running for a few miles and resting for a brief period, letting the horses drink during the breaks. The horses nibbled at grass when they stopped, but Samara could tell they were under stress.

As the sun dipped in the sky, they decided to stop for one last moment. Maddox tossed her some dried fruit to eat and she ate it slowly. Not even the sweet flavor cheered her up. The horses now lay on the ground, tired and breathing heavily. They were nearly home and needed to make as much progress back to Casimir as they could before night fell. The horses could stumble in the dark, which would be detrimental to getting Casimir the aid he needed.

Samara examined Taiga's legs and cleaned out his hooves, making sure nothing was wrong.

Maddox approached her. "We'd better get moving. Casimir is in bad shape."

These last few miles felt like the final stroke of an executioner's blade. Once they made it to the house, they would collect the plants they needed and race back. Samara would have no other moment to say goodbye to Taiga.

When Maddox saw the tears in her eyes, he put an arm around her shoulder. "Taiga has been a wonderful companion." He pulled her into a hug. "I am sorry about all of this."

A sob broke through her composure. "I'm not ready to lose my horse, Maddox. I can't even bear the thought."

Maddox released her, then knelt and put a hand on Taiga's nose. He spoke in soothing tones while Samara worked up the courage to continue their journey. Sensing it was time, the horses stood. Maddox and Samara mounted.

"We need to get back as soon as we can. Fewer stops," Maddox said gravely.

Samara could only nod.

Maddox dug his heels into Tristan's horse and Samara followed his lead. They raced through the woods the last few miles to her home. As the path curved, the bridge came into view. The clip-clop of their horses' hooves thundered across, but they headed straight for the garden.

Their search did not take long. The plants grew in the same area and were unmistakable in appearance. The yellow honey oat flower was small with six thin petals. The center was white, and the stems were dark green. The sandslip stem held ten cup-shaped white flowers. Inside each cup were thin streaks of pink so light they almost weren't visible. Samara and Maddox grabbed a handful of each, placed them carefully in a satchel, and ran back for their horses. They raced out of the courtyard without so much as a glance back at the house.

"Samara!" her father's familiar voice called as they ran over the bridge.

They didn't stop. They couldn't. If they delayed any longer, it could cost Casimir his life. They disappeared down the path and rode through the sunset until the trees turned into shadow against a backdrop of reddish-orange hues. As the sky darkened, Taiga never slowed. His steps pounded the earth as if he knew Casimir's life depended on it. He followed Samara's commands at every moment and often she leaned down to talk to him, to console him. She knew he was in pain, and tears threatened to cloud her vision.

They came around a bend and the others came into view. The team had made some progress and were closer to home than before. Seeing them, Taiga sensed the end of the mission and his legs gave out, unable to take one more step. Samara cried out as she and the horse flew to the ground.

"Samara!" Maddox called.

He jumped off his horse as he, too, fell to the ground, exhausted. Maddox ran to check on her. Taiga had barely missed landing on top of her, and she crawled to his side. "Help me! Help me get him up." Her voice trembled; her hands shook.

"Samara—"

"No!" She grabbed at Taiga's body and tried to heave him up. The horse neighed weakly. Maddox just stood there.

"Help me!" she cried again. "Please, get up, boy."

Maddox put a hand around her shoulders. "Samara, he's not going to stand, even if we help him."

She looked at Tristan, who knelt beside his horse. She looked at Casimir, who lay still on the ground. Danson, Rawlins, and Maddox watched her, all with solemn expressions. Helplessly, she looked at Taiga; his body heaved with the deep, painful breaths he took.

"Taiga," she sang his name. She rubbed his neck and continued to sing to him.

Tristan suddenly stood. "The plants?"

Maddox handed him the satchel. Tristan and Danson sorted through the collection of plants and prepared them for Casimir. They pulled the petals from the flowers and put them in a bowl. With careful movements they crushed them with a stone. The stems they broke in half and eased any juices into the same bowl. With a little water, they created a mixture.

Samara kept one hand on Taiga and both eyes on her team as they worked. Her heart was burdened by the worry she felt for Casimir and for her horse. Maddox never left her side as she continued to sooth and calm Taiga. With Casimir's condition deteriorating rapidly, Taiga and his brother dying, and Samara and Tristan saddened by their losses, the feeling over the camp was somber. Maddox rubbed Samara's shoulder helplessly and Samara in turn continued to rub Taiga.

"Casimir needs to drink the mixture," Tristan said. "My practice in Hungau poisons is not as fresh as it used to be, but I think this is right."

"I'm sure it's fine," Danson said, then grit his teeth in an effort to remain calm.

The Gardiens drew a collective, uncertain breath. A long pause followed as the bowl touched Casimir's lips. Samara watched, with incredible anxiety, for the effects the cure would have on their longtime friend.

The first dribble of liquid went down his throat. Casimir immediately coughed and the cure sputtered out of his mouth.

"Hold him still!" Tristan ordered. Danson and Rawlins took

hold of Casimir's body as Tristan tried again. Casimir's breathing became labored.

"Casimir, you stay with me," Danson demanded as Tristan poured more of the mixture down his throat.

All color from Casimir's face suddenly drained, and with one last, slow breath, his chest stopped moving.

"No!" Danson cried. "Casimir? Casimir, wake up."

Maddox fled to his friend's side. Samara fell to the ground, her eyes fixed on Casimir's still form. The air around her felt hot and sticky and her vision blurred as her mind tried to make sense of what had just happened.

They had raced to get the cure. They had it in their hands.

And Casimir was dead.

Compassionate, strong Casimir did not move. He looked different, cold. Samara slowly stood and reached for a blanket to cover her dear friend. She put it over him, helpless to know why the cure hadn't worked. Seeing him lifeless and empty, she sank to her knees. Casimir's tunic absorbed her tears, and when she looked at Danson, she saw that he, too, was crying. She reached out and pulled him into a hug. Danson, capable and strong in the face of battle, but quiet in nature and less prone to emotional upheaval, shouted in agony.

He had just lost his brother, and his anguish was plain to see. Seeing it made Samara realize how broken her heart was in that moment. She clutched to him as he trembled with the grief of their loss, though she didn't feel she had any comfort to give.

Maddox stood stone still. He stared at Casimir like he wasn't sure what to do. His face was pale, and his eyes glistened with the sheen of unfallen tears. Tristan still held the bowl of mixture in his hands, but it sagged and spilled uselessly to the ground. Rawlins responded to this new hurt with a stiff jaw and an angry furrow of his brow. His eyes never strayed from Casimir.

For a long moment, no one moved.

For what purpose had they gone into Eagle's Bay? They had all been ready to give their lives in the fight against the Hungau if it meant they could save others and stop the enemy from their unjust crusade. But this mission had only resulted in immense loss. They had gained nothing.

Samara released Danson and wiped the tears from his cheeks. He seemed to need her hold, so she pulled him back in and embraced him.

"Casimir is dead," he said. "Casimir is dead."

Maddox blinked at Danson's painful words. As if he needed to see for himself, he crossed to where Casimir lay and put his ear to his face. He then put his ear to Casimir's heart.

"There is no breath," Maddox said quietly. "No heartbeat."

Something about his tone caused Samara to turn and look at him. He sounded confused, like there was no way Casimir could be dead. Maddox then fell to his knees and the reality of his grief subdued him. Tears fell down his face, and Samara realized it was the first time she had seen him cry in a very long time. The last time was when they had received word of her mother's death.

She held out her arm and invited him into their circle. Maddox fell into it willingly and Rawlins followed. Tristan wasn't far behind.

Danson, at the center of their embrace, suddenly stilled. When Samara looked up at him, she found him looking at his brother.

"Our parents—" he began, then shook his head in sorrow.

"They'll want to see him." Tristan's eyes watered. "I am so sorry, Danson. The cure—"

"We did all we could," Danson interrupted. "We were just too late."

Samara's shoulders sagged at his words. "I should have run faster. I should have made it back sooner."

"It's not your fault, Samara," Danson said while looking into her eyes. "Don't blame yourself for Casimir's death. Please, he wouldn't have wanted it."

Samara hugged him again, and the team fell quiet once more. Tristan and Danson took to wrapping Casimir securely in a couple of blankets so they could carry him back home, his body as protected as it could be. Samara moved to be by Taiga's side, and there she stayed.

Rawlins was one of the first to speak. "The horses are in pain," he explained to Maddox. "Tristan's is on the verge of death."

Samara looked into Taiga's big black eyes; she, too, was amazed he was still alive. "What are you suggesting?"

"We need to get Casimir home."

Samara sensed there was more he wasn't saying. "What else, Rawlins?"

Rawlins swallowed and tugged at the neck of his tunic. "The horses are in pain," he said again. "It's cruel to let them suffer more than they already have."

Samara felt sudden annoyance toward Rawlins. Apparently, so did Maddox. "Really, Rawlins? Right now?"

"What? We need to get Casimir home, and we could end their suffering."

Maddox didn't respond. The somber, black feelings of death surrounded them.

"Go, then," Samara said. "All of you. I am going to stay with Taiga. I can make it home on foot. Tristan, if you want to stay with me, you can."

Tristan nodded his agreement.

"Maddox, lead them all home. This way none of you will have to carry extra passengers. There is no way I'm going to shoot my horse," Samara said, and glared at Rawlins.

Taiga exhaled a huge breath and Samara felt a groan underneath her hand.

"Taiga?" she pled. She opened his huge eyes and saw nothing but a blank stare. "No!" Before she could stop them, more tears spilled onto her cheeks. Maddox gently took her by the arms and helped her stand. He let her cry, wrapping his arms around her and gripping her in a tight hug. The rest of the team averted their eyes and moved closer to the fire that still burned.

A distressed whinny drew Samara's eyes to where Tristan's

horse lay. Tristan soothed his horse, and just as he reached for a bow, his horse exhaled one last time and stopped moving.

Anguish squeezed her heart. She couldn't stop crying, and the sudden emptiness in her chest made her realize how much she already missed Casimir and Taiga. Their deaths were unfair and had all been for nothing. If only she could have had a clear shot, Casimir would still be alive, and Taiga wouldn't have had to run himself to death.

"I hate Algernon Montcroix," she hissed through her tears. "He asked for the impossible."

"I know," Maddox replied. "I know."

After a while, Samara had cried herself out. She was mentally, physically, and emotionally exhausted and could not bring herself to care anymore. Numbness washed over her mind and settled. In these early moments of grief, anger toward the king also settled in her heart.

He had blood on his hands.

Maddox released her and wiped the tears off her face. Rawlins had taken the responsibilities of cleaning up their camp, and Samara saw there was nothing left to do but move.

"All of us ready?" Maddox asked in a low voice. He looked at Samara. "You should ride with us now."

Samara gave a quick nod of her head but let her eyes linger on Taiga.

"Samara, you ride with me. Tristan, you can ride Casimir's horse, and Danson will carry Casimir," Maddox advised.

He reached down a hand to help Samara onto his horse. She climbed on and grabbed Maddox's waist. With one last look at her beautiful, black horse, she turned her head away from him, never to see him again.

Moving homeward brought thoughts of her father. She was certain he was worried, but he knew she was safe. He would learn of Casimir's fate and the safety of the others soon enough. The nerves she felt in facing him—for all she had done and all she had failed—became her relentless companion.

They quickly moved home. Samara barely noticed where they were, but as the familiar path drew her closer to the borders of her father's manor, her desire for his comfort and wisdom pulled at her. Gardien warriors soon appeared all around them. Their faces showed happiness that they were all home, but as soon as their eyes landed on Casimir's draped form, shock replaced their expressions.

The peaceful forests of her home usually made Samara calm and happy, but now they did nothing for her as she struggled with her losses. As they crossed the bridge in the darkness of night, the Gardiens who had come to greet them sank to their knees when they realized their party was one short.

Samara searched the crowd for two faces. When she saw them, their eyes lighted on Danson. They searched each face for their other son. When their mother finally found Casimir, her eyes widened, and she cried out in pain. She and their father rushed to Danson and helped remove Casimir's body from the horse.

Dagan stepped through the crowd and Samara watched him take in the news. His eyes stayed on Casimir's mother, who now knelt on the ground beside her son. She had pulled the blankets back to expose his face and she held his cheeks as she cried.

Samara couldn't look at him. His skin was the wrong color and the spirit and humor that had always been there were missing. She averted her eyes and met her father's gaze. He swiftly moved toward her and caught her up in a hug. She cried anew in his arms.

"I failed him," she whispered. "I failed Casimir."

Her father didn't respond, so she pulled back and looked at him. His eyes were wet with tears, but his expression was comforting.

"You are not responsible for Casimir's death. Whatever happened is not yours to shoulder." He turned to Casimir and Danson's parents. "Bring him inside. We shall prepare him for the dead."

Maddox, Rawlins, Danson, Tristan, Dagan, and Casimir's

father gently lifted the body that had been Casimir and carried it inside. Samara went to his mother's side and helped her into the house. As they entered, Samara was surprised to see Nickson coming down the stairs. With so much sadness in her heart, any excitement she would have had at his presence could not be summoned.

Nickson's eyes landed on Casimir and stayed there for a long moment. When Samara drew closer, he looked at Casimir's mother. "I am sorry," he said. "Casimir was a good man."

"Thank you, Your Highness," she said, though her voice held a hint of resentment. She left Samara's side and followed the others to a back room under the stairs.

Samara turned to Nickson. "Your Highness."

"Samara, I am so sorry about Casimir."

She had cried enough; she didn't want to continue feeling this pain. She took a deep breath and willed the tears to stay put. "We did not get the evidence you requested," she said in a clipped tone.

He reached a hand toward her, but she found herself pulling away. His hand dropped awkwardly back to his side. "I am sorry," he whispered. "This is my fault."

Casimir needed her, and she moved past the prince to attend to his burial preparations. Then, remembering Casimir's compassion for others, she stopped.

She put a hand on Nickson's arm. "This isn't your fault," she said. "If anyone is to be blamed, it's me." She suppressed the shuddering sob that surfaced at her declaration and moved quickly to one of the rooms behind the stairs to help the others.

CHAPTER FIFTEEN

Casimir's body had been placed on a table. The room for burial preparations was in Dagan's manor, in a room in the back hallway under the stairs. This sacred space was used for the dead, and Dagan himself oversaw the preparations for each and every Gardien warrior who passed. His love for his people, and the service he gave to them because of that love, had always been apparent. As Samara watched her father with Casimir now, she was again reminded of how important each person was.

As a member of the Gardien Council, Casimir was irreplaceable. A few tears escaped her eyes again as she watched her father help Casimir's parents dress him in his finest burial clothes. The Gardiens believed in a quick burial, so the individual could rest in peace. After a bit of sleep last night, which was greatly needed by the entire team, they gathered in the morning to prepare for the funeral.

Maddox stood beside her, his arms crossed and his expression somber. Rawlins and Danson were there too. None of them seemed ready to leave Casimir's side. Maddox's eyes were fixed on Casimir. "I miss him."

Dagan's eyes fell on their fallen friend. "I understand the feeling."

Danson moved to be with his parents. Rawlins' jaw had remained tense through the preparations and he suddenly turned and walked out. When Samara moved to go after him, Maddox stopped her.

"Let him be. He's angry with the crown, and I'm going to let him take as long as he needs." Maddox furrowed his brow.

Casimir's parents approached where they stood. "We're ready for the burial," his father said. He looked worn out, and Samara knew they had been up all night with their dead son.

Dagan hugged them both. "Casimir is greatly missed. He was a good man and a good warrior."

Rawlins was asked to return and the group of them, Samara and Casimir's mother included, helped to carry Casimir's body outside on their shoulders. They moved slowly, in a solemn procession of respect for the passing of their friend and leader. The Gardiens had gathered again, each with a yellow Cascadian rose in their hand. As the team passed, they each fell in line to follow.

The morning was cooler than it had been of late. The trees swayed in the breeze and the sun shone through the forest canopy. Samara preferred the morning—the night had brought horrors she never imagined would happen.

They continued their march through the forest. Casimir's final resting place would be in the Gardien burial grounds where all their warriors were buried.

Samara turned and saw Nickson amongst the crowd. He held a flower, too, and was watching Casimir with the saddest look of regret she had ever seen. When their eyes met, she nodded respectfully to him. He nodded in return.

The burial mounds were a quiet, reverent place. The sun shone brilliantly upon it, as the area had been cleared of trees. Grassy, green mounds flourished, along with many kinds of wildflowers from the abundant access to the sun. It was peaceful despite its purpose.

While they had prepped the body during the night, a site had been dug for Casimir. This section of the burial ground held warriors who had died in battle. As a member of the Gardien Council and a military leader, Casimir would be buried amongst his comrades.

They reached his final resting place and lowered him into the ground. Somewhere in the crowd a voice sang out the haunting, yet calming, melody of the Gardien burial song. Others joined, and soon the entire gathering had joined in the tune of mourning. As Samara sang, tears streamed down her face.

O, Gardien proud,
Come here to rest!
Your last arr'w flown;
Your battle's passed.

Leave now to us
The charge to keep.
We take the watch,
So you can sleep.

Through the trees,
Our Father's come
On silent wings
To bear you home.

Maddox handed Samara a rose, and with one last look at her dear friend, she placed the flower into Casimir's grave. She moved aside and let every Gardien take their turn. By tradition, Casmir's parents would be the last to place their flowers—the first to meet him when he was born, and the last to say goodbye at his death. There were many Gardiens, and they humbly watched everyone pay their respects.

When Nickson approached, he knelt before Casimir and said something only the dead would hear. He dropped his rose in with the others and moved to Samara's side.

Though her feelings were tumultuous, his presence was comforting. She turned and looked up at him. "Thank you," she said, and took a step closer to him.

He nodded and watched with her until the last roses had been placed. Maddox, Danson, and Rawlins saw to covering Casimir with dirt. When the deed was finally done, the Gardiens dispersed and went to mourn in their own ways.

Samara returned with her father to their home, and the others followed, none of them wishing to be alone. Without coordinating, they went to the dining room and took their places around the table. Danson, however, went to his parents' home.

Nickson hesitated at the door.

"Come in," Samara encouraged him. "The respects you paid Casimir were kind."

Nickson motioned toward Rawlins and lowered his voice so the others couldn't hear. "I don't think he wants me here."

"That may be true, but you are here. Come in with us."

Convinced, he moved to the table and took a seat next to her.

"I need a drink," Maddox said, even though it was only late morning.

Tristan entered with tankards for all. "I thought we all would."

Samara declined, as did Nickson and her father, but the rest indulged.

"What happened?" Dagan asked quietly.

No one answered.

Rawlins slammed his cup down on the table. "Casimir's dead. That's what happened."

Maddox clenched his jaw. "I still can't believe he's gone."

Samara met her father's gaze. She swallowed hard and started at the beginning. "I followed the team to Eagle's Bay." She explained what happened to her while she was there. She explained what happened to Casimir, unable to keep her tears in check, and how the tree had blocked her shot. She told her father everything and how she pushed for everyone's flight out of Eagle's Bay. As she started on Taiga's race to his death, she couldn't continue, and Maddox took over the tale. Tristan and Rawlins added their own perspectives, and by the time they finished, Samara was exhausted. Dagan had risen from his chair to stand with his face toward the wall.

"All we have to show for our mission," Rawlins said bitterly, "is a dead friend and two dead horses. What are we supposed to do now?"

Dagan turned to Nickson. "I suppose your father still wants his evidence?"

Nickson spoke for the first time. "What my father wants, and what I want, are two different things. But yes, I imagine he will still demand evidence."

Rawlins stood and glowered at the prince. "We lost a dear friend trying to get what your father wanted. I refuse to be used in this way by the crown."

"I'm with Rawlins on this," Maddox said and folded his arms. "It nearly cost the rest of us our lives. I'm not certain another attempt would be wise."

"Without this evidence, the king won't move to strike against the Hungau," Samara said. "All of Cascadia's villages will be left unprotected unless we can prove the Hungau's intent."

Rawlins steepled his fingers over his nose in frustration. "So, we try again, and lose how many more? Me? Samara? The Hungau know it was us who entered their forests. Will they retaliate?"

"Father, do you think they would?" Samara asked.

"If they do, I do not see the king stepping in to assist us," Dagan said, with a pointed look at the prince.

Nickson stood to his full height. "My father is unwilling to move forward without the evidence. I can't change his mind, but I can help you. However you wish to proceed, you have my sword and allegiance."

"How should we proceed? Our mission was a complete failure." Maddox blinked and averted his gaze to a far wall. Tears came to his eyes. "And we lost Casimir."

Samara sank back in her chair and thought of their best friend buried now in the earth. A wave of sorrow overwhelmed her, and she stood quickly. "I am sorry," she said to her family. "Casimir's blood is on my hands, and I will never be rid of this guilt."

She fled.

It was the only thing she could do. She ran to escape her pain, the reality of her loss, and her footsteps carried her to the stables where her dear horse would have been waiting for her. Many years of habit stopped her in her tracks at the stable door. Taiga's stall was empty.

Another wave of sorrow wrapped around her heart. It squeezed uncomfortably and a sob escaped her. Taiga was gone.

Forced to saddle another horse, she chose Casimir's mount—a chestnut mare with a red mane and tail. Ember was the name given to her fiery appearance. As Samara pulled her out of the stable and took her seat in the saddle, a familiar anger filled her. The horse's temperament—feisty and eager—seemed just what she needed. She dug in her heels and took off over the bridge.

She had no destination in mind, but as she drove the horse deeper into the woods, she thought of the Great Falls.

The Great Falls created a division in the Forests of the North. Still under Dagan's rule, the falls separated the upper bench from the lower valley. It was here she often went to go swimming and find solitude.

The falls fell to the bottom of a large pool, which fed a river that led out of the forest and eventually out to the sea. Several trees and a couple of giant boulders circled the ground around the water, giving the illusion of privacy. At this time of the season, wildflowers would surround the pool and river. Samara could imagine the mystical quality the scene created and the peace she could find there.

She reached her destination, and the familiar rocks that sprang up along the waterfall beckoned to her. The giant pool below was deep enough that one could dive from these rocks with plenty of clearance. While she normally enjoyed the recreation, today she needed stillness and time to think through her failures as a Gardien. As a friend.

She pulled Ember to a stop and was about to dismount when something up the path drew her attention. She lifted her gaze, and her stomach dropped to her feet.

A Hungau warrior looked right at her.

The drive of competition flowed through her veins. Anger at the warrior, deeply rooted in all the harm the Hungau had inflicted on her family, cast any fear aside. Ember sensed the change and pranced anxiously underneath her. She was battle-trained and understood what was about to happen. Samara pulled out her dagger.

The Hungau warrior moved closer, and Samara could see she was female. Her hair was long like Samara's, and it hung free in dark waves down her back with small twists and braids scattered throughout. It was wild around her face, which was covered in paints and mud for camouflage.

She met Samara's gaze and fiercely held it, then turned and pulled her seax from the sheath on her back. The woman crouched, prepared to fight. Her left shoulder, now visible to Samara, held the Hungau symbol. The red X with a circle around it clearly identified the woman's loyalties, and a flare of hatred ignited inside Samara at the sight of it.

Her bow would have been a better choice at this distance, but she had left it at her father's house. Her dagger would not do well against the seax, but she had to try. With a flick of her wrist, she launched the dagger across the distance between them. Her aim was true, and it sailed directly for the Hungau's face.

Right before it hit, the woman struck it down with her seax. Samara hid her surprise at the woman's quick reaction, but Samara was now weaponless. She was about to turn Ember to run, when the woman sheathed her seax and held up her hands in surrender.

"I mean you no harm," the Hungau said, her voice strong and clear.

Samara did not believe her. She had no reason to trust a Hungau warrior, and she wasn't foolish enough to pretend this warrior was any different than the others.

So, why did her voice pierce Samara to the very core?

The warrior was about as tall as she was. Samara looked more closely at the woman and tried to see past the mess of paints covering her skin. The neat, chiseled look of her jawbone and the high cheekbones made her face vaguely familiar. Samara noted her hair again and somehow knew it would feel soft like her own when washed and combed.

"Who are you?" Samara asked. "I've seen you before."

A need to know who this woman was pulled at her so strongly, she dismounted her horse and moved closer. The air between them was tense, but the woman hadn't moved to kill her. Not yet.

Samara locked her gaze on the Hungau warrior. The strange sensation that she was looking in a mirror flooded her with confusion.

"Who are you?" she asked again, demanding an answer.

The strange woman raised her arm and in response Samara halted. Expecting a weapon of some kind, she immediately saw she was mistaken. What she had thought was a weapon was not a weapon at all. In the Hungau's hand was a long, cylindrical tube. Attached to the brown tube was a leather strap.

The warrior held it up to her. Samara watched this woman, fascinated that she hadn't tried to kill her. When Samara made no motion for the cylinder, the woman threw it to her. Samara caught it.

"What is this?"

The woman motioned for her to open it. Samara opened the lid. Inside were papers, maps, and battle plans. The evidence.

Samara looked up at the warrior, awestruck.

"Take them," the woman said. "Take them to Dagan."

Shock froze Samara's feet to the ground. She looked at the woman's long black hair and the familiar shade of her blue eyes. She had heard that voice before.

Samara's mouth fell open.

The woman suddenly shook her head and pain fell upon her features. "Go!" she said. "Take them!"

Before Samara could get a word out, the woman turned into the trees and fled. Samara felt the urge to follow, but the weight of the tube in her hands reminded her of the importance of what she carried.

She retrieved her dagger and swiftly mounted Ember. With the precious cargo draped across her back, Samara raced back toward her father's home. Her mind focused on the cylinder draped across her body. She thought of the Hungau who had given it to her. She did not understand why a Hungau would not kill her, let alone help her. The Hungau warrior had turned over the evidence that would justify a war between their people and the whole of Cascadia.

Surely the woman had known this. So why would she do it?

Samara saw the woman in her mind's eye. She looked so familiar—her blue eyes, her fair skin, her long dark hair. Features Samara saw every day in the mirror.

With each hoofbeat, with each heavy breath, Samara's heart screamed what her mind would not accept. The two faces that had haunted her life could not be erased—one bright, kind, and loving; the other black, shriveled, and burned. As Samara ran, tears poured down her cheeks despite her attempts to stop them. Reality was not what it had appeared to be.

As she rode, a memory from her childhood surfaced. The face of her mother, beautiful and kind, smiled at her as she stood in her lovely garden. It was the garden just outside her home, where her mother's grave was.

She ran outside. "Mother!"

"Out here!" Her mother was bent over a giant yellow rosebush, clipping the longest ones. She placed them in a basket. "Come help me." She smiled.

Samara ran to her and grabbed one of the roses. The rose pricked her finger and made her cry.

Her mother chuckled. "Be careful, Samara. The roses have thorns. See?" She pointed to one and Samara looked at it curiously, and stuck her tongue out at it.

Calida laughed and grabbed Samara's stinging finger. She kissed the tip. "There, all better."

Samara laughed with her mother.

Another memory replaced the first, but this one held a face hardly recognizable.

Four dead bodies, burned and murdered, were all that remained of her mother's team. Three she recognized, but the fourth was so badly mutilated it made Samara sick to her stomach.

She sank to her knees in agony, then retched violently into the grass.

Her mother, once beautiful and full of life, was nothing but a charred piece of nothing. A scream escaped her lips at the sight.

Her mother was burning.

She ran to the pole and attempted to put out the flames. Maddox pulled her away.

Her mother wasn't dead. She couldn't be.

She couldn't stop staring at her face.

Her beautiful face was blackened and charred.

Samara retched again.

The tears were relentless. This was the last memory Samara had of her mother, but as she crossed the forest, a new face floated behind her eyes. This face, covered in green and brown paints, was hardened. It was the face of the enemy. The face of a traitor.

She flung herself from her seat atop Ember and rushed inside to her father. She pushed open the door and nearly plowed into Maddox.

"Samara? Where have you been?"

"Where is Father?"

Her friend held her shoulders. "What happened? Why are you crying?"

"I need to speak to my father. Now."

"He's in the dining room with all the others." He pointed.

She marched in. Everyone was seated at the table. Tristan, Danson, Rawlins, her father, and Nickson. They were all there.

How would she tell her father what now caused her soul to ache? How would the Gardiens comprehend that one of their own had betrayed them?

But had she betrayed them? She gave Samara the papers, after all. Why had she not identified herself? She obviously knew who Samara was and wished to help her. How would her father handle this?

Samara asked herself endless questions, none of which had a satisfying answer. Each brought on a series of more questions, and she felt like her mind would be swallowed up in the deep chasm of all she did not know.

"Samara? Are you all right?"

Her eyes focused again on her father. "Father, a Hungau—" She couldn't finish her sentence. She suddenly felt lightheaded.

"What about a Hungau?" Her father stood. "What is it?"

She looked at him, and a sudden wave of exhaustion, both mental and physical, overwhelmed her. "Something happened out there."

"Are you hurt?" Maddox asked, his voice full of concern.

"No! I'm not. I'm certain—" She focused on the Hungau woman now miles away. "I mean I think I'm sure—"

"What are you talking about?" Dagan approached her.

Nickson also stood, his expression full of worry.

"I feel very strange." She fell forward. Maddox caught her and helped her to the table.

She sat, closed her eyes, and took a deep breath, unsure where she should begin.

"What is that tube?" Rawlins asked.

Without a word she stood and removed the cylinder from her shoulders. Taking a few steps to her father, she handed it to him. Dagan looked at her, confused. "What is this?"

"The evidence," she said wearily.

The team looked at her in surprise, speechless at their sudden success. Then everyone began to talk at once.

"How did you get this?" Rawlins asked.

"We can give this to the king," Danson added.

"A Hungau warrior was in the Forests," Samara tried, but she was quickly interrupted.

"A Hungau?" Maddox asked. "Are you hurt?"

Samara fought a growing headache. "No, I'm not hurt. I have something I need to tell you."

"Where is the Hungau now?" Dagan asked.

"They crossed into your borders," Nickson observed.

"We need to look these over at once," Dagan said. "Samara, you still look tired. Are you sure you're all right?"

"Yes, I'm tired," Samara explained. "But—"

Everyone continued to talk. Maddox was the only one who seemed to notice Samara's distress. He moved to her side and watched her intently. The headache roared and pounded against her ears. The barrage of questions and voices raised her level of irritation until she could take no more. "Stop!" she cried.

Everyone went silent.

"There is something I'm trying to tell you!" Tears again began to fall to her cheeks.

She sank to her chair once more and then looked up at her father, certain her news would devastate him. "A female Hungau warrior just handed me this tube. She looked just like me."

Samara took a deep, shaky breath.

"Father, Mom's alive."

Chapter Sixteen

Six shocked faces stared at Samara in silence. Nobody moved.

With this sort of news, she expected her father to say something: *No, you're lying. Are you positive? You saw your mother on the stake.* Samara anticipated any of these responses. Instead, her father stared at her, his mouth open and eyes blank, face as white as a linen sheet.

Perhaps this was the most appropriate response.

She opened her mouth to say something, but decided against it. She had already had time to work through this; her father needed to let it sink in as well. As she watched her father's eyes, she could see the truth hit him. She watched the emotions work: shock, then surprise, then anger, sadness, and disbelief. Finally, his eyes found the emotion he had settled on, one Samara did not understand.

Was it pity? Or regret? Regret for what, and pity for whom? As she watched him, it occurred to her that he did not display any inner turmoil. He looked at *her*, and his pity was for her and her alone.

Perhaps he took pity on her for thinking such outlandish things and regretted that he would have to inform her it was untrue. Perhaps he pitied her crazy wish for her mother to still be alive. Perhaps . . . Samara's thoughts trailed off. Her heart was pounding.

"Father, why are you looking at me like that?"

"Samara, your mother is dead," Maddox responded slowly, as if she had lost her mind.

She could not tear her eyes away from her father.

"Why are you looking at me like that?" she demanded more firmly.

Dagan took a step toward her. She surprised herself when she took one step away.

He reached for her. "Samara."

Samara stared at the man she had always trusted. Their entire relationship suddenly felt different. Her head spun. "You knew. You knew all along."

"Samara, let me explain," Dagan pled.

She glared at him, and her breath came in quick gasps. "And you didn't tell me? You didn't tell your own daughter her mother was still alive?"

"Your father had his reasons," Tristan said.

She whipped her head to look at her uncle. She looked back at her father and then at Tristan again, and pointed her finger at him. "You knew too?"

Tristan nodded.

Samara didn't know where to turn. Nickson looked flabbergasted, Maddox stared at Dagan in disbelief—everyone else was in shock.

"It was for your own protection," Dagan tried to explain.

"You knew," she whispered again, unable to believe it. Her father stepped forward and touched her elbow. "Don't touch me," she whispered as she took a step back. "How long have you known?"

Dagan looked heartbroken. "I found out shortly after the incident," he explained. "She contacted me."

Samara shook her head in disbelief. "You've been keeping this from me for four years? I don't believe it."

"It's true," Tristan piped in. "We kept it from you to protect you."

"Protect me from what?"

Dagan and Tristan exchanged a glance.

"There is a lot to explain," Dagan said. "For starters, your mother is our Hungau contact. She's the one who has been warning us about the attacks."

"Calida Wells is Hungau?" Nickson asked in surprise as the pieces of the puzzle came together.

"And she's alive?" Maddox added.

Samara took a deep breath. "I need . . . time. To process this, all of it."

"Please, don't be angry," Dagan begged.

Samara looked at her pleading father. "I am already angry. You've allowed me to mourn all this time for nothing." She turned to Maddox. "So far you, Rawlins, Danson, and Nickson are the only people who have not lied to me. Is there anything, anything at all, you have never told me?"

Maddox looked Samara in the eye. "I have no secrets from you."

She turned to Nickson. "I don't know you nearly enough, but do you have anything to add?"

"Remember who you're talking to," Dagan corrected.

"No," Samara shot back. "You failed to acknowledge that rule in every moment a word was shared between us. You failed to remember your daughter, and you *failed* to tell her she still had a mother."

Her father looked hurt, but Samara ignored his pain. She turned to Nickson. "Well?"

"No secrets from me," Nickson said.

Marginally satisfied, she turned on her father again. "Explain. Now."

The air between them was strained in a way it had never been before. Samara waited, impatiently, for her father to justify all of this. She couldn't fathom any good reason to keep the truth from her.

"I understand why you're angry," he said. "I did it for your own protection."

"You said that already."

Dagan took a deep, slow breath. "You are much wiser and stronger than I give you credit for. I thought I was doing you a service, keeping certain things from you, but I can see I was wrong. So, let me go back to the beginning. When your mother first came to our forests after she abandoned her life with the Hungau, it didn't take long for the Gardiens to like her. We didn't say she was Hungau, but people caught on quickly." Dagan smiled at the memory. "To protect her identity from the Hungau, we changed her name from Calista to Calida. When you were born you brought such joy to our home. Life was good for our people, politically and personally. The Hungau were active, but they were quiet, and we kept our eyes on them for many years with few problems.

"Four years ago, everything changed. When our scouts reported Hungau activity, we thought about sending Tristan as the team leader, but it was out of the question—he hadn't changed much. For your mother, disguise was one of her many fine skills. So, she changed her look and they headed into Hungau land to see if the reports were true. They found evidence—the Hungau were planning to attack our eastern border. On their way home, they decided to head south and come in from that direction. They wanted to survey that side of the border, and it seemed as good a time as any to do so. That is where the Hungau ambushed them." Dagan took his daughter's hand. "But here is where the story differs from what you know."

Samara took a deep breath. "Go on."

Dagan swallowed hard. "When the fighting was over and the team was forced to surrender, your mother removed her disguise, hoping it would save her team members' lives. She couldn't have been more wrong. They seemed eager to have the heir to their people return, but they killed the others, burning them alive. Your mother felt guilty for their deaths, even though she couldn't have done any more than she had. Most of the Hungau were willing to take her back, but she still had to convince her father and several other leaders that she was still loyal to the Hungau ways. Somehow she was able to convince the Hungau that she had been held captive by the Gardiens the entire twenty years she was with us." Dagan looked into his daughter's eyes. "By lying to them, she kept her marriage a complete secret. And by keeping her marriage a secret, the Hungau had no idea she had a daughter."

Samara thought about this. If her mother had been able to convince the Hungau she was a hostage, they wouldn't have killed her. They would have let her assume her rightful place as heir and leader.

"Why doesn't she try to escape and come home?" she asked. "Does she not want to be here anymore? Why didn't she make herself known to me?"

"Sometimes knowledge makes you a target. I refused to let you go on missions because if you were captured, I didn't want the Hungau to know who you were. I didn't want them to find out that Calida had a Gardien daughter. She didn't make herself known because if the Hungau knew about you, they would kill you both. Your mother stayed away because she wanted to prevent a war." Dagan smiled, though only faintly. "As soon as she had a chance, she made contact with me. By this time, of course, I believed as you had—that Calida was dead. We had identified three bodies of the team; it only made sense the fourth was your mother."

"Who was the other person they killed?" Samara asked.

"Some other Hungau warrior. He had committed a crime, and for his punishment they killed him and positioned him as the fourth member. You see, they were hoping to keep Calida's survival a secret. They thought we would attempt to reclaim our hostage since she is the daughter of Hungau leaders."

"I hate to pry into family matters," Nickson said dumbfounded. "But is your wife the heir and leader to the Hungau nation?"

Dagan nodded. "Yes, Your Highness."

"Why would she lead them in a revolt against the crown?" He leaned against the table; his brow furrowed.

Samara's anger surged. "And what about Treewell and Bender Village?" Her jaw clenched. "She has betrayed us."

Dagan's eyes widened. "Samara, you mustn't think that. Calida was forced to return to the Hungau to keep us safe. Your mother is the leader of the Hungau, but she does not hold the title alone. Others work with her. Your grandfather, for one, led the Hungau until two years ago when he passed. She has too many years of Hungau ideology working against her. So, she did what she could and informed us so we could help save the villages."

Samara processed what her father was saying. "And she's been our contact this whole time."

"Yes. Little do they know her loyalty still lies with us, the Gardiens." He beamed.

Her father's words exonerated her mother, but her anger refused to subside. "Then why doesn't she return home? Let the Hungau attack, but at least she'd be with us."

"Your mother will never risk our safety, because she is the key to our protection. If the Hungau realize their heir is a Gardien, they wouldn't hesitate to attack."

Samara clearly saw the red Hungau X on her mother's shoulder. "So I'm supposed to accept that my mother is with the enemy? She couldn't let *me* know she was still alive?"

"We agreed not to tell you any of this."

"I know it was to keep me safe, but how would keeping the truth from me prevent the Hungau from finding out?" she pressed.

Dagan looked sorrowful. "Samara, I don't know how to say this, but it isn't just about the Hungau finding out. Will knowing your mother is alive change our lives? What we do?"

At first, she did not understand. She took a moment to work it through in her head. Her mother had not tried to make herself known and had left as soon as the evidence had been delivered. Her mother had not tried to make contact since then, and it seemed evident she would never try—simply because she never *could* try.

An anguish, so complete, washed over her. "We will never see her again, will we?"

Dagan shook his head. "No, Samara, I'm afraid not. It's too dangerous to risk it. The Hungau have no idea she has a family, and your mother would rather die than see either of us fall into their hands."

"Is it so easy for her to just leave us alone?"

Dagan hugged his daughter. "Never think that. In her last contact to me she said she loved you very much and wished she could be here for you. She said many tender and precious things about you and the memories she has of you. You are her pride and joy!" he exclaimed with a tear in his eye.

More tears fell. Samara was tired of crying, and she was ready to stop feeling so sad. Her mother, though still alive, would never see them again. It would be as if she really was dead—at least that was how she would have to view it.

Her father's eyes were now on her as she processed what he had told her. Everyone seemed to need time to make sense of it in their own way. Samara looked at Maddox and couldn't remember another time when her friend had looked as livid as he did then. He normally expressed his emotions without inhibition. For him to be so silent was unusual.

"You kept this from the entire Gardien Council," Samara broke the silence. "You and Tristan have been lying to all of us."

"Now you know everything," Dagan said. "When your time comes to rule these forests, you will realize that certain hard decisions have to be made. It pains me to know I have hurt you, Samara. Please, forgive me. Forgive your mother."

Samara had always been able to forgive people when she gained understanding, but she couldn't fight the feeling that if her mother truly loved her, she would have found a way to remain with the Gardiens. Anything would have been better than siding with the Hungau. Her mother had returned to the enemy and Samara would never see her again.

Samara was suddenly disgusted with herself. She had Hungau

blood running through her veins. She turned to Nickson. "Now you know I'm half Hungau," she said to him. "I haven't been completely honest with you, and I'm sorry."

Nickson met her gaze, but the disappointment she saw there was more than she could bear.

She turned to her father. "And I can't believe you would ever dream of being dishonest with me."

Without waiting for his response, she turned and walked out of the dining room. For the second time that day she felt the need to flee. Her life had become complex in the last few days and it weighed her down.

How could her father have not mentioned this? *This*, as if *this* were nothing more than forgetting to tell someone the horses needed to be fed. At the thought of horses, she marched toward the stables. Taiga's empty stall again reminded her of his absence, and she cursed her ingrained habits. She was always ready to let him out and take him for a ride; it would be hard to stop.

Casimir's absence was also everywhere she looked. A sob built its way up to her chest and she clutched at her throat to keep it from coming out. She leaned against the stable wall and focused on breathing deeply.

This was too much to take in.

When she had calmed, she prepped Ember and took off riding for the Great Falls again. Her home, usually a place of peace and safety, was so full of strife she didn't want to be there. She was mad her father lied. She was mad her mother was a Hungau and that she'd never see her again.

Her thoughts wandered to the evidence her mother had given her. If she was the Gardiens' Hungau contact, she took great risk coming into the Forests to give it to them. Her concern for her mother warred with her feelings of betrayal, but in the end her thoughts only led to more tears.

She arrived at her favorite place in the Forests and dismounted. Stepping onto the cool, green grass around the falls, Samara removed her shoes and picked out a giant rock to sit on. She dangled her feet in the water and listened to the water rushing down to the rocks and pool below.

The falls were where she often went to ponder her life and feel close to her mother. With no mother to help guide her, Samara, as the only woman in her family, sometimes felt alone. Now she knew her mother was alive, yet she felt more alone than ever.

There were no reasons valid enough for her father to keep this from her. There were no reasons for her mother, either. Father said she had contacted him; why had she not contacted her daughter?

A tear trickled down her cheek. This was not a turn she had expected her life to take. With a deep breath, her resolve shuddered, and the tears burst from her eyes. Her life was a complete lie!

With a sudden wave of anger, she lifted her face to the sky and shouted, "Why does it hurt so much?"

"I wish it didn't," a voice behind her said.

She turned at the voice, unashamed of her now tear-stained face. "My mother is alive, Nickson." The very idea of it sounded too fantastical to believe—she had seen her burnt body on the stake.

He dismounted Kalia and moved toward her. "I can't even imagine what you must be going through."

The water lapped around her ankles in gentle waves. It soothed her but did not heal her.

"May I join you?" Nickson asked.

"Have a seat."

He took a place next to her on the boulder but did not remove his shoes. Serenity cloaked them for a few moments. Samara felt more relaxed and the atmosphere of this peaceful place calmed her some.

"This is beautiful," Nickson commented.

Samara sighed. "It's one of my favorite locations."

She could sense Nickson had questions, but, respectfully, he did not ask. The very thought of explaining anything drained her, but there was also a need to talk about it.

"You must be surprised to find out my mother is Hungau."

"It was quite a shock, especially since they are your mortal enemies."

"I believe the beginning of the story will help you understand," Samara said. "My mother's death was a tragic one, but her life was happy. My mother and my uncle Tristan were born to the Hungau."

Images from the story she had heard a million times filled her head as she told the tale, but she fell into a rhythm and let the history of her parents echo across the afternoon air.

During one of the many skirmishes between the Gardiens and the Hungau, young Calista, as she was called before she became a Gardien, came head to head with Dagan. The fight lasted longer than they both thought it would, but soon Dagan's strength overpowered her. Struck by her beauty, he could not bring himself to kill her and he surrendered. Calista took pity on him, and as Hungau heir, enforced his status as prisoner. They kept him barely alive for months, and during that time, they fell in love. They could not let their relationship become known—the Hungau leader, Calista's father, would surely kill Dagan if he found out. One night, with Tristan's help, Calista broke Dagan out of the prison hold and escaped with him to the Forests of the North. Upon his return, Dagan took his rightful place as heir and leader of the Gardiens. He married Calista, and she kept her Hungau descent a secret. She changed her name to Calida. After a time, Samara was born, and trained in the ways of the Gardiens.

Calida never returned to the Hungau until four years ago. Gardien scouts on the eastern border observed the Hungau gathering for battle. It only seemed natural to assume they were preparing a strike against the Gardiens. Calida convinced Dagan that she should go. As someone who understood the land and the people, her knowledge would be invaluable, so she headed the team. Three other men accompanied her. As far as anyone knew, they were successful in their mission and would return after seven days with any information. What the Gardiens didn't know was that a specialty kill team of Hungau warriors had followed them. When Calida and the team reached the edge of the forests, the Hungau ambushed them.

The pain hit Samara anew. She took a deep breath.

"The ambush was a slaughter," she said through clenched teeth. "They fought a large party and killed half before the Hungau finally took them over. There was so much blood on that field." She had to suppress a chill.

"Word came quickly that there was trouble on the southeastern border, but by the time we got there, it was too late." Samara closed her eyes. "We assumed that because she had turned traitor against the Hungau, they did the most damage to her on purpose. Her death devastated us."

Nickson's expression fell with concern. "I can't believe you had to see her like that."

"I was part of the group that ran to the aid of that team. I was eighteen and well-trained and capable. Despite it being four years ago, my father refuses to let me go on missions, even now. I offered to go with Maddox and the others for this current trip but was overruled."

Nickson pursed his lips. "We might forever disagree on this, but your father was wise to keep you home."

"They are my brothers, Nickson. I couldn't let them go unprotected."

"What if you had died? Your father would have no one."

"I didn't die, so this is a moot argument."

"I know your father loves you and that the Hungau are dangerous." He tossed a rock into the water. "I couldn't imagine letting my daughter go, either, especially if I needed to protect her identity."

Samara looked at him. "Nickson, you don't understand. I had to help."

"Why?"

"At the time I thought it was to avenge my mother," she shrugged. "Now that I know she's alive . . ."

They were both quiet for a moment.

"I don't trust my father," she admitted. "I feel as if our whole relationship has been a lie."

"I'm sorry, Samara. Do you really believe that, though?"

"I just don't understand."

"Maybe he thought you were too weak to handle it."

Samara glared at him. When he smiled brilliantly she jabbed at his arm. "Very funny."

As she pulled her fist away, Nickson caught it unexpectedly and held her hand in his. "I know you're strong enough."

She looked at their entwined fingers. "You've been very friendly since my return."

His eyes sparked with mischief. "Are we not friends?"

"Friends don't hold hands," she pointed out.

Nickson stroked her palm. "They could," he ventured.

"Does a prince hold the hand of a Hungau? His enemy?" she asked him, changing tactics.

A hint of frustration played in his eyes before he looked into hers. "Does a Hungau hold hands with a Gardien?" His voice was hushed, but firm.

Samara did not know how to respond. The impossible had happened for her parents; why not for her? But when she analyzed her feelings she knew, deep down, she could never live in the castle. It was too far from home in many different ways.

"And yet, in the end, their differences pulled them apart." She pulled her hand free from his grasp.

Nickson's jaw clenched. "I do not mind that you have Hungau in your blood," he said. "I see there is more to you than that. My father has made poor choices, but you do not judge me for them, do you?"

He held out his hand again, but she hesitated to take it. As she stared at it, the desire to feel his hand in hers caused her to reach for him. His fingers encircled hers and her heart started to pound. "No," she answered. "I do not judge you for his choices."

"Nor do I judge you for your relations."

In the quiet, with her hand in his, Samara suddenly felt guilty. "I'm sorry I never told you about my mother being a Hungau. I'm sorry I lied to you about my connections to them."

Nickson's green eyes landed on hers. "You do not need to apologize. I understand why you kept it a secret. With what's happened in recent weeks, the citizens of Cascadia do not take kindly to the Hungau. Perhaps, since the future is unknown, it is best you tell no one else."

Samara reluctantly pulled her hand out of his. "Our differences really might be too great to overcome."

"Samara, no, I—"

"It's all right. You can't deny that, right now, it would be unwise to pursue a relationship with a Hungau. It would hinder everything we are trying to accomplish with your father."

"But you're a Gardien," he countered. His eyes pled with her.

"Until your father learns the truth. Then I'll be a Hungau, and you know that's what he'll say. No, it is better this way."

Nickson turned away from her, obviously frustrated by her unwillingness to consider the interest they had in one another.

He didn't know how hard it was for her to reject him. She had grown to admire and appreciate the prince, and rejecting him upset her tremendously. She knew she had offended and frustrated him, but she couldn't fight her fears. The differences between their lives would hinder anything they tried to establish. The dissimilitude of their worlds was not something they could overcome. Eventually, their worlds would collide—just like her parents' had.

Nickson reluctantly stood. "I suppose you are correct, my lady." His expression betrayed his disappointment in spite of his words. "I will leave you now."

"I can take you back," Samara offered.

"No." He raised his hand. "I can take myself if you'll point me in the right direction."

Samara would have smiled at this, but Nickson's hastiness to leave was evidence he was upset. "Head south and follow the path that snakes through the trees," she instructed. "Nickson, I—"

He held up his hands. "You don't need to explain, my lady."

She looked up and tried to ignore the pressing awkwardness suddenly between them. Apparently, the formalities were back. Samara bowed her head. "Your Highness."

Samara caught a glimmer of regret in his eyes. He still didn't want her to bow or address him as his title, but that seemed unimportant now. He dipped his head in a slight bow and retreated toward the trees.

Maddox suddenly appeared on the path. He bowed to Nickson as the prince passed, then continued to where Samara sat. With a last glance, Nickson met her gaze, and disappeared. As she watched him leave, another feeling of loss grated on her peace.

"Hello, Maddox."

"Dagan is looking for you."

"Apparently he found me," she muttered.

"I know you're upset with him." Maddox approached her. "But he loves you and is concerned about you."

"I'm sure." She folded her arms. "I don't want to see him just yet."

Maddox looked in the direction of the trail. "The prince seemed to be leaving in a hurry. What did you do?"

Samara glared at him. "Me?"

The sadness in his eyes belied his jest. "I'm only teasing. He did seem upset, though."

"Probably another thing I've ruined," was all she could bring herself to say.

Maddox grabbed her by the elbow. "Are you all right?"

Samara bit her trembling lip. "Not really, no."

"Come here." He pulled her to him and she gratefully accepted the hug.

"I'm hurt my father lied to me," she cried into his shoulder. "I'm hurt my mother is a Hungau once again, and no one told me she was still alive. Her position within the Hungau means I'll never get to see her again. I frustrated Nickson, and that's bothering me too."

"Is that all?" Maddox laughed.

"I miss Taiga," she whispered.

"You've got a full plate." He squeezed her tighter. "You have the right to feel frustrated, but I am here for you." He kissed her hair.

"Thank you, Maddox." She pulled away and looked up at him. "I feel so lost right now."

"I know how you feel." Maddox's face fell. "Calida being alive changes everything, and Dagan keeping it from us . . ." He clamped his teeth in frustration.

"I know," she said. "And Casimir."

Maddox blinked back tears. "He was like a brother to me. The entire council is my family. I can't believe he's gone."

Samara hugged her friend again. "I see that moment over and over in my head," she confessed.

"I do too."

A sorrowful silence enshrouded them. They sat there, side by side, for a long moment without saying a word. The trees swayed in the breeze and the water rippled as the air pushed at the surface. The crashing of the waterfall calmed her, and after a time she felt Maddox relax too. Samara's thoughts stayed on their friend and on her mother, certain they'd be there for a while before her heart could mend.

Finally, Maddox stood. "Your father wants to discuss the evidence."

"I figured he would."

"He told me he wants to give us time to adjust, but the problem with the crown is far from over."

"Do we ever get a break from life's hardships?" she pondered.

Maddox shook his head. "No, but what matters is how we rise to meet them. We're Gardiens, and we will never stay down for long."

Samara smiled a little. "Casimir said that once."

Maddox smiled back. "Yes, he did."

For the first time, Samara felt a hint of peace. Her sorrow was far from removed, but she was grateful Casimir's optimism could still affect her even though he was gone.

"Do you want to ride back together?"

"You go ahead," she said. "I need another moment before I face my father."

Maddox nodded in understanding. "I will tell him."

After he left, Samara was rejuvenated by the peace and quiet. She felt the tension leave her body as she breathed deeply and focused her thoughts elsewhere. She reveled in the solitude she could find at the pool and trusted nature to heal her as it had many times in the past.

A rustle in the bushes on the other side of the lake startled her. She looked carefully but saw nothing. An uneasy feeling came over her.

She donned her boots and slipped from her boulder. Heading away from the pool, she ducked into the forest and planted herself behind a tree to watch and listen. She had a clear view of the falls, but it was as she had left it. She heard nothing else, but she pulled her dagger out of its sheath just in case.

The bushes rustled again and the feel of the dagger in her hands brought some comfort. She held her breath and watched more closely. Something emerged from the cover of the trees.

Green-and-brown paint covering his arms and chest. Long hair cut short on the sides but pulled into a messy twist from the top of his head to the middle of his back. The very way he carried himself. All were unmistakable markers. Across his chest was a strap that fastened his bow to his body. Samara didn't need to look twice to know who it was that spied on her.

Samara held her breath.

For the second time that day, a Hungau had crossed over their borders. And she was in his line of sight.

Chapter Seventeen

Samara watched the Hungau spy, not daring to give away her position in case there were more. He walked to the pool's edge and dipped his finger in the water. He smelled it and looked at the surrounding ground as if he were tracking something. Samara wondered what it was he was tracking, when she realized the footprints he studied were her own.

He was tracking *her*.

She had been confident the Hungau had not seen her. When he approached the pool, he had been loud and careless, allowing the bushes to announce his position. The tree she was hiding behind was large enough to keep her hidden, but it was only a matter of moments before her tracks led the Hungau to her hiding spot.

The Hungau were fierce warriors, and with no one around to help her, Samara was on her own. She pushed these thoughts from her mind and instead studied his clothes: brown leather breeches and a pair of thick brown boots looked flexible and durable; this would give him speed and maneuverability. His sleeveless tunic accentuated the muscles in his arms. This Hungau was strong, and she mentally thanked Maddox for training her for such situations. She glanced in the direction her friend had gone, wishing she had left with him when she had the chance.

This warrior had not bothered with as much dye to camouflage his face, which Samara determined was a result of his confidence. On his shoulder was the clear, unmistakable mark of the red X.

A shudder went through her body and she inadvertently stepped back. The sound she heard next pierced her like an arrow: a twig beneath her snapped.

She froze.

The Hungau snapped his head up and looked in all directions. Samara sank behind the tree and took a deep breath. She counted to three before peeking around the trunk once more. The Hungau was looking directly at her.

He had spotted her.

She tightened her grip on the dagger in her hand and planted her feet more firmly on the ground. The Hungau took a step toward her, listening, watching. Her hands grew warm and sweaty as she moved back behind the tree. The Hungau had not moved his eyes from her spot.

She took a deep breath, sheathed her dagger, and drew an arrow from her quiver, which she connected to her bow. She was grateful she had been thoughtful enough to bring her weapons this time. She counted again in her head, and on three she lunged from behind the tree and pointed her arrow at where she knew the man had stood.

He wasn't there.

She looked around her and listened. There was not a sound, nothing. The birds had gone quiet and the deer had fled, leaving her alone with an enemy she had lost sight of. She fought the nervous turns of her stomach. Silence with a Hungau did not mean he was still—they were expert killers designed to move like the whisper of wind.

"Hungau!" she called.

No movement, not even a stir. She called again.

"Hungau!"

She hoped her presence had frightened the warrior away, but she could feel his eyes on her. She would make a run for it. If she could get close to home, the warrior would not follow, and she would have time to warn everyone else. She took a few steps back with her arrow pointed at the line of trees before her. She continued to retreat, but her progress was halted when she bumped into something hard. It was the Hungau man. Her eyes widened and, dropping her bow, she reached for her dagger. He was faster.

He caught her by the arm, stopping her strike. Locking her wrist in his talon-like grip, he studied her with a curious look. His eyes swept over her face, her eyes, and the rest of her features.

Her heart pounded, pumping her body full of energy, as she considered her options. The warrior continued to hold her in place, still studying, analyzing.

"You're Hungau," she said. She wanted him to know she knew who he was.

He nodded once and reached with his free hand to touch a piece of her dark hair. He felt it between his fingertips, then looked back at Samara's face.

"You're a Gardien." He tilted his head and his mouth curved into a smile.

She shuddered. Though she could feel her body preparing to fight, she couldn't bring herself to move or attack him. A hatred for this man started to build inside as he continued to study her. When he leaned in, she pulled away from him.

Still holding her wrist, he spun her around and threw her into the trunk of a tree. The brief moment her back faced the Hungau made her feel vulnerable and bare. She whipped around to face him and held out her dagger in preparation to fight. It was at this moment that she realized she was still armed. For some reason, he had failed to disarm her.

The Hungau stood before her with a seax in his hand. He sauntered from side to side but didn't attack. Samara thought of her mother; the hatred she felt for this man and all he represented momentarily overwhelmed her.

She charged. He caught her dagger with his blade and knocked her off balance, but she recovered and charged again, this time throwing her entire body into the warrior. She raised her dagger to strike at his head, but he blocked it and locked her in place. Their faces were a handsbreadth apart.

So quickly she didn't realize it had happened, the Hungau kept Samara's dagger in a lock with one hand and reached down with his other. She felt a slash of sudden pain in her arm. Crying out, she pushed him away and clutched at her elbow. Blood dripped down her arm.

The Hungau did not relax his defensive posture, nor Samara hers. He thrust his blade forward. She caught her breath and his seax with her dagger at the same time, spinning him around. She flicked her wrist and her dagger made contact with his cheek. He put his hand to the cut and looked at the blood that now covered his fingertips. He snarled and lunged at her again. Strike after strike she blocked him, but Samara realized right away something was amiss in their combative dance.

He's not moving very fast, she thought. *He's holding back. Why*?

He kept striking, until finally he stopped. He gave her one more venomous look and rushed her a final time, spinning her around so she was backed up against a tree.

Samara did not know what hit her. His hand was at her throat, though he squeezed only slightly. Her dagger was no longer in her hand. She clutched at his arm, knowing he could kill her with one flick of his powerful wrist.

"You're Hungau," she warned, "and not allowed on our land. If they find I'm dead, my people will hunt you down and kill you." Whether he cared or not, she didn't know, but it felt good to make some kind of a threat.

His grip lessened and she took a deep breath. He leaned his face in and sniffed again. The smile that had crossed his lips earlier spread across his face. "I'm looking for a friend of mine who entered your forests," he said with an accent.

Samara's thoughts flew to her mother. Her mother had risked entering the Forests to give them the evidence. If this man knew she had been here, Calida's life was in grave danger. Samara focused on keeping her face unreadable. "So, that's why you haven't killed me yet," she quipped. "Who is it?"

"That's not important. Where is she?"

She shifted under his grasp. "You're the only Hungau warrior I've seen."

The corner of his mouth raised. "I saw her enter these woods."

"If she's Hungau, and she entered our forest, you can bet she'd never make it out again."

His eyes narrowed, but he didn't respond.

She looked at his features; he was actually a handsome man with tan skin and dark hair. A scar ran down his jawline, and he seemed older than her by only a few years. It was strange to talk to someone who also knew her mother and would only know her by her Hungau name. This man could not discover Calida's true purpose for visiting the Forests of the North, and he definitely could not learn of her mother's true identity.

"I tracked her to this waterfall. Am I supposed to believe it's a coincidence you're here too?" he sneered.

"The only coincidence on which you have trespassed is that I'm a Gardien, and this is Gardien land."

He smirked again and released his hold on her neck. He backed up, keeping his eyes on Samara's face, until he reached the water's edge. He stared at her one more time before disappearing into the trees on the other side.

Samara had one person on her mind. Her mother's crossing into Gardien territory would only cast suspicion on her loyalties, and the Hungau wouldn't hesitate to remedy the breach.

Her gaze turned toward home, but there was no time. She would have to go after the Hungau alone before he learned that Calida had betrayed the Hungau.

She recovered her dagger, hooked her bow and quiver around her back, and took off at a run. She stopped once by a river to wash the blood off her arm. The cut from the warrior's knife was clean, but it measured from the middle of her arm to below her elbow, long and fairly deep. She ripped a portion of her clean sleeve and wrapped it around the wound, tying it tight. She took off running again.

With her mother's life in her hands, she would not fail. Not this time.

Nickson sat in the Gardien council hall with the others. He could see their morale had taken a hit with the death of Casimir and the information Dagan had kept secret. Rawlins, Danson, and Maddox seemed as loyal as ever to their leader, but the atmosphere was strained and Nickson felt like he had barged in on a private family matter.

Dagan stood behind his desk, facing away from them, hands clasped behind his back. His worry was evident, and he had not stopped glancing at the door in hopes Samara would walk through it.

Nickson understood the feeling; the way he and Samara had parted bothered him. His admiration for her had grown into something more, but with her belief that her Hungau heritage would hinder their work, he wouldn't have the opportunity to pursue it.

This bothered him. A lot.

He had to put his feelings aside, not because he agreed with Samara but because the Gardiens were under a lot of pressure. While they mourned the loss of their friend and leader, they were also mission-focused. The tube of evidence handed over by Samara's mother—a fact he still couldn't quite get over—lay on the table.

"Let's just open it," Rawlins said. "We can fill Samara in when she gets back."

Dagan turned, his face grim. "Why hasn't she returned yet?"

Maddox stood alone in the corner. He had barely said a word since he came from talking with Samara. "She needs time, Dagan. She said she'd come when she was ready."

Dagan sighed and made his way to his seat. "I am sorry I lied to all of you. It was for Calida's protection and Samara's."

Maddox's face softened. "We understand your reasons."

"But it doesn't lessen the blow, does it?" Tristan said and slapped the table.

Maddox rolled his eyes and hid a small smile, unaffected by Tristan's way. "What's done is done."

Danson stood and grabbed the tube. "Casimir died trying to get this evidence. Now that we have it, he'd want us to open it."

Rawlins put a hand on Danson's shoulder. "Yes, he would. I agree with Danson."

Dagan looked at Nickson. "Sire, if you agree, we will move forward."

Nickson nodded. "If this evidence will prove that my father needs to take action, then we shouldn't hesitate."

Dagan looked at the door one last time. "Samara will be informed when she returns. As we discuss the evidence, we can decide where we, as Gardiens of the Forests of the North, are to go from here. Now that all of you know Calida is alive, I do not need to remind you about secrecy. What is spoken in this room *stays* here." He turned to Danson. "Danson, would you do us the honors?"

Danson removed the lid of the tube and dumped the contents onto the table. Everyone stood to see. The biggest roll of paper was about as long as the tube. Danson unrolled it and Nickson immediately recognized it as a map.

"This is a map of Eagle's Bay," Maddox said in awe. "I know we have the map Calida drew hanging there," he pointed to a wall, "but this is it exactly."

Dagan studied it. "There are several landforms we do not have on ours. I will take this to be the most current. What else?"

Rawlins picked up another paper and studied it. "This looks like a communication." He hesitated and looked at Tristan. "It's in Hungau; I can't read it."

Tristan took the paper and silently read the words. "Looks like a letter from a man named Hadar. It doesn't say anything of great importance, but he writes about his plans to build up his armies."

"Calida wouldn't have included it if it wasn't important," Dagan said.

"Who's Hadar?" Nickson asked.

Tristan shrugged. "The name doesn't sound familiar, and I can't envision a face."

"He must be a leader of the Hungau who works with Calida if he's discussing Hungau armies," Maddox suggested.

Dagan frowned. "This concerns me. The Hungau follow rights of succession through their lineage, just like the royal family and the Gardiens do. I don't recall Calida mentioning any leader, potential or current, by that name."

"There wasn't one," Tristan replied.

"You said Samara's grandfather had died," Rawlins pointed out. "Perhaps they shifted from their tradition and appointed him."

Dagan nodded, still in deep thought. "That is a possibility. Let's keep this Hadar in our minds until we can find out more."

Nickson grabbed another rolled piece of paper and opened it up. As he stared at the markings, he knew he had found something big. "I've got it."

The council huddled around the table to see what he found. On the paper was a large circle. Scattered within the circle were several different symbols and between the symbols were lines.

"It's a map," Nickson explained. "See this here?" He pointed to a figure on the upper left-hand side. "That is the crest of the king, but moving eastward," his finger followed an invisible line, "you have the symbol of an eagle." He continued pointing. "These are the Mirror Mountains, and this is your forest."

"I see," Rawlins exclaimed. "Although it's not your traditional map."

"It's actually quite ingenious," Maddox said. "It looks more like a key of symbols than a map." He pointed to it. "See these lines here?"

"What are they?" Nickson asked.

Maddox stood straight with a gleam in his eye. "They are troop movement lines."

Dagan and the others leaned in to observe the strange marks.

"Troop movement lines?" Danson repeated.

Nickson looked where the lines led—some led from Eagle's Bay to a symbol he believed represented Pondwood, others led from

Pondwood to the Montcroix crest. Still others led straight from Eagle's Bay to the castle, and there were varying lengths and places to stop. He could see in his mind what the Hungau had planned.

"I see," he burst out. "Look at this line." He traced it with his finger. "See how it stops at Pondwood and a fresh line starts leading to the castle? They must have several regiments making these trips all at once."

"Troop movement lines," Dagan said. "We've got them." He wore a small but victorious smile.

"It looks like they are planning multiple attacks." Tristan studied the map. "To be carried out simultaneously?"

"No, there are phases," Maddox replied.

"What do you mean?" Nickson asked.

"The first set of lines starts out from Eagle's Bay Forest. They each hit a point where a new set then begins, creating a fan pattern," Maddox explained. "You were right about multiple regiments. If it were me in charge, I would keep a handful of men at each village I conquered, while sending out the rest to complete the next phase."

Nickson counted the phases with his finger. "There are three," he said. "One from Eagle's Bay to Leafland, Springside, and Lakeview. The second starts at those three locations and ends at Poolside and Pondwood. The third phase ends at the castle."

"There are four phases," Dagan said, suddenly stiff. "If the Hungau succeed in taking Leafland, Springside, Lakeview, Poolside, Pondwood, *and* the castle, that leaves one major territory unmarked and unaccounted for on this map."

"The Forests of the North," Maddox said through gritted teeth.

"So, is the castle just an afterthought?" Danson asked. "I think it's right to assume we are their number-one enemy. If these other attacks are to surround us for an ultimate attack, why bother with the castle? It would be harder to get at than our forests."

Everyone stopped to consider this. "He's right," Maddox said. "Going for the castle is a big risk. Obviously, we have a treaty with the royal family, but to hit it first? It could wipe out a huge portion of their army before they even had a chance to attack us."

"Maddox," Dagan responded. "What would we do if we found out the Hungau were attacking the castle?"

"We'd go and fight," Maddox said without hesitation.

"Exactly," Dagan confirmed. "The Forests of the North would be empty and for the taking."

Nickson felt the blood drain from his face. Things his father said came rushing back to him, and though he didn't have all the answers, something did not sit right.

"Your Highness, do you have something to add?" Maddox asked.

Nickson silently cursed the Gardien's observational skills, but he couldn't hide the truth much longer. He clenched his hands into fists and stared at the castle point on the map. Since his acquaintance with the Gardiens, his uncertainty about his father's role in this mess had plagued him.

He stared at the troop movement lines. The third phase, the lines leading to the castle, didn't look like an attack. They looked like a meeting point. The players remained a mystery, but everything seemed to lead him back to his own father.

Nickson slowly stood. The group watched him expectantly as he worked up the courage to tell them what he had kept secret. He clenched his jaw and pursed his lips together. He did not want to say what he knew; the Gardiens had been through enough as it was.

"What is it?" Dagan asked.

Nickson could not look anyone in the eye. Instead he spoke to the table, his head down. "My father lied. The king lied to me, and he lied to you about his knowledge of the attacks. He does know about the Hungau being involved, and my instincts fear the reason isn't good. This evidence proves an attack on the castle has been planned," he turned to Maddox, "but your concern they will be decimated before they hit the Forests may not be necessary. I decided that if my investigation led me to the conclusion that my kingdom is corrupt, I would not allow the Gardiens to fight."

"Because it isn't war with the Hungau." Dagan met his gaze. "It would be war against the crown."

Nickson pushed away from the table and walked to a far wall where he stared at a painting. "I am not certain to what extent the king is involved, but at this point his words don't line up with his actions."

A grave silence settled over the room.

"War against the crown? That's treason," Danson said. He sank into his chair. "What connection have you made between the crown and the Hungau?"

Nickson shook his head. "None yet, but my instincts tell me something is very much amiss."

"Did Samara know your father lied?" Maddox asked.

Nickson met his eye. "Yes. When she came to the castle, the king confessed his knowledge about the attacks. I asked her not to say anything until I could piece things together."

Rawlins cursed. "He knew all along and still sent us to Eagle's Bay. What do we do now?"

Dagan clasped his hands together. "It looks like we need some more information. We need to find out the truth. Your Highness, Samara will accompany you to the castle—as will Danson as a bodyguard—and we'll turn over our evidence to the king." He turned to the rest of the council. "Are you up for a game of covert work?"

Danson nodded firmly. "I'll do it for Casimir."

Maddox clenched his fists with excitement. "I would love to investigate the royal family."

"That is," Dagan turned, "if it is all right with you, Your Highness."

Nickson did not respond right away. The problems coming from his home, his court, and his family infuriated him, but their next course of action was clear. "You think the answers are at my home," he stated carefully. "And I agree things have been strange as of late."

"There must be a weak link for them to have any hope of their campaign succeeding," Maddox added, "but it doesn't mean it is the king. It could be anyone in the castle."

Nickson appreciated Maddox's attempt to give his father the benefit of the doubt, but it was hard to ignore the holes in his story. "We must do what needs to be done."

Rawlins and Danson jumped up from their seats.

"I comply only because as leader of this nation I, too, must do what is right." Nickson glared at Maddox. "This may be a Gardien mission, but I make the rules. You will be in my world."

Maddox stared hard at Nickson for a long moment. "Fine. And I request that Samara stays home. Someone else can go in her place."

Nickson clenched his jaw. This wasn't the first time Maddox was unwilling to let Samara go to the castle, and the accusation Maddox had laid at Nickson's feet still annoyed him. What Maddox had against him, he didn't know. "I think I have proven that Samara will be perfectly safe in my home."

"Samara has grown into a capable warrior, Maddox. Her actions the last few days alone have proven that," Dagan said. "But before we gear up for another mission, let's check the rest of these papers for any more evidence. Sire, when do you wish to leave?"

"As soon as possible. Tomorrow morning will be fine," he replied.

"Where is Samara? She needs to be filled in and she needs to prepare for her journey," Dagan said.

Maddox looked toward the door and Nickson could see he was still concerned. Nickson moved around the table and stood beside him. "Samara is perfectly safe with me." He pursed his lips.

Maddox lowered his voice. "I would hope so, but it's not always about you. Samara is the princess of our people and the only sister I've ever had. It hasn't escaped my notice that you admire her." His eyes moved to the door again. "I'm also wondering why she hasn't returned yet."

Nickson's eyes also fell on the door. "She has not returned as quickly as I expected," he agreed. He wondered if she was more hurt than she had initially confessed. Nickson met Maddox's gaze. "Would she do anything rash?"

Maddox shook his head. "She's not rash by nature, but she said she would be right behind me."

"She did take off for Eagle's Bay," Nickson reminded him.

Maddox pursed his lips and stood. "Dagan, I'm going to go find Samara."

"Please," Dagan said. "We'll get things ready on our end for your journey."

"I'll go with him." Nickson also stood.

Nickson wasn't worried she was in any danger, but Samara felt things deeply and he was worried about how she was handling things. He could see her spending the rest of the day at the falls feeling sorrowful, not that he would blame her. Perhaps a friend or two would be helpful. As he rode toward the Great Falls with Maddox, he hoped he could be a good enough friend to cheer her up.

Friendship was only the beginning of what he wanted, but for now, it would have to be enough.

Chapter Eighteen

Nickson and Maddox made good time getting to the falls, but when they arrived, Samara was nowhere in sight.

"Maybe she headed home," Nickson suggested.

Maddox looked confused. "We would have seen her on the way. I wonder if—" He stopped, his gaze fixed firmly on the ground before his horse. He quickly dismounted and moved his horse away from the water's edge, where he studied the ground.

"What is it?"

Maddox pointed. "These tracks. They aren't Samara's."

"Whose are they?"

Maddox moved over to the right, still analyzing the faint imprints. "They're bigger. Like a man's."

Nickson's heart nearly stopped. "Please tell me it was another Gardien."

"No way to tell."

Maddox kept working. He pointed to the rock where they had sat earlier. "She jumped down here and moved . . ." He looked south, toward the nearby trees. "She moved in that direction. The other tracks stopped at the lake, went around, and disappeared to the south."

Maddox followed Samara's ghost of a trail. Nickson waited, rather impatiently, for him to get answers or, better yet, to find Samara hiding among the trees. The trail led them to a cluster of woods to the south. "She backed up here, and then . . ."

Nickson studied the ground but could not see what Maddox saw. The Gardien was an expert tracker, and if Nickson's concern hadn't grown, he would have been impressed. His eyes suddenly caught sight of something in the dirt. He bent down and put his finger to it. It was red, wet, and looked a lot like . . .

"Blood," Maddox whispered. "She fought the man, and there is blood."

Nickson cursed.

A sense of urgency fell over them and Maddox followed the tracks to wherever they led next. "She went this way."

"She went north? Away from home?" Nickson asked, truly worried now.

"She must have pursued him."

"Could she have been taken?"

Maddox shook his head. "There are two sets of tracks, and they are separate from one another."

Nickson breathed a little. "Well, let's go."

They mounted their horses and followed the trail to where he hoped they would find Samara.

Alive and well.

Samara ran through the woods. The Hungau warrior wasn't far ahead; he knew he was being pursued, but he didn't stop to engage her. The only thing that kept Samara from collapsing in exhaustion was her mother's safety. She didn't know how much information the Hungau had or what he would do if he got it, but she wouldn't risk finding out.

They finally came through a small clearing surrounded by dense foliage. The Hungau warrior stopped and turned around, breathing deeply.

"You cannot run from me," Samara said between breaths.

"Begs me to question why you're chasing me in the first place."

"You trespassed."

He snickered. "I followed her trail to the lake. I found you. This trail we've been running was the path she took to get home. She made it out. Why didn't you chase her?"

"I never saw her."

The Hungau straightened his shoulders. "The leader of the Hungau would be hard not to notice."

Samara feigned surprise. "Calista is the person you're tracking?"

"She was a prisoner here for twenty years. Why would she come back?"

"Why did you feel the need to follow her?"

"She slipped away, and I wanted to know where she was going." Suspicion clouded his eyes. "I wanted to know why she would enter the Forests of the North."

Her mother had done a good thing, getting the evidence to her father, but she had been foolish to risk it. This warrior would not be convinced by any lie Samara could tell. He had decided upon his own truth, but he was right. The only thing he didn't know was that Calida had given them the evidence.

"What was her business here?" he demanded.

"I told you I don't know."

He cocked his head. The way he studied her made Samara nervous. What he saw as he stared at her she could only guess, but she did not like the way he analyzed her appearance.

She and her mother looked exactly alike.

There was nothing but hatred in his eyes. She hoped it meant he still didn't know who she was.

"Who are you?" he asked her.

"A Gardien."

"Don't toy with me, *thianti*."

She didn't know what *thianti* meant, but it was only a matter of time before he pieced together that she was Calida's daughter. He already knew too much. Seeing Calida enter Gardien territory was enough to condemn her. Samara pulled out her dagger.

The warrior smirked. "Now we get to the truth, don't we? What would cause you to enforce my silence with the sword?"

"A great many things. Your people have blood on your hands. You killed my friend Casimir."

"No, that's not it," he mused. "Calista is disloyal. I knew it."

Samara stepped to her right and tightened her grip on her dagger. The warrior responded by pulling out his own blade.

"Why did she meet with you?"

He was taunting her, but Samara didn't answer. Instead, she lunged. He parried and sidestepped her next strike. Their blades met with a clang and Samara kicked, spun, and kicked again.

The warrior was well trained, but so was Samara. It wasn't until he connected a fist to the side of her torso that she faltered. She groaned and clutched her side. He grabbed her by the arm where he had cut her before, and squeezed. Hard.

Crying out, she shrugged away from him and looked at her arm. Fresh blood soaked the cloth she had tied earlier.

"You'd better take care of that," he sneered.

Samara stepped forward, but her feet felt unstable as the ground beneath her swayed. She had lost some blood, she knew that, but the pain caused a pulsing in her ears and momentary loss of steadiness.

She waited to regain her balance. Then, with a well-timed kick, she knocked the warrior's blade from his hand. Sheathing her dagger, she engaged him in hand-to-hand. He was skilled and suddenly he had her backed up against a tree again. His hands clutched her throat and she couldn't free herself.

She longed for a breath, but the air would not come. She struggled against his grip until he pulled her toward him and spun her. He now stood behind her, one hand still around her throat, the other restraining her arms.

"Tell me why she came here," he hissed in her ear.

There was nothing else Samara could do, so she opted for the element of surprise. She could only hope it would work. She opened her mouth to speak, his hold loosening enough so she could form words. "Because Calista is a Gardien," she spat. "She's been working for us all along."

His grip tightened.

"There's more," she got out.

"What?" He jerked her. "What else is there?"

With her left hand she reached for the dagger at her waist. Her fingers barely brushed the handle. She couldn't quite reach it, but if she could just pull it out, she could free herself from his grasp.

"What is it?" he yelled at her.

She tried for her dagger again and missed. His hold was too firm. Desperate now, she opted for more surprise. "Calista has a daughter. A Gardien daughter."

He reacted just as she hoped. His shock caused his grip to loosen, and as it did, her left arm moved freely and she gripped the dagger in her hand. She yanked it off her belt and adjusted her grip. With a quick backward thrust, she lodged the dagger in the man's stomach.

She turned to face him.

On his face was a look of complete shock as his hand circled the hilt of her dagger. He sank to his knees as blood came up through his mouth and his teeth became stained.

"At least tell me who it is," he rasped. "Who is Calista's daughter?"

Samara bent down, put a hand on his shoulder, and looked right into his eyes. "Me."

His eyes widened, and as she pulled the dagger out of his body, he collapsed into the dirt. Samara's confession and the truth of her mother's identity would die with him.

Suddenly exhausted, she sank to her knees. The wound on her arm had soaked the linen and she ripped her other sleeve to stop the bleeding. To be sure he was dead, she went over to the body of the Hungau warrior to check his breathing and check his heart. He was gone.

The sound of horses met her ears and she turned at the sound. She saw Maddox's horse first, but Nickson wasn't far behind. The prince's regal air immediately caught her attention. She couldn't help but notice him and everything he was. Their last conversation had not been ideal, and she wouldn't be surprised if he retained the formalities they had parted with. When he saw her, he immediately dismounted and approached her.

"Samara, are you all right?" Nickson asked.

She almost smiled when he used her name. "I'm all right."

Maddox saw the warrior on the ground behind her. He dismounted and approached the body. Once he, too, confirmed the man was dead, he turned to face her. "What happened?"

"He's Hungau," was all she could get out through her labored breathing.

Maddox stared wide-eyed at her disheveled appearance. "What was he doing here?"

"Your tunic is ripped," Nickson observed.

Samara was hesitant to tell them everything that happened. Her father worried enough about her that she didn't want to worry her friend, too. "I saw him at the Great Falls and followed him here."

"Were there any more?" Maddox asked.

"Just him. He was tracking my mother's trail."

"All the way from Eagle's Bay?" Nickson's eyes strayed to the dead warrior.

"These men are excellent trackers," Samara explained. "And once they learn something, they rarely forget."

Her own words scared her more than she realized, and she repeated them in her head over and over. *Once they learn something, they rarely forget*. Had he been allowed to return to Eagle's Bay with the information he held, the Hungau would have destroyed her mother. She was surprised she had told the man about her connection to Calida, but it seemed the right thing to do at the time.

"If they were tracking Calida, you were right to kill him." Maddox studied her carefully. "Are you hurt?"

Her elbow started to burn. The pain rose up her arm and she resisted every urge to hold it. "Not seriously."

"Samara, you have blood all over your tunic," Maddox said.

She shook her head. Her thoughts clouded and were hard to pinpoint. "I'm fine."

"Maddox is an amazing tracker," Nickson complimented her friend. "And he saw what really happened by the falls." He turned accusing eyes toward her.

Samara knew a lost battle when she saw one. She lifted the bloodied sleeve and showed them her wrapped wound. "He got me."

"All that blood was yours?" Maddox moved toward her. "Let me see it."

She slowly unwrapped the linens and exposed the cut. Maddox swallowed hard at the sight, but he kept his demeanor even and calm. "We need to stitch that."

"I knew you'd worry," she said. "It's just a cut."

"Of course I'm going to worry, Samara. A cut from a Hungau blade is concerning. Don't be so stubborn that you'd keep something like this from me, your friend *and* commander. We'll have Tristan take a look at it."

She put a hand to her head. She was suddenly very tired. "You're right. Now you know. I'm exhausted, and we should get back."

"We'll pick up your horse on the way," Maddox said, still studying her with concern.

She nodded.

"I'll carry this Hungau back with us. Dagan will want to know what happened, and maybe Tristan can identify who he is," Maddox added.

"Samara, you can ride with me until we get to your horse," Nickson offered.

Samara climbed on Kalia behind the prince. She put her arms around him, and as they rode through the forest, she rested her head on his back. Earlier she had claimed it would be unwise to pursue anything with him, but she couldn't resist, and she loved the feel of her arms around him.

She closed her eyes and let herself feel comforted by his

presence. Even after they returned to the falls, she didn't switch horses. No one seemed to mind, and she was too tired to make the change.

"Thank you," she said quietly to the prince.

"For what?" He looked back at her.

"For coming to find me."

Nickson covered her hand with his own, but the gesture was hesitant and brief. He squeezed her hand. "I was worried."

She smiled at the action but frowned when he let her hand go. "I'm sorry if I upset you earlier."

They pulled up in front of her home. Nickson helped her down and locked his gaze on hers. "I'm not upset with *you*," he clarified.

"What happened?" Dagan's worried voice came across the courtyard. "Samara, are you all right?"

Thankfully, Maddox stepped in to explain. "She fought this warrior. Said he was tracking Calida through the Forests."

"You fought him alone?" her father asked, eyes moving to the blood covering her tunic.

She nodded and leaned into Nickson for support. She was so very tired. "I couldn't let him go or Mother's life would have been in danger."

Tristan helped Maddox remove the Hungau's body from the horse and looked at the man's face. "He looks like the son of one of the leaders," he said grimly.

Maddox cursed. "Why would they send an heir?"

Tristan shrugged and turned to Samara. "If he was tracking Calida, he may have entered on his suspicions alone."

"I had to kill him," Samara explained. "He was suspicious about Mother."

Dagan straightened and pointed east toward Eagle's Bay. "At most," he barked, "we have three days before they realize their warrior is not going to return." He eyed everyone carefully. "Three days," he shouted. "I want command to be set up in the council hall. Maddox, go and prepare our fighters for the possibility of an attack."

"I'm sorry, Father. I had to do it."

Dagan turned to her; his expression remained fierce. "I know. I only wished it wouldn't have turned out this way. We trespassed into their lands, they killed Casimir, they'll discover their missing evidence eventually, and now we killed one of their own. It could be the catalyst for war, and sooner than we anticipated." Dagan barked orders to Danson and Rawlins. "Get a perimeter around the forest. Ready our defenses and close all other openings to the home except the main gate. Get everyone inside here and safe."

Everyone scurried to obey. Time was of the essence.

Her father approached her. "You sure you're all right?" Dagan asked.

"I'm fine," she said, but her voice was weak, even to her own ears.

"She has a wound that needs to be addressed, but she fought well," Nickson informed Dagan.

Dagan nodded. "Sire, would you mind taking charge of my daughter? I want her kept safe."

"Absolutely, sir. Whatever you need," Nickson replied.

Dagan stared at her. "I am sorry, Samara, for lying to you about your mother."

Too tired to think on it and not sure she was ready to respond, she only nodded. She let him give her a kiss before he rushed off to help secure their people.

Nickson and Tristan guided her inside and Samara explained to her uncle what happened. Tristan removed the bandages and looked carefully at the wound. With cleansing ointment and balm for infection, he washed it out and prepared to stitch it up.

"Are you feeling anything else besides pain?" Tristan asked.

She shook her head. "Mostly tired."

"It's a fairly good cut. You've lost some blood. You ready?"

She turned away and found Nickson's gaze. "Go ahead."

Tristan sewed her skin together in careful, neat stitches. She flinched here and there, but mostly found comfort in Nickson's deep-green eyes. When the sewing was complete, she sat up slowly.

"If you start to get a headache or feel anything out of the ordinary, please let me know," her uncle advised.

"Thank you."

Tristan disappeared and Nickson helped her stand. "Are you sure you're all right?" he asked.

"I think so. I haven't had much rest since returning from Eagle's Bay. I think I need to lie down for a moment."

Nickson helped her to her room and then left her. She felt so incredibly tired, but she found enough energy to remove her weapons and change her bloody clothes. Her body felt tight and all she wanted was sleep. Freshly changed, she lay back on her bed and her eyes closed immediately. Sleep was instantaneous, but it was filled with strange dreams.

She dreamed horrible things. Nickson's castle had been attacked and was burning. As she approached, she heard screams coming from inside. Everyone was trapped—Mary, Constance, and the king. She called frantically for Nickson but never received an answer. She couldn't save the servants no matter how hard she tried; every entrance she found would erupt in flames and send her flying through the air.

The flames began to take on an abnormal shape and move. No, dance. They danced toward her. She watched them curiously and laughed to herself; they were amusing. The flames phased again into a face she recognized. This face, beautiful and kind, smiled at her and soon she found herself in a lovely garden. Her mother was there, planting cures for Hungau poisons. All too quickly the scene changed again and her mother disappeared. Samara ran in endless circles searching for her lost parent.

"Mother? Where did you go?" Her mother was lost. "Mother!"

Fading between memories and another dream, her nightmare became warm and uncomfortable. Samara sensed a hot presence behind her. The heat on the back of her head made her neck sweaty and she reached back to wipe it away. When she looked at her hand, it was covered in blood. Before she could scream, she turned around and saw, nailed to four stakes, four people burning. Among them was her mother.

"No!" Samara cried and ran forward. "Stop! No!" No matter how hard she ran, she could never reach the stakes. She could not save her mother.

As abruptly as it came, the scene whisked away and standing before her now was the female Hungau warrior.

"You killed my mother!" she cried out. She leaped through the air, and just as she was about to tackle the Hungau, the Hungau disappeared and Samara fell into a black abyss.

She sat up and gasped.

It was dark outside, but the sun was beginning to rise. She must have slept the rest of the day and the whole of the night. She flinched when she moved and her elbow pulsed in pain, but she got out of bed and made her way into the hall. The torches were lit, which meant others were already up.

She could barely get her feet steady underneath her, and she half stumbled down the stairs to where she heard voices in the dining hall. By the time she reached it, her mind was clearer and she had regained her balance.

Everyone was relaxed and eating when she entered. Nickson stood and bowed, as did her father. Dagan was still hesitant to approach her, but she moved to his side to reassure him. Now that she had some rest, she could make some sense of all the things that had happened to her.

"Father," she began. "I understand why you did it."

"Do you?"

"Yes. It still hurts, but having to kill mother's tracker made me understand what you meant about hard choices. I don't know how I feel about knowing Mom's alive, but it was hard seeing her dressed like the Hungau."

Dagan's expression turned sympathetic. "I understand. It isn't easy to reconcile her position within that nation, but there is little else we can do."

She hugged him. "You must miss her."

He squeezed her back. "I miss her more than you'll ever know."

Feeling better now, she turned to face her friends. Nickson stood for her and she smiled at him.

"We're discussing the Hungau," Rawlins informed her as he hugged her. "How are you feeling?"

"Still tired, but better, I think. Any news?"

"No movement yet," Maddox said. "But they won't know their warrior is missing for some time."

Samara sank into her chair. "I hope I have not brought the entire Hungau upon us," she sighed. "I can't seem to make a sound decision."

"You were right to kill him," Maddox said. "He would have returned to tell the Hungau about Calida, and they would have killed her. Not only would we really have lost your mother, but our contact within the Hungau. We'd be completely blind."

"He's right," Nickson agreed. "You did well out there."

"What's the tentative plan?" she asked.

"We're trying to decide if we should attack the Hungau first," Danson replied. "Before they attack us."

"We can't let them attack our forests," Samara prohibited. "In the last two years, many children have been born. Some of our women are in varying degrees of recovery. All the men are trained, but we can't let them breach our defenses."

"Strategically, our forests would give us an advantage. We know the terrain better than anyone else, but there is also greater chance for ambush," Maddox stated.

"I agree with both of you," Dagan said. "We must draw them away."

"Hold the battle elsewhere?" Danson asked.

Dagan gave a curt nod. "I'm afraid the only way we can ensure this possibility is if we attack them first."

Maddox's face dropped as he considered the consequences. "How big is their army?"

Rawlins answered, "Double what they were twenty ago years ago."

"How is that even possible?" Samara asked.

Rawlins shrugged. "They've been steadily building for decades. In the letter from the man Hadar, he discusses their success."

Nickson looked irritated. "So, in estimate, how many warriors are we talking about?"

"Minus the ones Samara killed on our mission and the one by the falls," Maddox pretended to do the math, "they are down to three thousand nine hundred and ninety."

A light roll of laugher sailed through the room, lightening the heavy mood ever so slightly.

"Unlike the mission," Dagan responded, "Samara will not be fighting."

Samara looked at her father with surprise. "Father, I am helping. I can fight."

"No," Dagan responded. "You can fight, but I'm not letting you."

Samara stared at her father in disbelief. "You would keep me from fighting alongside my people? You cannot be serious."

"I am." Her father's tone was final.

Samara looked at Maddox for help, but he only stared at the table. She looked at Nickson, who gave her an apologetic look.

"Father—" she began.

"Samara," he stopped her. "We will discuss this later. Now is not the time. You still need to go to the castle and get more information, and a battle with the Hungau hasn't truly been decided."

She glared at him and left the table without dismissing herself. Her feet carried her down the hall, up the stairs, and back into her bedroom. She stood in the middle of the floor and looked in her body-length mirror, which stood on a rolling stand on the far wall. She resembled her mother and had the same stamina and strength, as well as the same feisty attitude. Since she was unable, she wished her mother were still here to speak sense into her father.

She thought of the dressings around her elbow and in so doing forgot her anger. She focused on the pain and analyzed how it thumped in her elbow. It moved up her arm, where it burned and ached. She rolled up the sleeve to her tunic and undid the dressings so she could examine the wound in the mirror. A giant black-and-purple bruise sat on the elbow joint, and red and blue marks spread over her arm and lower forearm. She touched the bruises gently but withdrew her hand as they stung. She cringed and studied the place where her skin stretched open. The stitches had somehow been melted away, like a rope stretched over a fire, and were barely keeping the skin closed. The laceration had not had time to close properly, but it had stopped bleeding long ago.

Overall, it looked much worse.

From her wound kit, she grabbed a clean rag and some cleansing ointment. She placed the ointment-covered rag over the injured area and clenched her teeth as the pain stung and grated at her nerves. Letting out a little groan, she continued to hold the rag in place. Just when she thought she could take no more, there was a knock on her door.

She practically jumped out of her boots and dropped the rag. "Who is it?"

"Nickson."

She pulled the sleeve of her tunic back down and made her way to the door. Out of habit, she opened the door with her injured arm and nearly collapsed with the pain. It felt like her elbow was torn from its place, but she forced a smile as she greeted him.

"Yes, Nickson?"

"Are you okay?" Nickson looked concerned and took a step toward her.

"I'm fine," she said, feeling a little dizzy as the pain kept pounding. "Does my father need me?"

Nickson smiled. "No, I came up to talk."

She opened the door wider. He entered and took a seat at the table.

She crossed her arms. "What do you need to talk about?"

"What your father said. He's wrong and should let you fight."

Samara's face brightened. "I'm glad you agree with me."

Nickson wrinkled his nose. "I also see his point," he confessed, and Samara threw him an accusatory glare. "I talked to him about it and I understand where he's coming from."

"And me?"

"I definitely understand where you're coming from." He smiled.

"I'm tired of being coddled. No matter what happens, he feels the need to protect me."

"I can imagine how frustrating that must be."

"But what is your counterargument?"

He gave her a sheepish smile. "I have none."

Suddenly curious, she eyed him closely. "Why did you come up here?"

He looked uncertain. "I know you've made your decision about me, but I just can't seem to keep my distance. I worry about you when you're not near."

"I'm a staircase away," she teased.

His eyes got a familiar twinkle and her breath caught in her throat.

"Even so," he whispered.

"Nickson, we agreed now would not be a good time."

"I didn't technically agree." He shrugged a shoulder. "But I know."

"And yet here you are."

"I may be a prince but I'm still a man, and an imperfect one at that."

She smiled at his confession. "I'll be sure to keep your imperfections a secret from your subjects."

He smiled. "I would appreciate that."

He stepped closer and she instantly became aware of his strength. Even if physical prowess were not a factor, she couldn't deny his kind heart and his gentle way. She couldn't ignore his fierce loyalty or his proficient ability to lead and guide. She let her admiration for Nickson wash over her completely. She hesitated only a moment before she took a step toward him to close the distance.

"I have to be honest and admit that I admire you, Nickson."

Nickson smiled and reached out to take one of her hands. With his other hand he pulled her toward him. Her heart started to beat frantically. The pain in her elbow began to subside as a much happier and relaxed feeling sailed through her body. She completely forgot about the injury.

Until he grabbed it.

Samara let out a shriek and clutched at her elbow. The pain was so great that a headache throbbed at her temples. She let herself collapse; she couldn't hold herself up any longer. Nickson helped her to the ground as concern filled his face, and when he asked her what was wrong, she couldn't answer.

Seeing her hand at her elbow, he grabbed her sleeve and pulled it up to see what had happened. When he saw the elbow he froze, a momentary look of horror on his face. Eyes wide, he looked at Samara.

"What happened to the stitches?" he demanded.

She still couldn't answer; her breaths became raspy and shallow. She focused hard on steadying her breath, but the pain was intense.

"Samara, talk to me." Worry and concern dripped from his tone.

She gritted her teeth. "The Hungau," she was able to spit out. A burning sensation crept down her forearm and into her hand. The muscles cramped and the never-dulling pain seemed to escalate.

"Dagan!" Samara heard Nickson yell. She felt herself being lifted from the hard ground, and the soft and cushiony sensation of her mattress welcomed her. All she wanted to do was close her eyes and sleep. At least it would take her away from the pain.

Dagan, followed by Maddox and Tristan, came into the room.

"I heard her scream. What happened?" Dagan started, but he saw Samara's elbow. His face went pale and his eyes jerked to Tristan.

Tristan froze, unable to move at the sight of her injury.

Dagan rushed to Samara's side. "Samara," he whispered roughly. "Tell me what you're feeling." His voice was urgent and his hand shook as he put it on her forehead. "She's breaking into a cold sweat," he muttered helplessly. "Maddox, go to my bedchamber and find Calida's book of poisons. Now!"

Maddox didn't hesitate. He fled the room to do as Dagan ordered.

"She said it was the Hungau," Nickson said with a helpless wave of his hand. "This is the cut she got during their fight."

"The Hungau must have lined his blade with poison," Tristan muttered under his breath. "I was afraid this would happen."

"Poisoned like Casimir," Nickson pointed out.

"What poison is it, Tristan?" Dagan asked.

Samara felt cold fingers touch her elbow as Tristan examined the wound. She shrieked again as a fresh wave of nauseating pain permeated her left shoulder and chest. She coiled into a ball and fought against the throbbing pulse that originated at her elbow. She let out a scream. Tears soaked her cheeks.

"It hurts," she whimpered.

Nickson knelt beside her with a pained expression. "We'll fix it, Samara." He pushed some sweat-soaked hair away from her face, then he turned to Tristan. "Well?"

Tristan shook his head. "I need to consult Calida's book. It could be anything."

The pounding of their voices made Samara's head hurt. She couldn't focus on what they were saying; the pain from her wound was at the forefront of her mind. All she wanted was to sleep. She closed her eyes.

"No, Samara!" Tristan warned. "Stay with us."

"No," she said, but obeyed and opened her eyes.

Tristan cursed. "It's Hungau poison," he snarled. "If she falls asleep, she'll succumb and we may not get her back."

Nickson winced.

Maddox returned with the book and handed it to Tristan. He moved to Samara's side and gripped her hand. "Samara, you stay with me."

"We need to find a cure, and fast." Tristan flipped frantically through the pages of the book. He landed on a certain page, his eyes darting from one end of the page to the other. "The pain caused by the poison will burn her from the inside out. Her heart won't be able to take the stress and it will give out."

Dagan moaned in anguish.

"How is the poison attacking her?" Maddox asked.

"It attacks the muscles. Right now, the pain should still be centralized in her elbow. But give it until the afternoon and she'll be in pain all over." Tristan shuddered.

"Why did it take so long to manifest?" Nickson asked.

"That's how this poison works. It stays in the fresh wound for a period as the heart works double time to pump it loose. She's probably been very fatigued, and that's why she slept so long. Once the heart releases the poison from the entry point, it spreads to each limb where it gets saturated into the muscles and tissue."

"The Hungau cut her knowing there was poison on the dagger," Dagan snapped.

Tristan looked at his brother-in-law. "We Hungau are ruthless killers. I'm sorry."

Dagan crossed his arms and turned away from his daughter. "How do we fix it?"

Tristan didn't answer.

"Tristan!" Nickson shouted. "How do we fix this?"

"We can't lose Samara and Casimir within a few days from each other. Is there no way?" Maddox demanded.

Tristan looked helpless. "Not here," he confirmed, and pointed to a page in the book.

Dagan spun around. "What do you mean 'not here'?"

"Based on how the wound looks, I think the cure for this poison is only in Eagle's Bay."

"The Hungau will give it to us," Dagan said.

"Dagan, there isn't time to go to the Hungau, beg politely for a cure, and ride back. The poison will have killed her long before we even get to Eagle's Bay."

Dagan glared. "I will not sit here and do nothing while the Hungau claim yet another life from my family."

"What is the cure? What exactly are we looking for?" Nickson asked, his tone impatient.

Tristan placed a wet rag on Samara's forehead. "The poison is derived from a plant called *wintag*—it means death in Hungau. The Hungau brought it with them from a distant land. They found that if you crush the fresh plant, it emits an unpleasant odor. Inhaling the fumes for too long causes headaches and nausea, but if you boil the plant, you can create a thick, soupy cream. Once the cream turns dark, it is finished. They applied it to the lips of one of their test subjects and he died instantly. They discovered that if you water it down, it takes longer for the poison to affect its victim. The antidote is derived from a rare, strange plant."

"What is it called?" Maddox asked.

"*Almat.* It means life. The plant is pure white in color—white roots, white stems, and white flowers. It is the only plant we know of that completely reverses the effects of *wintag*. Something in *almat* attacks the *wintag's* poison and neutralizes it. It could cure Samara in a matter of moments."

"That fast?" Nickson asked.

"Yes," Tristan confirmed.

"Does Calida not have this cure in her garden?" Maddox asked.

Tristan shook his head. "*Almat* is very rare. The Hungau will have grown it in their forests, but it has been brought here. It does not grow naturally in Cascadia."

Dagan looked at his daughter. "She is all I have," he said in a hushed voice. "How can I get this plant in time?"

Maddox put his hand on Dagan's shoulder. "We could ride for Eagle's Bay—"

"There isn't time," Tristan interrupted. "She needs it right now."

"But it's the only plant that will save her," Nickson pressed. He turned to Dagan. "Is there any way your scouts can set up a relay?

If we can get a message to her mother, then maybe she can get the cure and meet us halfway."

Dagan thought quickly. "We'd have to send out riders and they would have to ride fast."

"I'll go," Nickson volunteered.

Maddox stood and looked at the prince. "I will ride with you."

Nickson nodded.

At that moment, the pain in Samara's shoulder began to spread through her chest. She yelled and clutched at her heart. "Make it stop!" she cried. "I want to sleep."

Dagan's face turned fierce. "Ride hard," he pleaded.

Maddox left the room to prep the message for the first relay.

Nickson grabbed Tristan's shoulder. "You keep her awake," he ordered. "I don't care how much she screams; you keep her alive."

Tristan put his hand on Nickson's arm. "You can count on me."

Nickson gave him a small, tense smile and turned to Dagan. "Leave the room. It will not do you any good to sit and listen to her this way. Go with Maddox to set up the relay; I will go and prep our horses."

Dagan took one last look at his daughter before leaving the room.

Nickson knelt beside the bed. "Samara," he whispered, "we'll be back soon. Stay with us."

Samara felt a warm hand clutch at her own. Wanting it to stay, she tightened her squeeze. She whimpered when he pulled away and let out another scream as the pain burned her chest.

"Go!" Tristan whispered urgently. "I'll keep her awake."

Nickson stared at Samara for a moment longer. "I hate to leave her."

Tristan gave him a sympathetic look. "You'll see her when you get back."

Samara watched Nickson slip out of the room. Her heart pricked at his departure and a sudden pressure filled her chest. Her body shook as the pain fought with her to succumb. Her eyes moved toward the open window as the thunder of hoofbeats echoed across the bridge. As they died away, she felt herself slip into darkness. She was all alone, save for the pain and the strange thumping that throbbed at her ears. As the pain surged around her chest, the dull beat slowed dangerously.

She focused on this drum, somehow aware that it was important to maintain. It continued to slow until finally she could focus no more. The pain flared, she heard a scream, and the thumping ceased.

All she saw was blackness.

ACKNOWLEDGMENTS

I would like to thank the BookLogix staff who made all of this possible! From the beginning, your guidance has been invaluable to me. Thank you for making this dream become a reality. I would also like to thank Kyilee for her incredible artwork and how she made the story come to life. My children deserve a shout-out for the many hours they let me write and work on my stories. And finally, to my friends and family who have encouraged me, despite my own doubts, to move forward.

About the Author

Originally from Salt Lake City, Susan Shepard has moved all around the United States with her husband and their four children. She is a twenty-five-year student of the piano and a classically trained vocalist, with a deep love for musical arts. More than anything else, Susan loves spending time with her family exploring the outdoors.